THE MARATHON MURDERS

THE MARATHON MURDERS

A GREG MCKENZIE MYSTERY

CHESTER D. CAMPBELL

NIGHT
SHADOWS PRESS

First Edition

10 9 8 7 6 5 4 3 2 1

Cover design by Katie Small

Printed in the United States of America

Library of Congress Control Number: 2007938171

ISBN 978-0-9799167-0-0

Night Shadows Press, LLC
8987 E. Tanque Verde #309-135
Tucson, AZ 85749-9399

Dedicated to the memory of those great teachers at East Nashville High School who stirred my imagination and taught me the elements of writing. May they rest in well-deserved peace.

Other Greg McKenzie Mysteries
by Chester D. Campbell

Deadly Illusions
Designed to Kill
Secret of the Scroll

ACKNOWLEDGMENTS

THE IDEA FOR THIS BOOK came from a suggestion by a neighbor, Kathleen Mays, who had recently visited Marathon Village, the restored plant and offices of the company that gave Nashville its claim to automotive fame—home of the only car completely built in the South. Her father, Joe O'Mara, had worked in the Chassis Department in 1914, the year the plant closed. Kathleen suggested I write something about Marathon in my next book.

I need to thank several other people for their help with various facets of the book. First, of course, is Barry Walker, the intrepid entrepreneur who took on the task of salvaging two decrepit, decaying industrial buildings and turning them into historical landmarks. In the small county of Trousdale, I had the help of Chief Deputy Sheriff Wayland Cothron. Providing valuable insights into the workings of the Tennessee Bureau of Investigation were Law Enforcement Information Coordinator Jim Green, Special Agent Dan Royse of the Forensics Division, and Director of Communications Jennifer Johnson. I consulted with the mystery writer's favorite forensics guru, Dr. D. P. (Doug) Lyle, in hopes of getting my medical facts straight.

Also, thanks to avid reader/fan Wayne Fought, who won a contest and contributed his name to the TBI agent in the story.

A special word of appreciation to Bob Middlelmiss, the editor who has guided me through four Greg McKenzie mysteries. And last, but hardly least, thanks as always to my live-in assistant, wife Sarah. You're the greatest.

Having said all that, I take full responsibility for any discrepancies that might have crept in.

1

I NEVER IMAGINED how much destruction a ninety-year-old car could cause until I got involved with the Marathon Motor Works case. I had tackled my share of strange investigations over the years, but this one had more twists and turns than a Tennessee mountain road. It rumbled onto the scene one scorching August afternoon when digital signs above Nashville's major highways warned of dangerous air quality, a circumstance the TV weather folks insisted senior citizens and children should beware of. That seniors tag included Jill and me, of course, though we had little time to worry about it after the phone rang.

"McKenzie Investigations," I answered. "Greg McKenzie speaking."

"Retired Lieutenant Colonel Greg McKenzie?" asked a voice that resonated from somewhere in my past.

I hesitated. "That would be me. Who's this?"

"Colonel Warren Jarvis."

A flood of images played out on my internal memory screen as I glanced at Jill sitting behind her desk. "Did you finish your tour in Israel, Colonel?"

"I did. And you're a private eye now. I thought this had to be you."

"Jill and I have been in business about eight months. Retirement turned out to be a pain in the butt. Are you in Nashville?"

"Right. I was on my way to Arnold Air Force Base for a speech when I got sidetracked. It's a bit of a complicated story. And a rather puzzling one, I might add. We may need your services."

"We?"

"Remember my telling you about a lady named Abby Farrell, who I worked with on the Raptor Project?"

"The lady who disappeared? Don't tell me you finally found her?"

"Yesterday. Can we come over and talk?"

THIRTY MINUTES LATER, we met the elusive Miss Farrell at our less-than-sumptuous office suite in a suburban shopping center (for "suite," think former beauty shop). Only it wasn't Miss Farrell now.

"Jill and Greg McKenzie," said a smiling Warren Jarvis, "meet Kelli—spelled with an *i*—Kane. And that's K-A-N-E."

"Nice to meet you, Kelli-with-an-*i*," I said, shaking her hand.

She gave me an indulgent grin. "My pleasure, I'm sure."

Jill invited them to occupy the client chairs that faced our twin desks. Dressed in trim designer jeans and a white shirt, Kelli Kane moved with the easy grace of someone accustomed to traveling in sophisticated circles. Long black tresses accompanied a pleasant smile accented by hazel eyes that had a striking starburst effect. I guessed her age at early to mid-forties. That made her at least twenty years younger than Jill or me. On the outside, she had the look of a successful businesswoman on a relaxing vacation. My sixth sense told me there was a lot more going on inside.

I turned to Jarvis, a handsome man who made no attempt to hide that precursor of aging, gray around the temples. "After what you did for us in Israel, Warren, we could hardly refuse our help."

"We're not looking for charity, Greg."

"Point taken. So what's the problem? I hope it isn't too serious."

He glanced at Kelli. "That remains to be seen. It could involve a ninety-year-old murder."

"Ninety?" Jill's brown eyes sprang open wide. "Wow, talk about your cold cases."

Jarvis shifted in his chair. "True. But it appears to be heating up."

Kelli spoke, her expression clouded. "Before we go any further, we need to agree on some ground rules."

As a retired agent with the Air Force's Office of Special Investigations, I could write a book on dealing with confidential sources.

Considering Colonel Jarvis's earlier description of Abby as having apparently operated under deep cover, I wasn't surprised at her conditional response.

"I've never been a big fan of rules," I said. "But let's see if we can live with yours."

"Warren has told me about his previous conversation with you. Forget Abby Farrell. She no longer exists. That's really all you need to know of my background. Kelli Kane is the name I was born with in Seattle forty-plus years ago. And that's a fact."

Seeing the perplexed look on my wife's face, I smiled. "My partner doesn't understand these things. I'll explain it later."

Jill's eyes narrowed. "That would be appreciated."

"Now, you or the colonel needs to tell us what this is all about, and how we might be able to help."

Kelli crossed her legs, folding strong, slim hands over one knee. "When I spoke with my grandfather a few days ago, he asked if I could come to Nashville. He was scheduled to meet with a man named Pierce Bradley, a construction supervisor who related a rather strange story on the phone. Grandpa wanted me there to hear all the details when they met."

Bradley, she related, was job foreman for a contractor involved in renovating an old brick building near downtown Nashville that had once housed Marathon Motor Works. Bradley had a bundle of papers that contained the name of Kelli's great-great-grandfather, Sydney Liggett, who was Marathon's assistant treasurer. A carpenter discovered them stashed behind the paneling of an old wall he was restoring.

The foreman thumbed through the papers and found they were Marathon Motors records dated in 1914. A handwritten note attached indicated Liggett planned to turn them over to the District Attorney. An enterprising fellow, Bradley made a few calls in the business community and learned that Sydney Liggett's grandson, Arthur Liggett, had been admitted recently to a nursing home on the northeast side of town.

"Your grandfather is Arthur Liggett?" I asked.

"Yes. I had been out of the country and wasn't aware he'd gone into the nursing home. He's eighty-four."

Jill donned a sympathetic frown. "Was it the result of an illness?"

"No, though he has emphysema."

"So why the nursing home?" I asked.

"He fell at home and fractured his leg in a couple of places. He's coming along. I think he'll make it okay, but it will take a while. I had just completed an assignment and was ready to take some accrued leave when I called to check on him. That's when he told me about Mr. Bradley."

I turned to Jarvis. "What's the deal on this ninety-year-old murder, Warren?"

"Sydney Liggett disappeared around the time that note was written." A trim, muscular man still capable of handling the controls of the Air Force's hottest jet fighters, Jarvis squared his jaw. "They accused him of running off with some company funds."

"Did he ever turn up?"

"They found him five years later . . . dead," Kelli said. "Grandpa says the family never believed he took any money or left of his own volition."

It had the sound of a tragic story, but I didn't see where Jill and I fit in. "Have you talked with Mr. Bradley?"

A grim look crossed Kelli's face. "We were supposed to meet with him last night. He didn't show."

"Did he give any reason why?"

Jarvis tapped his fingertips. "We haven't been able to locate him."

"If he's a supervisor, you'd think he would be on the job."

"You would think so, but they haven't heard from him over at the Marathon project. They say he doesn't show up there every day, but he hasn't been by the contractor's office, either."

"Does he have a wife?" Jill asked.

Kelli opened her handbag and pulled out a cigarette pack. "Mind if I smoke?"

Jill gave her a polite smile. "We'd rather you didn't."

Jarvis looked at me and grinned. "Did your wife prod you back off the cancer sticks?"

"She prodded with a vengeance. I found it pretty tough at the start, but I gritted my teeth and hung in there. Regarding this Mr.

Bradley, did you make an effort to check with his family?"

"He's a single man," Kelli said. "Lives alone over in another county."

"That's why we're here," Jarvis said. "We don't have a lot of time. We want to hire you to find him and recover those papers."

Kelli stuck the cigarettes back in her bag and dropped it to the floor with a pronounced clunk. I took that to mean she wasn't too thrilled with the house rules. But she hid it well as she spoke in an impassioned voice.

"My grandfather thinks those papers may provide the proof that Sydney Liggett was no embezzler. They could show he was framed, possibly murdered. Grandpa feels the erroneous allegations have left a permanent stain on the family name, one that should have been erased long ago. This is very important to him. He's in poor health. I want to do what he'd do if he could. I have some investigative talents, and I'll do whatever you'd like me to. But this is your territory. I'm sure you can do the job much better and much quicker."

I hoped she was right on both counts. From her description, it sounded like a no-brainer. I had a bad feeling, though. Brush aside something that looked no more complicated than a twist of rope, and the next thing you knew it could pop up as a coiled snake and take a bite out of your behind.

But we owed Warren Jarvis. Whatever it took, I was determined to track down those errant records.

2

A FTER JARVIS AND Kelli left for the nursing home, Jill pulled her chair over to my desk. "I don't suppose the police would consider Mr. Bradley a missing person," she said.

"You don't suppose correctly."

"So what happened?"

"It's a nice Tuesday afternoon in August. He probably went fishing."

"That's not what happened to me two years ago."

"True." No way I could forget that. "But I found out pretty quickly you'd been kidnapped. Until we get some positive evidence that it's otherwise, we have to assume Mr. Bradley, for whatever reason, simply chose not to keep an appointment."

"So how do we find him, boss?"

That "boss" bit was delivered tongue-in-cheek. Although Jill held a license as an apprentice investigator under my supervision, she considered herself a full partner in the firm. Which she was, of course, though I sometimes wondered why I let her talk me into pursuing this wacky profession in a partnership. Anyway, I suppose you could say I qualified as the lead investigator on this case.

"We start with Mr. Bradley's boss. Where are your notes with the contractor's name?"

After consulting the notes, I called Allied Construction and got the owner's secretary, a Mrs. Nelson. Her voice reminded me of my mother's, laced with overtones of patience and tolerance. When I explained my problem, she gave a musical laugh.

"I'm not all that surprised. His transportation probably played out on him. Pierce Bradley is a stubborn young man. He insists on driving an antique Jeep."

"An old Cherokee?" That's the Jeep I had driven the past few years.

"Heavens, no. It's a real Jeep. You know, that military color."

"Olive drab."

"That's it. Looks like surplus from some ancient war."

I knew about ancient wars, too, having served an Air Force tour in Vietnam. "Does it break down often?"

"I wouldn't say often. But a lot oftener than he'd like, I'm sure."

"I've had experience with Jeeps like that. Where does Bradley live?"

"In Walnut Grove. It's a wide spot in the road up in Trousdale County, about forty miles northeast of Nashville. I think he'd like to move down here, but he's got some problems. Would you like his phone numbers?"

"Sure."

She gave me both home and cell numbers. I thanked her and turned to Jill. "Mr. Bradley probably had car trouble. He drives what sounds like a Vietnam-era model of what Jeep now calls a Wrangler."

She fixed me with a wary frown. "Why didn't he call and tell somebody?"

Good point, but I played devil's advocate. "If he didn't have anything pressing, he probably didn't feel it necessary."

"I heard you repeating phone numbers. We should try calling him, right?"

"Right."

"Shall we divvy up?"

"You try at home. I'll try the cell."

We were big on serendipity, economy of effort, all that good organizational stuff.

Neither of us got an answer, which was troubling. We left messages on both phones to call us, regardless of the hour.

It was almost time to close shop when Jarvis called back.

"Having any luck?"

"Not so far. How's Mr. Liggett?"

"He's doing fairly well, but the pain medication leaves him a little confused at times. I think it would be profitable for you to come over and hear his story, though."

"And you want him to see that we're on the job."

"Might improve his outlook."

"When is a good time for us to make our appearance?"

"He's eating supper now."

"Why don't Jill and I get a bite, then we'll drop by."

"Sounds good. Kelli and I'll be here. I don't have to be down at Arnold for my talk until in the morning."

Jarvis's current assignment was with the Defense Intelligence Agency at the Pentagon. He had flown into Nashville to rent a car en route to Arnold Air Force Base near Tullahoma, seventy-five miles to the south. He planned to brief delegates attending a conference at Arnold Engineering Development Center, the Air Force's big supersonic wind tunnel facility capable of testing most anything that flew, on the situation in the Middle East.

OUR STOREFRONT OFFICE in a suburban strip center had acquired a little more dignity since we'd covered the plate glass windows with a mural depicting the Gardens of Versailles. Quite a step up for an ex-beauty salon. Being the daughter of a symphony violinist, Jill had insisted on a classical look. That, however, marked the extent of our elegance. The rest was strictly utilitarian, more in tune with my Scottish roots——a couple of green metal filing cabinets, a well-stocked bookshelf, a paper shredder, and a table with printer, fax, copier, and a small TV.

I had found the location ideal for a guy who likes to eat, being convenient to numerous restaurants. We stopped at a nearby ribs place and ordered a pile of food that would embarrass a porker. I had just cleaned the last bone of its barbeque sauce-slathered meat when Jill gave me her be-prepared-to-duck look.

"After eating all that, you'd better be ready to march in the morning, Colonel McKenzie. Considering what you put away, you may have a stomach cramp, but that won't work as an excuse."

Most mornings we trekked the neighborhood on a two-mile jaunt before breakfast. We'd shower and eat and head for the office around eight. This morning I had begged off walking because of a leg cramp.

"Okay, babe," I said. "I'll be ready. I guar-ahn-tee it. You can cancel the whip-cracking routine."

My bride of nearly forty years had become a firm taskmaster of late when it came to my maintaining a healthy lifestyle. I tend to gravitate to what is politely called hefty. She not always politely reminds me to back away from the table.

AFTERNOON RUSH HOUR traffic had subsided, although a conglomeration of cars and trucks cluttered Old Hickory Boulevard as we took the circumferential highway to the north. It led past President Andrew Jackson's restored Hermitage mansion, for which our community was named, through an area called Old Hickory, another Jacksonian reference, and the tiny incorporated village of Lakewood. The traffic slowed to a decent 45 miles per hour there, thanks to its reputation as a speed trap.

I had never been to this particular nursing home. We found it in a fashionable neighborhood of large post World War II houses built on sizeable lots with brawny oaks and maples and lawns as smooth as golf course greens. Though I couldn't say if it was a conscious effort to stash away the ranks of the infirm, the facility lay hidden behind a woodsy façade. We would have missed it except for the modest Safe Harbor sign at the driveway entrance.

A nurse wearing a colorful smock directed us down a tiled corridor infused with a pervasive antiseptic odor. We passed a huddled woman in a wheelchair, a few wisps of gray hair clinging to her bowed head. She talked to herself in low, unintelligible tones. It left me with a hollow feeling inside, a feeling I should do something to help her but without the vaguest idea of what I could do. It was similar to what I felt when encountering a homeless guy on the street. I usually gave them a buck and hoped it would be spent in some useful manner, if not a wise one.

We found Arthur Liggett's name beside the door to a room not a lot more spacious than a broom closet. It housed a bed, a lounge chair, and a three-drawer wooden chest. A few aluminum stack chairs had been squeezed in for our benefit.

A large man with thinning white hair, Liggett had a full face and a silvery mustache in need of trimming. I suspected his granddaughter would get around to that shortly. Hooded eyes gave him a lethargic look. Small oxygen tubes fed into his nose, a circumstance that struck me as demeaning, though necessary. Neither age nor physical impairment had lessened his desire to maintain the formality of years in management, however. He wore a white shirt with red tie beneath the blue sweater donned to combat the robust air-conditioning system. My approach to retirement had taken the opposite tack. After a lifetime of being forced to dress up in coats and ties, I took pains to avoid them except when an absolute necessity, and never during a mid-August heat wave.

After introductions, I shook Mr. Liggett's large, gnarled hand and took a chair beside the battleship gray wall. "What in the world are you doing here, Mr. Liggett?" I asked. "You look like you're ready to run a marathon."

He leaned his head against the lounge chair and gazed out through thick oval lenses, the bare hint of a smile tilting a corner of his mouth. "You can't see the gruesome part . . . under this blanket covering my legs. I never did run too fast, though. Maybe it won't matter."

He spoke in a low, breathy voice, the words coming slowly.

"As long as I've known him, he's never been a complainer," Kelli said.

I wondered about that "as long as I've known him" but let it pass.

"You were a hospital administrator?" I asked.

"Yes. You'd think I'd seen enough of this sort of environment, that I'd figure out how to avoid it in any way possible."

"How long were you in the hospital business?"

He took a deep breath, looked up at the ceiling, then back at me. "Practically all my life. I served in the Army Medical Corps during the war. Went to work in a hospital after my discharge. I only needed a year to finish college. They were generous enough to let me do that while I was working."

Kelli leaned forward. "He was manager of one of the city's largest hospitals when he retired at seventy-plus."

"You've spent a long in the trenches," Jill said. "Time for you to get a rest."

"Hmph. Only rest I'm likely to get's in the grave. Kelli says you're detectives. I hope you can find out what's going on."

"Tell us how this came about," I said.

"A few days ago I got a call." He glanced at the phone on the bedside table. "Fellow said—what was his name?"

"Pierce Bradley," Kelli prompted.

"Yes, Pierce Bradley called. Said he was a foreman with a contractor rehabbing the old Marathon Motors buildings on Clinton Street. It's just beyond downtown, near the Inner Loop. I knew the place, of course. That's where my grandfather worked years ago. Werthan Bag Company used the buildings in its operations for a while, but they'd been vacant a long time."

"Somebody new had bought them?" I asked.

"Yes. A fellow making office space for photographers and artists and musicians. Don't remember his name. Anyway, this—Bradley, was it?—said one of his workers had found a sheaf of papers behind some wood paneling. It was addressed to the Davidson County District Attorney General."

"The worker gave the papers to Bradley?"

"That's right."

"Did Bradley show them to anybody else?"

"I don't think so. Said they were obviously quite old. The building had been vacant for years. Derelicts had trashed the place. Bradley said he started to throw the papers away but decided to take a look first. He's not a financial type of fellow. He wasn't sure what to make of it. But he talked to the building's owner and lerarned of Marathon's bankruptcy. He knew there had been a lot of controversy. Then he saw my grandfather's name, that he was the assistant treasurer."

"How did Bradley connect it with you?" I asked.

"I think he started with the Chamber of Commerce. They suggested he contact somebody else. After a few calls, he came up with my name."

"I imagine you're pretty well known in the Nashville business community," Jill said.

He allowed a full smile for the first time. It had a touch of shyness to it. "You could probably say that."

I looked up from the notes I was jotting in my lap. "That part about the District Attorney sounds like your grandfather thought something criminal was involved. Did Mr. Bradley give you any clue as to what the records contained?"

Liggett took another deep breath before replying. "I don't think he really had any idea. He didn't know anything about Sydney Liggett's disappearance."

"Tell us about that."

Liggett shifted in his chair, a beefy hand smoothing his tie. "It's one of those things you'd rather forget, but can't. The first I knew about it was when I was in the first or second grade. This uppity boy got mad at me one day and said, 'Your granddaddy was a thief.' I thought he was just inventing an insult until I got home and told my mother. She sat me down and told me not to believe such things. My grandfather had been accused of taking money from the company, but the family was convinced he didn't do it."

"That was a terrible way to learn about it," Jill said.

"It was. My mother told me Grandpa Liggett had disappeared. They found nothing but bones when they discovered his body several years later. The legal system ruled him guilty, but his wife and son, my dad, always believed in his innocence." Albert Liggett rubbed his eyes. "I'd like to be able to prove that, and these papers sound like they just might do it."

Jill leaned over and whispered in my ear. "He's getting tired."

I agreed. I stuck my little notebook in my pocket and stood. "We certainly enjoyed meeting you, Mr. Liggett. This little chat should help get us off to a good start. You take it easy now and get well. I'm sure we'll see you again soon."

"Just find that fellow and get me those papers," Liggett said, removing his glasses and pinching the bridge of his nose.

Kelli and Jarvis followed us into the corridor. "What do you think, Greg?" Jarvis asked.

"I think we'd better go camp on Mr. Bradley's doorstep. I hope he's just gone fishing. It would certainly make things a lot simpler."

We had just returned to the car when my cell phone rang.

"Hello," I answered.

"Who's this?"

I don't take well to that sort of question on the telephone. "Who wants to know?"

The voice was a young man's, with a good ol' boy twang. "Well, I found this here cell phone with a message on it to call you. I figured you'd know whose phone it was."

I checked the number on the caller ID. It looked familiar. I opened my note pad. "It belongs to Mr. Pierce Bradley. Where did you find it?"

"On Carey Lane, just off Highway 25."

"What's that near?"

"Near?"

I shook my head. "Is there a town somewhere around?"

"Walnut Grove," he said, "but it ain't zackly what I'd call a town."

3

E HIT BUSY VIETNAM Veterans Parkway shortly after seven o'clock, by-passing the upscale suburban town of Hendersonville as the sun dropped behind us into a smorgasbord of clouds, shooting out rays that exploded into a kaleidoscope of color. I hoped the light show was a good omen, but I didn't count on it after that phone call. Merging onto 31E, we passed the mushrooming, high-ticket subdivisions of neighboring Sumner County, turned onto Highway 25 and cruised through the less hectic historic center of Gallatin. It was hardly fifteen miles across rolling farmland to the rural community of Walnut Grove.

On the way Jill checked with a phone company source and learned that Pierce Bradley lived on Carey Lane, where the cell phone had been found, just inside Trousdale County.

The multi-hued sunset was fading to black by the time we pulled into a convenience store/service station at a four-way stop where two main highways crossed. Bright lights welcomed us to the small oasis in a darkening world of cow pastures and cornfields. The farmhand who found Bradley's cell phone said he would leave it at the market.

I parked beside two vintage cars and a pair of dusty pickups. We walked inside to find two young boys ogling a candy display like a couple of small barn owls eyeing a pack of field mice. Nearby, two bearded guys chatted with a lanky younger man who stood behind a counter laden with overpriced knick-knacks. A youthful customer with a crew cut and baggy jeans that appeared in danger of sliding off his backside strolled up and plunked a six pack beside the cash register.

The clerk cast a curious gaze at Jill and me. I speculated that he was gauging the possibility of our being clandestine inspectors from the Beer Board. He turned to the boy and said, "You sure you're old enough to buy that beer?"

The boy frowned and pulled a card from his pocket. "This says I'm twenty-one."

The clerk looked at the card and grinned. "You make this one yourself or buy it somewhere?"

The boy grabbed the pack and stomped toward the beer display. "To hell with you! Damned if I'll trade here anymore."

"Watch your language, sonny. There's a lady in the store." The clerk gave a tentative shake of his bushy head and turned to us. "What can I get for you?"

"Am I old enough for a six pack?"

"I'd have to check your ID."

I grinned. "I'm Greg McKenzie. A fellow was supposed to leave a cell phone here for me."

He reached under the counter and pulled out a small flip-top phone. Instead of handing it over, though, he gripped it in his hand. "The guy said this belongs to Pierce Bradley. What's your interest in it?"

"I'm headed for Pierce's. I intend to give it to him."

"Where're you from?"

"Nashville." I took out a business card and handed it to him. "He has some information for us. I know he lives on Carey Lane, but I'm not sure exactly where his house is. Could you help us out?"

"How come he didn't tell you?"

I'm a pro at bluffing my way around. I gave him a disarming smile. "We called his home but he doesn't answer. On a night like this, he's probably outside in the hammock."

One of the bearded men laughed. He had the look of a life spent outdoors—gray hair, tanned, muscular arms, a weathered face. I could picture him out in the field astride a chugging John Deere.

"Pierce ain't got no hammock," he said. "Anyways, the skeeters would eat him alive laying out there tonight. More'n likely he's somewhere with his coon dog."

"Is that Reba's boy?" asked the other man. He was slightly stooped, with a corncob pipe sticking out of his blue work shirt pocket.

"Yeah. Don't live too far from my place." He nodded to his friend, then turned back to me. "Carey's the next road toward Hartsville. Take a right. Go down about a mile, maybe a little more, till you see a fancy brick entrance gate on the left. A school bus'll be parked in the driveway of the next house. The one after that is Pierce Bradley's. It's a nice looking double-wide."

"Thanks," I said. I held out my hand to the clerk, who grudgingly parted with the cell phone.

Jill and I got back into my black Jeep Grand Cherokee and headed for Carey Lane.

"How did that man happen to find Bradley's phone?" Jill asked.

I'd neglected to tell her. "He pulled up to a stop sign at Carey Lane and noticed a buzzard pecking at something by the side of the road. When the sun reflected off a shiny object, he took a closer look and saw it was a cell phone."

"How do you think it got there?"

"Excellent question, babe. I don't have the slightest idea, and I can't think of a logical explanation for how it could have happened."

"Makes me wonder if he's all right."

The headlights caught Bradley's name on a mailbox right where the old farmer said we would find it. I turned into the driveway past the one with the school bus and pulled up to the house. Clouds had obscured the moon, leaving no clear view of the place. As best we could see, he had a well-kept yard and a few blooming plants around the front steps. There were no lights visible inside and no sign of the vintage Jeep.

The coon dog barked from his pen in back. Otherwise, the place appeared deserted. I rang the doorbell to make sure.

"Looks like we scored a zero," Jill said.

I had spent nights on stakeouts in places a lot more lonely and deserted than this, but it had been a long time since one left me with the uneasiness I felt here.

Jill locked her arm in mine as we paused on the small stoop, then turned back toward the driveway. As if to remind us we had invaded alien territory, a sudden gust assaulted us with a disgusting whiff of manure from a nearby pasture. Cicadas buzzed and tree frogs serenaded us with their rattling croaks. The sounds magnified the eerie mood that pervaded this forlorn place and the moonless night that closed in like the walls of a cave. Jill obviously sensed something, too. She shuddered against my arm.

"I have a bad feeling about this, Greg."

I tugged her toward the car, unwilling to voice my own sentiments. "Not much we can do around here in the dark. Let's call it a night and see what we can turn up tomorrow in the daylight."

4

WE HEARD THE PHONE ringing as we entered McKenzie Investigations Wednesday morning at eight, refreshed by our two-mile walk before the sun rose high enough to bake us like a couple of breakfast croissants. Jill skittered across to her desk and answered it.

"Good morning, Kelli," she said, motioning for me to pick up my extension.

"Did you find Mr. Bradley?" Kelli asked.

"I'm sorry, we didn't," Jill said. "Greg is on the line with us. We found Bradley's place out in the country, but his coon dog was the only one at home."

"Damn," she said softly. "Where do you suppose he is?"

"Considering the circumstances," I said, "I'm not too sure we're going to find him."

"Why would he run?"

I glanced at Jill with my try-again look. "I don't know if he's done a disappearing act, but it looks like he could be in trouble." I hesitated, then put it out there. "Somebody else may be after him besides us."

There was disbelief in her voice. "Over a ninety-year-old murder?"

"I'm talking about the papers." I told her about Bradley's cell phone being found in Trousdale County. "There could always be some other explanation, but maybe somebody else wants those papers as much as your grandfather."

"Who else would even know about it?" Kelli asked.

She hit on a question that was already bugging me. "That's

something I intend to find out. Your grandfather said he thought Bradley began making inquiries at the Chamber of Commerce. That sounds like a good place to start. Has he said anything else about what might be the significance of those papers?"

"Just that they might show how Sydney Liggett was framed. Grandpa's father was only about fifteen when the murder took place, if that's what it was. They found Sydney's remains in his car in an abandoned barn a year before Grandpa was born. And since all the bad publicity was so painful, it was rarely mentioned as he grew older. He told me his father would never say a word about it."

"That probably means there aren't any old family records around that might enlighten us," Jill said.

Kelli sighed. "I doubt it. But while Warren is down at Arnold today, I plan to dig around the house here and see if I might turn up anything."

"We plan to look into a couple of things here," I said. "Then we'll head back to Trousdale County and see how the situation looks in the daylight. Good luck on your digging foray around there. Check with you later."

Jill switched on the computer to download our email, and I glanced at my calendar. We had a few minor tasks in the works but nothing pressing. I took out Pierce Bradley's cell phone and checked the numbers in his contact list. He either had a new phone or few close acquaintances. I recognized the number for Allied Construction. Marathon was listed and someone named Pat. That was about it.

I turned to Jill. "Find anything interesting in the mailbox?"

"Somebody wants to refinance our non-existent loans, several people propose to sell us a bunch of pills we don't need, and there's the usual suggestion of how to enlarge your manhood. Since I have no complaints in that department, I guess we can delete it, too."

"Thanks for that vote of confidence," I said with a Groucho Marx flutter of my brows.

"You mentioned the Chamber of Commerce to Kelli. Shall we head downtown?"

I leaned back in my chair and tapped my fingers on the desk. "Why don't we split up. You're a much better library researcher. How about you head for the Nashville Room to see what you can find out about Marathon Motors. I'll check the Chamber for any leads there."

She gave an exaggerated imitation of a pout. "You hog all the choice assignments. I get the dregs."

"What's so choice about a visit to the Chamber?"

She planted her hands on her hips and did her Lucille Ball impression. "You don't fool me, old boy. You're going down to check out the shapely young things who answer the phones, while I get a headache with my face buried in a microfilm reader."

I laughed as I walked over and popped her on the bottom. "You're the youngest shapely thing I'm interested in, babe."

My wife was amply endowed, and I would put her up against a lot of women half her age. I gave her a peck on the cheek to emphasize the point.

It was around nine o'clock when we turned into the garage that adjoined the main library downtown, the asphalt already feeling mushy beneath an impassioned sun. I still wasn't convinced about global warming, but our little corner of the globe was damned sure doing its part today.

Jill took the escalator up to the library while I literally sweated out the three-block jaunt down Commerce Street to Third Avenue. The Nashville Area Chamber of Commerce, which I had recently heard was the third largest chamber in the U.S., had its swanky suite of offices in the Commerce Center Building. The location bordered on The District, a quaint nickname for the row of Victorian commercial structures along Second Avenue that had been converted to prime tourist territory. It included the Wildhorse Saloon, the big dining, dancing and live country music emporium that was part of the Opryland Hotel empire.

I strolled into the Chamber lobby and approached the young woman at the front desk. She had long blonde tresses partially obscuring the one blue eye. Her teeth could have graced some dentist's whitening ad. As I gazed at the twinkling eyes and coquettish smile, I remembered Jill's comment about my checking out the shapely young things. I smiled in return.

"I'm Greg McKenzie, one of your members," I said. I handed her my card.

She glanced at the inscription. "Hi, Mr. McKenzie. What can I do for you this fine summer morning?"

"This fine sweltry morning." I fanned my face with the small note pad I always carried in my shirt pocket. "I have a little question for you. If somebody called looking for information about a local businessman from many years ago, who would you refer them to?"

"That's an easy one. I'd turn them over to Craig Audain."

"Who's he?"

"He works under the senior vice president for Business Services. He's been around the Nashville business community forever."

Audain sounded like my kind of guy. "Is he in?"

"Sorry. He's out of town."

"Is there some way I can get in touch with him?"

"Not that I'm aware of." She brushed the blonde hair from over her eye. It promptly fell back into position, a Veronica Lake hairdo, if anyone remembers Veronica. "He's on a business recruiting trip that's so hush-hush I don't even know where he went."

I twisted my face into what must have appeared a frown of frustration. She hastened to add, "I'm really sorry. If you'd like, I'll make a point of giving him your card just as soon as he gets back."

"Is there someone else the caller might have been referred to?" I asked.

"Who was the person they were inquiring about?"

"A man named Sydney Liggett. He was assistant treasurer of the old Marathon Motor Works."

Her face brightened. "I remember that. It was just a few days ago. And I did switch the call to Mr. Audain."

Just my luck. Industry recruiters could be as secretive as Pentagon spooks. I'd need more than bloodhounds to track him down. "When do you expect him back?"

"In the next few days."

"Then I'd certainly appreciate your asking him to call me just as soon as possible."

I left the Chamber, jerked my Titans cap down on my forehead, and walked toward the library, fuming over this unexpected setback. I had counted on the Chamber contact pointing me toward anyone else who had knowledge of the Marathon papers discovery. I saw two possibilities. Maybe I could turn up someone who had a reason to want those papers. Or, perhaps I'd find somebody with a better take on what they might concern.

I strode up the sidewalk almost oblivious to the blare of horns along the street and the hickory smoke wafting from a restaurant whose sign I nearly collided with. A trickle of sweat down my back kept me from ignoring the fiery red ball that peeped around downtown Nashville's most prominent landmark, the Batman Building—actually the BellSouth Tower, its twin spires rising skyward like Batman's ears.

I hated having to confess to Jill that I had struck out on our only promising lead. As I mulled over what little we knew about Pierce Bradley, I realized we had yet to establish any family connections. Since he seemed to be well known around Walnut Grove, he must have parents or siblings in the area. The farmer type with the corncob pipe in his pocket at the convenience market had mentioned something about "Reba's boy." His mother must live nearby.

When I got to the Nashville Room, where comfortable chairs invited curious minds to lounge and absorb a wealth of knowledge about the local scene, I found Jill at a table with a book-like file of clippings, jotting notes on a ruled pad. She looked up as I scooted onto the chair beside her.

"This is fascinating," she said. "I'm a native Nashvillian, but I'd never heard of an automobile called Marathon. Southern Engine and Boiler Works built the car originally down in West Tennessee, in Jackson. Marathon Motor Works split off in 1910 and moved here. They bought a factory and built an office building on Clinton Street. By 1912, the plant was producing sixty cars a month. It was the only car completely manufactured in the South and was sold in every major American city, as well as in Europe, South Africa, South America and Australia."

"Impressive. What were the cars like?"

She pushed a sheet toward me. "Here's a picture."

Photographed beside Nashville's full-size replica of the Athenian Parthenon in Centennial Park, the Marathon was a sleek black touring car. With the top down, the flat, rectangular adjustable windshield was slanted at a rakish angle above the steering wheel. It had gas head-lamps and two side oil lights. An online engine gave it a long high hood you could lean against.

"What did it sell for?" I asked.

She flipped a few pages. "Based on an Olympic theme, they had three models. The Champion sold for eighteen hundred dollars as a seven-passenger touring car. The Winner was thirteen-fifty, the el cheapo Runner, nine-fifty."

"A tad less than my Jeep."

"About twenty thousand cheaper than my little red Camry. I haven't found the whole story on what happened to the company, but there were mentions of mismanagement that brought on lawsuits by suppliers."

"Did you find anything about the current rehab?"

She looked down at her notes. "A fellow named Mike Geary bought the buildings and has been restoring them. He's rented suites to musicians, photographers, artists, and such. His office is in the old Marathon administration building. He calls his development Marathon Village."

My cell phone rang. I moved to a corner beside the windows as I caught a disapproving glance from a librarian behind the nearby counter.

"I've found something that might be interesting," Kelli Kane said. Up to this point she hadn't exhibited a great deal of emotion, but I caught a touch of excitement in her voice now.

"What do you have?"

"A packet of letters dating back to the nineteen teens and twen-ties. They appear to be from my great-great-grandmother, Grace Liggett, to her sister in Texas. She writes in a beautiful script. I haven't read much yet, but she talks about Sydney's problems at work. Before I go any further, I thought I'd visit Grandpa and ask him about them."

"Let us know what you turn up," I said and switched off the phone.

I relayed the message to Jill, who nodded as she gathered up the clipping book and stuck it back in its place on a nearby shelf. "They have stuff on every local business you can imagine in these volumes," she said. "What did you find at the Chamber?"

"The guy we need to talk to is out of town. Incommunicado." I explained the situation.

"Bummer. Where does that leave us?"

"I need to call Mrs. Nelson at Allied Construction and see what she knows about Pierce Bradley's next-of-kin."

"You make it sound like he's no longer with us." She gathered up her note pad and pen, shoving them into her large handbag.

"Not necessarily. True, next-of-kin is an old military expression with that connotation, but us civilians use it in a lot of contexts, too."

"Okay. Let's get out of here so you can call her without raising too many eyebrows."

When we got down to the garage, I checked my call list and re-dialed Allied Construction. I asked the secretary if she had heard anything from Pierce Bradley. She hadn't. I asked what she knew of Bradley's family.

"I'm not sure about his mother," she said, "but I think his father died recently. He has a sister in Hartsville. She's called here for him a couple of times."

"Do you have her name?"

She asked me to hold while she looked for it. A minute or two later she came back on. "It's Patricia Cook. That's Mrs. A. B. Cook."

I shut off the phone. "We have a name. I'll bet it's the Pat I found in his cell phone. Let's head for the office and check her out. Then we can hit the road to Trousdale County."

"Good. I've been worrying about Bradley's dog out back. If he's not being cared for, you know something has happened to Bradley."

We had just taken the I-40 exit to Hermitage when the phone rang. Jill pulled it out of the small scabbard attached to my belt and answered.

"What?" It carried the sound of disbelief. "Here, tell Greg about it."

I took the phone and stuck it to my ear. "What's happened?"

"I was followed over here to the nursing home," Kelli said. "The guy was pretty sharp. I'm trained for anti-surveillance, and I tried a couple of elemental maneuvers to shake him. He stuck right with me. I didn't want it to be obvious that he'd been made. Since I didn't care who knew where I was going, I ignored him as long as possible. I tried to get a license number, but he wouldn't cooperate."

"Do you have any idea who it was?"

"None whatever." The words came across knife-edge sharp. "But I'd sure as hell like to find out."

5

"WHAT DO YOU MAKE of it?" Jill asked as we pulled into the parking lot near our office. "Who could it have been?"

"I don't know, unless Warren has some competition."

"Be serious, Greg."

"Okay. It could relate to this case, of course. But knowing her background, it might be something else entirely."

"You say 'knowing her background,' but what do we really know about her?"

I smiled as I got out of the car and went around to open her door. "You ask good questions, babe. I think it's time we learned who Miss Kelli Kane really is."

Back in the office, I got on the computer and did a quick check for Kelli Kane in Seattle. It brought up nothing.

"Her mother must have been a Liggett and married a Kane," Jill said. "Could we track it from this end?"

"If Kelli's forty-five, that would probably put her parents' marriage back in the late fifties. We could ask our newspaper buddy, Wes Knight, to look into it, but I doubt their computerized files go back that far."

"What if we just ask him to do a search on Kelli Kane?"

"If she grew up in Seattle, they won't likely have anything, unless it has a Nashville tie-in. But it's worth a try."

I caught Wes at the newspaper office, and he agreed to do a search for any stories involving Kelli Kane. I had fed him enough news tips that he was usually willing to help us out.

While waiting to hear back from Wes, we ran a check on Pierce Bradley's sister, Patricia Cook. We found her at a Hartsville address. Her husband, A. B. Cook, was listed as an officer at the local bank. I called the Cook's home number, which was the one listed in Bradley's cell phone. Patricia answered. I identified myself and asked if she might be able to help me find her brother.

"Why's a detective looking for him?" she asked. "He in trouble?"

"No, ma'am."

"What's he done?"

"Nothing that I know of. I just need to get some information from him."

"Well, I can't help you. I have no idea where he is."

Her tone indicated she not only didn't know where he was, she didn't give a damn, either.

"Mind telling me when you last saw him, Mrs. Cook?"

"Mr. McKenzie, it's a personal matter that I don't care to go into, but my brother and I have not been on very good terms of late. The last I saw of him was when he stormed out of here Monday afternoon."

"You haven't heard from him since and have no idea where he went?"

"That is correct."

Obviously, this was getting nowhere. I thanked her and hung up. When I repeated the conversation for Jill, she shook her head.

"That could be the reason he didn't show up at the nursing home Monday night."

I agreed. "If he was all bent out of shape, he might have decided to hell with it, cut out and got soused."

"If he was a drinker."

I'd had some less than stellar experiences with alcohol during my younger days, but I had long since learned imbibing was best pursued in moderation. Not everyone followed that course, though. I thought about contacting Mrs. Nelson at Allied Construction again, but she probably didn't know anymore about Bradley's drinking habits than she did my own. While Jill and I were discussing the possibilities, Wes Knight called with the results of his file search.

"I found something for you. A Kelli Kane, the granddaughter of Arthur Liggett, a Nashville hospital administrator, came to Nashville in nineteen eighty-four. She helped set up a congressional hearing on public housing."

"Who was she working for?"

"Congressman Gerald Minchie of Seattle, Washington. She was a staff assistant."

"Interesting. Did you find anything else?"

"Looks like that's about it, Greg."

"Thanks, Wes. I really appreciate it."

"No problem. Anything here I might use in a story?"

"Sorry, it's just a routine thing."

"Well, keep me in mind next time you turn up something juicy."

I gave him a bit of a chuckle. "Wes, you're on my speed dial under J for Juicy."

Jill digested that bit of news while tapping a carefully manicured finger against her chin. My wife believes a successful businesswoman pays close attention to her grooming. And though she doesn't pack her closet with expensive clothing, she keeps a careful watch on things like fingernails and hair. Of course, the charter air service she ran during my Air Force career didn't require her to do a great deal of dressing up.

"Do you want to try Seattle or Washington next?" she asked.

"Washington," I said, feeling it offered more fertile ground.

We hit pay dirt at *The Washington Post* web site. A search on Kelli Kane not only fleshed out her career as a congressional aide following graduation from the University of Washington, it revealed her marriage in 1985 to a young diplomatic officer, John Hunter. A search on Hunter turned up postings around Europe until 1996, when he was killed during a terrorist incident in Italy. The trail ended for Kelli Kane Hunter about the same time. It made sense. After her husband died at the hands of terrorists, she was ripe for recruiting by a clandestine agency. It would take more than our best reference channels to ferret out which shadowy group had coaxed her into its ranks.

At least now we knew a bit more about the young woman whose ancestor we had been hired to track. I still had one nagging question

——what had Kelli meant by her "as long as I've known him" comment about Arthur Liggett?

I was still stewing around over that one when Kelli called back, this time furious.

"Now I know what that bastard was doing!" She almost shouted into the phone.

"Who?"

"The louse who tailed me to the nursing home."

"What was he doing?"

"Making certain I was out of the way. I'm glad I found these letters before I left. There's no telling what would have become of them."

"What happened?" I motioned for Jill to get on the line.

"Drawers dumped out on the floor, cushions pulled off chairs and sofas, sheets stripped off the beds. I'd bet they were looking for those papers Mr. Bradley promised to bring to us."

She may have been right, but what in those1914 files could have prompted someone to go to such lengths was beyond my imagination.

"Have you called the police?" Jill asked.

Her reply came in a terse, "No. And don't you even think about calling them."

Jill's eyes popped open wide. "But——"

"I suspect Kelli's employer wouldn't be too happy if her name appeared in a police report," I said.

"You've got that right. Especially if it could lead to a newspaper story. Please keep in mind that I want absolutely no publicity to come out of this."

I switched on my most reassuring tone. "We always keep our clients' identities confidential, unless they agree to have it otherwise."

"There will be no otherwise in this case."

I reached for a pen and pad. "I think we'd better come take a look. What's the address?"

6

ARTHUR LIGGETT LIVED in a large two-story brick off Blair Boulevard, a main artery into an area of once genteel homes not far from the sprawling Vanderbilt University campus. Liggett was one of the few long-time residents who had not fled to the suburbs in various waves of migration that followed World War II. Renters or upwardly mobile singles and families who had bought in during recent decades occupied most of the picturesque old houses.

A squarish, three-story yellow brick with a porch that ran the full width in front, its roof anchored by six white Ionic columns, Grandpa Liggett's house featured a small, flat-roofed projection with two windows that likely opened onto a partial top floor. In contrast to most of the homes along the street, this one boasted a driveway of two concrete strips at one side. I parked my Grand Cherokee behind Kelli's rental car shortly after noon. We headed for the front steps.

Pressing a button beside the oversize mahogany door produced the sound of chimes. A Kelli Kane different from the one we had encountered earlier opened the door. This was probably closer to the real Kelli, shorn of the suave public demeanor. She wore a sweat-dampened, faded Yellowstone National Park tee shirt over well-worn brown jeans. Floppy sandals adorned a strong pair of feet with bright red toenails. I suspected the earthy young woman with a certain natural charm was seldom seen in the clandestine world she occupied before coming to Nashville. At the moment, however, the charm appeared a bit bent out of shape, as evidenced by the anger that darkened her eyes.

"Come on in," she said, waving a hand. "I've been searching for identity clues they might have left behind."

I looked past her into the room. "What did you find?"

"Zilch."

A strong smell of tobacco smoke greeted us just inside the door. Now that I had become a confirmed non-smoker, the smell was enough to bring a twitch to my nose. It also told me the origin of Arthur Liggett's emphysema. In the living room, elaborate ornamentation on the chairs and a large sofa struck me as French provincial, though I admit I'm no authority on period furniture styles. I knew Jill would straighten me out if I had it wrong. Tapestries bearing ancient Roman scenes hung on the walls. I suspected the décor had not been altered in many years. The only modern touch was a large screen TV at one side of the room. A massive brass umbrella stand with some kind of figure on top stood near the door.

"The worst mess is in here," Kelli said, leading us down a hallway papered in subdued brown stripes to a room her grandfather used as an office. She moved with an athletic grace that hinted at a strict fitness regimen. I had worked out with fitness machines at an earlier stage in life. Now the closest I got to weights was in weight watching.

Drawers had been pulled out of a file cabinet, their contents dumped on the floor. Books and papers were strewn about, swept from shelves along one wall. It looked like the aftermath of a hurricane down in the neighborhood of our Florida condo, but it didn't appear to be the work of professionals. For one thing, the chair and sofa cushions in the living room hadn't been cut open.

"I'll have to get this cleaned up before Grandpa comes home," she said, shaking her head. "I'd hate for him to see what they've done. He's an exceptionally neat and organized person. This would kill him."

"By the way," I said, "yesterday you made the comment that as long as you'd known him, your grandfather had never been a complainer. That sounds like you haven't known him all that long. What's the story?"

She arched a well-sculptured eyebrow. "You're quite perceptive, Greg. Warren told me you had the reputation of being an excellent investigator. I can see why."

"Be careful you don't give him the big head," Jill said, grinning as she folded her arms.

Kelli leaned against her grandfather's large oak roll-top desk, its pigeonholes now bare thanks to the burglar's handiwork. "My dad, Vincent Kane, ran a liquor store. That made him persona non grata to the Liggetts, particularly my grandmother, who was a straight-laced Southern Baptist. She would have nothing to do with him and absolutely forbade my mother to marry him."

Jill gave me a knowing look. "I can sympathize with your mother. My father tried to talk me out of marrying Greg. He didn't have a very high regard for career military men. He finally gave in when I refused to budge. Obviously, your mom ignored her mother's protests, too."

"She did, but Grandma refused to relent. Mom and Dad wound up eloping and moving to Seattle. I had no contact with my grandparents until after I graduated from college."

"And went to work for the congressman," I said without thinking.

Her glance bore an icy sheen. "I thought we had a deal."

"We only checked a couple of open sources," I said with a shrug. "Newspapers, to be exact. You were chronicled in the press for several years. Practically a minor celebrity."

Her frown deepened. "Then I'm sure you found out about John Hunter."

"And his death at the hands of terrorists. We noticed that Kelli Kane Hunter faded from the headlines after that. I saw no reason to look any further."

She gave a mirthless laugh. "You would have found nothing. Unfortunately, there was no way to erase my past. My parents were killed in the San Francisco earthquake in 1989. Not long after that, my grandmother died. Grandpa Liggett retired a couple of years later. He tried to stay in touch with me after that. I was living in Europe at the time, but I kept in contact as best I could. It's been more difficult in recent years."

Kelli brushed supple fingers across her damp forehead and turned toward the doorway. "Damn this heat. Would you like something cold to drink? I think I'll run up Grandpa's electric bill and keep the air conditioner running full blast."

Compared to outside, it felt fine in here. She stopped to adjust the thermostat as we followed her into a large traditional kitchen that hadn't been trashed like the office. A few dish towels lay where they had been tossed from a cabinet drawer.

"Grandpa obviously doesn't do a lot of cooking," Kelli said. She opened a refrigerator that looked almost bare and took out three soft drink cans. Jill chose a Coke. Being a non-cola person, I took the Sprite. Kelli set them on the table and brought us glasses. "Let's just sit here and talk, if you don't mind."

Jill and I joined her at a vintage kitchen table with a plastic top that reminded me of one I ate at as a wartime tyke in St. Louis. Kelli scored several points with me when she moved a crowded ash tray from the table to a counter. Opening a cardboard box filled with letter-sized envelopes, she pulled one out.

"These are the letters I found in the attic, the ones from my great-great-grandmother. Her younger sister had bundled them up and stored them. Grandpa said a cousin found the box when her mother died. She recently mailed it to him, but he hadn't had time to read any of them."

"Do they date back to the time Sydney disappeared?" Jill asked.

"Right." She glanced at the envelope in her hand. "This one sets the stage. It was written early in 1914."

She opened the flap and pulled out a brittle sheet of paper filled with dainty penmanship in blue-black ink. She read:

"Dearest Sister,

"Things have not been going at all well in Nashville. As you know, Sydney does not like to talk business at home. He spends much of his time tinkering with his woodworking hobby, building cabinets and that sort of thing. But he has been so gloomy of late that I finally prodded him into telling me something about what was wrong. Still, he would only say some things were being done at the company that were not right, and he was afraid Marathon may not survive. I asked what sort of things and he would only say it involved money, what else? I got the impression his boss was doing something that he didn't approve of.

"It is affecting young Henry, too. His father has been too preoccupied to take him hunting, which he always loved to do. I am quite worried. I hope things get resolved for the better soon. I look forward to your reply.

"Your loving sister, Grace."

"Henry was Albert's father, right?" Jill asked.

"Yes. He was about fifteen years old then. He must have married at nineteen or twenty. Grandpa was born in 1920." She thumbed through the envelopes. "Look at these four-cent stamps with Jefferson and Washington on them. Quite a difference from what we have to pay today."

"The letters were written with an old nib pen, too," Jill said. "I'll bet you never used one of those."

Kelli looked up. "My mother had a fountain pen when I was little, but I cut my writing teeth on a ballpoint." She pulled out another envelope. "This is from one written a week after the disappearance."

She opened the letter and read:

"We still have no word from Sydney. They're saying awful things about him. His boss at Marathon claims he took a lot of money and some papers from company files. They say he embezzled funds and ran off, but that's preposterous. The day before he disappeared, he told me he had found something terribly disturbing. He wasn't sure who to tell about it, things were in such a mess."

Kelli looked up. "She must have been referring to those papers that Pierce Bradley had."

I leaned an elbow on the table. "That would be my guess."

"Have you read all the letters?" Jill asked.

"No. There are quite a number of them. I'll check out the rest as soon as I can."

I glanced at my watch, saw it was around one. "We'd better get moving. We need to take another look around Bradley's place up in Trousdale County. Could you make copies of any letters that discuss Sydney's disappearance or the problems at Marathon Motors? They should help us with some background."

"Sure. Warren will be back this afternoon. I'd imagine we can find a Kinko's somewhere nearby."

I took a final swig of my Sprite and pushed back from the table.

"Have you met any of the neighbors around here? Maybe one of them saw somebody snooping about while you were gone. A car in the driveway . . . ."

"I haven't met any of the neighbors, but I think they're young couples who work."

"We'll knock on a couple of doors, then head for Walnut Grove and see what we can unearth about Mr. Bradley. We should be able to get a better reading on his house in the daylight."

Kelli joined Jill and me as we started toward the front of the house. I noticed the air conditioner had kicked in full blast, dampening the pervasive smell of tobacco smoke, and lending a touch of cold storage locker to the living room. Her mood turned gloomy as we approached the front door.

"Grandpa is having a difficult time with this nursing home stay. I sure hope you can give him some good news soon on this Marathon Motors business."

I hoped so, too, though at the moment that task seemed on a par with attempting to start a ninety-year-old touring car.

7

AFTER GETTING NO response to our knocks at the houses flanking Arthur Liggett's, we headed across town to Gallatin Road. With Jill complaining of the tummy rumbles, I stopped at one of a dozen assorted restaurants in the area around RiverGate Mall in Madison. I had no objections, of course, since the pressure of a difficult case always ratcheted up my appetite. Jill could be counted on to call my hand if I tried to overdo it.

We chose one of those places where the patrons tossed peanut hulls on the floor. I hated crunching through all that litter but knew the food would make up for it. Wrong. After we were seated, Jill glanced at the menu, then tilted her head.

"Why don't we eat light and I'll fix us something good for supper."

I'd been thinking about a nice chunk of prime rib, but with my private gourmet chef making such an offer, I couldn't refuse. While we waited for salads and half a sandwich, Jill targeted in on the problem at hand.

"After talking to his sister," she said, "do you still think somebody with an interest in those papers got to Bradley?"

I leaned back in the booth and crossed my arms. "Let's consider the alternative. I suppose if he left his sister's in a rage, he might have been mad enough to toss his cell phone out the window. But he has a responsible job and sounds like an intelligent man. Doesn't strike me as something a normal person would do."

"I suppose not. Other than that cell phone and his not being home last night, though, we really don't have anything to suggest that something out of the ordinary has happened, do we?"

"We have a strong hunch, but hunches have to be backed up with facts. Let's reserve judgment until we get a good look at his house. If we don't find anything there, we can check the hospital or the sheriff."

I got high marks for not ordering dessert, and we headed toward Trousdale County around two. The sun beamed down like the red-hot eye on an electric stove, but my trusty Jeep's air conditioner proved adequate to the challenge. By contrast, the passing parade of luckless cows had to get by with only their tails for fans. Most clustered under shade trees like Fourth of July picnickers or tested the waters of nearby ponds.

We made it to Walnut Grove with no delays. Pulling into Bradley's driveway, I noticed the not-too-distant sky seeded with cumulus clouds that had blossomed into towering thunderheads.

"Typical August build-ups," Jill said. "Not a good time for flying."

Holder of a commercial pilot's license she had used in her charter air service, Jill still owned a Cessna 172 that she flew regularly, sometimes on McKenzie Investigations business.

In the daylight, Bradley's double-wide looked much more inviting. The neatly kept lawn bordered on a walkway lined with multicolored rows of impatiens and begonias. Beige drapes covered the windows. I wondered momentarily about that but noted the house faced westward. We also kept our drapes closed against the afternoon sun. I saw no vehicles around the place.

As we headed across the concrete walk toward the front door, I noticed the drapes at one window had been left with a small gap at the bottom.

"Let's check this out," I said, moving toward the window.

Jill walked up behind me as I peered inside. "Look at this, babe." I motioned to her.

Staring into the living room, we saw a straight chair turned onto its side. Papers lay scattered about the carpet. Except for the overturned chair, it resembled the shambles we had seen at Arthur Liggett's.

"Oh, my God," Jill whispered. "This doesn't look good at all."

I pushed up the bill of my Titan's cap. "That's for damned sure."

I hurried to the door and banged on it. After waiting a few

moments, I took out my handkerchief, covered the knob and gently turned it. The door opened. I took a step inside and looked around. Other pieces of furniture appeared to have been shoved about and papers, magazines, books, anything that might have provided a hiding place, littered the floor. A range hood light had been left on in the kitchen. Its glow illuminated a dark, rusty splotch on the carpet in the doorway leading from the living room.

I turned to Jill. "Stay right here. This has the look of a crime scene. Let me check closer on one thing."

I walked carefully across to the doorway and squatted beside what appeared to be a bloody spot just outside the kitchen. If there had been blood on the vinyl floor, someone had cleaned it up. I didn't venture any farther. The implications left me with a deepening unease. Our case was about to get out of hand. As I turned toward the front door, I spotted another item that stopped me. A heavy wooden walking stick topped by what looked like a doorknob lay on the floor. There appeared to be blood on it, too.

I stepped outside and closed the door.

"What did you find?" Jill asked.

I told her about the blood and the walking stick. Then I pulled out my cell phone. "I'm calling the sheriff."

I punched in 911 and soon had the dispatcher. I identified myself and asked to speak to the sheriff.

"Sheriff Driscoll isn't here."

"Is there somewhere I could find him? I have some important information I need to get to him."

"You'll have to head out to the lake then, around Pine Cove. That's where he and most of the deputies are."

"Has there been a drowning?"

"Right. And a car in the water."

It wasn't what I wanted to hear. "Do you know what kind of car?"

"They said it was an old military-style Jeep."

8

FOLLOWING THE DISPATCHER'S directions, we headed back to Highway 25 and turned toward Hartsville. After half a mile, Old Highway 25, a narrow two-lane road, angled off to the right and wound through green swaths of pasture and woodland. Jill quizzed me as I drove.

"If it's Bradley's Jeep, how did it get from his house to the lake?"

"Somebody could have driven it there with him tied up in back." I was already stewing over the possibilities, certain in my mind that the Jeep in the lake was Bradley's and his body was inside.

"How did the driver get back?"

"It would have taken two people, one in another car."

"So we'd have a murderer and an accomplice."

"Looks that way. You're thinking like a detective, but let's not get too far ahead of ourselves."

We soon crossed a bridge where a rain-swollen creek fed into the end of the lake. After passing several scattered houses, we turned onto Boat Dock Road, then Boat Dock Lane. We finally found the gravel road that was unmarked except for a crude sign nailed to a tree. From there it was downhill the rest of the way to the lake. Not far past a small frame house that seemed to have been squeezed into the heavily wooded area, two white patrol cars sat at the side of the road. Just beyond, a narrow trail led through the trees. Looking around at all the tall evergreens, it wasn't difficult to see why this area had been named Pine Cove.

I pulled off as far as I could and parked behind one of the patrol cars, which had METRO SHERIFF painted on the side, along with Hartsville/Trousdale County. Although the smallest county in the state area-wise, and one of the least populated, Trousdale had established a metropolitan form of government a couple of years ago with its county seat, Hartsville. We heard voices coming from the lake as we got out.

"Looks like a small clearing back through the trees," Jill said.

"Yeah. And what appears to be a tow truck backed up to the water." I checked the ground as we walked past the patrol cars. "I hate to tell you, babe, but this trail looks wet and rough."

The rain must have hit this area before we arrived. After some unpleasant experiences traipsing about muddy scenes in dress shoes, Jill had learned to keep a pair of walking shoes in the Jeep. I waited while she changed.

Fresh tire tracks plowed through the soft ground, leading us past knee-high weeds and an occasional mud puddle. After passing a few towering oaks and sycamores that provided a leafy canopy overhead, we saw two other white police cruisers off to the side.

A hefty man in a tan uniform and white hat stood near the water, bellowing and waving off a couple of power boats out in the lake. "Get those damn things away from here!"

A choppy wake washed up near the shore.

Approaching him, I called, "Sheriff Driscoll?"

He turned, a frown on his tanned, leathery face. I took him to be late fifties, a muscular man with a fringe of gray peeking out beneath the hat brim.

"That's me," he said. "Who would you be?"

I introduced Jill and myself and handed him a business card.

"Got a license?"

I showed that to him, also. "We've been looking for Pierce Bradley the past couple of days. I was told you had a Jeep in the water here, and I just wondered—"

"It's Bradley," he said. "Why were you looking for him?"

"He had some papers he was supposed to bring to a client of ours."

"Well, if he hadn't driven that fool Jeep into the lake, he might have given them to you."

Judging by that description, the sheriff thought Bradley had accidentally blundered into the water. I wasn't so sure.

"Sheriff, there's something you need to know," I said. "We just came from Bradley's house. We found the door unlocked. When I looked inside, there appeared to be some blood on the carpet in the living room. I also saw a large walking stick with possible blood stains. The place looked like the scene of a struggle, with furniture knocked around."

He gave me a grim look. "Are you an ex-cop?"

"Retired Special Agent in Charge with the Air Force Office of Special Investigations." I said it casually. Say it in a formal manner and it sounds pretentious, a turnoff.

He glanced back at the card, eyes widening. "McKenzie. You the guy was involved in that Federal Reserve chairman's murder case a few months back?"

I nodded. "That was me. It got sort of hairy there at the end."

The sheriff lifted his hat and swiped a hand across his brow. "I read the newspaper reports. A friend in Nashville told me you had a lot more to do with solving the case than the stories told."

"Maybe I'd better hire your friend to handle my public relations," I said, grinning.

A diver's head cleared the surface of the lake, his face mask glinting in the sun. "Hey, Sheriff," he yelled. "I got the chains hooked. She's ready to go."

"Listen up, everybody," Driscoll called out. "I don't want anybody touching anything else. We're treating this as a crime scene. I'll get on the phone to Wayne Fought. Looks like we got ourselves a TBI case."

He spoke on his cell phone for a minute, then sent one deputy to secure Bradley's house and ordered another out to the road to stop anyone attempting to come in. A third deputy brought out a roll of crime scene tape and began to cordon off the area. When Driscoll appeared satisfied everything was being done to secure the scene, he walked back to where Jill and I stood.

"Tell me more about your interest in Pierce Bradley," he said.

I explained about the papers found at the old Marathon Motors

Works and Bradley's failure to bring them in Monday night.

"That's 'cause he probably wound up in the lake here Monday night," Driscoll said.

He grinned at the surprised looks Jill and I gave him.

"Pretty good detective work, huh? Actually, a fisherman reported seeing the vehicle in the water this afternoon. It triggered one of those moments of enlightenment with one of my deputies. His mother lives just up the road. She had told him about hearing cars going in and out of here late Monday night. She thought it sounded like two going in and only one coming out. He figured it was fishermen and the other one didn't come out until after she'd gone to bed. But looks like she was right in the first place."

That dove-tailed with Jill's speculation on a murderer and an accomplice. Could it have had anything to do with the Marathon papers? I decided to press for the sheriff's take on possible explanations.

"If it turns out to be something other than an accident, do you have any idea who might have wanted him dead?"

"Oh, yeah. I could probably come up with several. I'd hate to think any of them really did it, but I wouldn't rule anybody out."

Jill broke her silence. "Would his sister, Mrs. Cook, be one of them?"

Driscoll frowned, his eyes alert beneath the brim of his white Stetson. "What do you know about her?"

"Greg talked to her earlier today. She indicated they'd been having some trouble. She said the last she saw of him was when he stormed out of her house Monday afternoon."

"Interesting." He turned to me. "How much do you know about Bradley?"

"Very little," I said. "Just that he was a supervisor for Allied Construction." I watched him ease his holster.

"No use standing around here," he said. "Come on over and sit in my car while we wait for the TBI agent and his crew. They should be on the way."

As we walked over to his car, he told us about Bradley's service as an A-10 pilot in Desert Storm. I'd had a little contact with Warthog crews during my OSI career. They were a daring lot, flying low level close air support of ground forces.

I let Jill take the passenger seat next to the sheriff, while I lounged on the prisoner side of the divide.

"When did he get out of the Air Force?" I asked.

"Around ninety-two. His father had a large farm west of Hartsville. Had a big tobacco allotment, plus a sizeable herd of Black Angus. Pierce came back home and helped his dad for a few years. He bought a Piper Apache and put in a landing strip on the farm. He's helped me out several times when we needed some air surveillance."

"How long has he been in the construction business?" Jill asked.

Driscoll listened to a burst of radio traffic squawking over his portable. "I think he went with Allied Construction in the late nineties," he said after a moment. "Pierce was planning to buy into ownership of the company. He got that double-wide in 2000 and moved off the farm."

I squirmed closer to the window and tugged at my collar. The sheriff had left the windows open, but despite the shade of the forest I'd have sworn a layer of hot coals had been dumped on the roof. "Any idea what the trouble was between Pierce and his sister?"

"Their mother died shortly after he moved out. Mr. Bradley passed on earlier this year. The old man left the two kids equal shares. Pat wanted to sell the place and get the money. Her husband's a banker. But Pierce didn't want to sell. I don't think he wanted to give up that airstrip. She said he could buy her out, but all his money was committed to getting a chunk of Allied Construction. I understand she threatened to go to court and force the sale."

"That's probably what the argument was about at Mrs. Cook's place Monday afternoon," Jill said.

The sheriff spread his hands. "Could be. Pierce was a personable guy, but he's always had a hot temper. I had to save his ass, pardon the expression, when he got in a fight with the manager at Cumberland Farm Supplies. The man got a little too aggressive over money he claimed Pierce's father owed. On another occasion, Pierce got in a scuffle and broke a guy's arm after he caught him messing around his airplane."

"Sounds like any number of people could have harbored a grudge against him," I said.

"Right. And there's another possibility I hadn't thought of until now. I can't tell you anything about it because it concerns an ongoing investigation that involves other agencies. Could have been retaliation for some of that aerial spying I told you about."

I didn't like the sound of that. Too many complicating factors could make it difficult to get the sheriff or the Tennessee Bureau of Investigation to give much thought to our problem. Particularly since we only had a strong hunch, no solid evidence, that could tie the missing Marathon papers into Bradley's death.

Driscoll was a likeable guy, bordering on garrulous, as were most politically-minded sheriffs. He regaled us with several of his escapades and was well into a tale about how he'd busted a family with a meth lab in their barn when my peripheral vision caught a man walking down the trail. I saw him heading for our car. Jill and I followed Driscoll as he climbed out to greet the new arrival, a man about my height, five-ten, with a bit less around the middle than me.

"Hi, Wayne," the sheriff said. "You made good time."

"I was just finishing up some paper work in Lebanon when you called. I headed right up 231. Didn't take long. Say you have a body in the water?"

This was obviously Wayne Fought, the TBI agent. He looked around forty, dressed in a short sleeve sport shirt and khaki pants, a Glock 40 holstered at his belt. He had the blunted nose of a boxer and almost black eyes that showed no emotion as he gave Jill and me the once-over.

"It's a fellow named Pierce Bradley," said Driscoll. "He's pretty well known around Hartsville. The diver says he's still in his Jeep where it landed."

"You said it looks like murder. What makes you think that?"

The sheriff turned toward us. "You need to meet the McKenzies."

He made the introductions and I shook the agent's hand, getting a firm grip and a wary eye in the process.

"They're private investigators out of Nashville," the sheriff said. "I'll let Mr. McKenzie tell you what they saw."

I briefly related our interest in Bradley and told Agent Fought what we found at the house on Carey Lane.

His forehead furrowed as he asked in a voice that snapped, "Did you touch anything inside the house?"

"No. I used a handkerchief on the door knob. I moved carefully across the living room and only looked at the blood stains. I'm a retired Special Agent in Charge with the Air Force Office of Special Investigations. I was likely handling crime scenes while you were still in diapers." No way to win friends, but his patronizing tone had grated.

The look I got said it all. Of course, I could have smudged any fingerprints on the doorknob, but the chances of lifting usable prints in a situation like that are slim.

If Fought was impressed by my professional credits, he did a good job of hiding it. He looked around the area and turned back to Sheriff Driscoll. "I knew your boys had already beaten a path down here. I hope they left us some undamaged tire tracks."

"I'd have secured the area from the start," Driscoll said, "but I thought we were dealing with a simple accident."

Fought glanced at his watch. "Our investigators are on the way from Nashville. Probably be close to five o'clock before they get here." He turned to Jill and me. "It's our version of CSI. We call it a Violent Crime Response Team."

"You have a great crime lab," I said. "I visited your headquarters when I did a stint as an investigator for the DA in Nashville after I retired."

A little flattery never hurt. This small foray seemed to put me in a little better graces. Though it warmed him up a bit, we were still far from getting admission to the inner circle.

"I'm sure you folks have other business to attend to," he said. "I'll need to get a detailed statement from you, but we can do that later. You have a card?"

I gave it to him. "We can be available whenever you need us. Look, we'll stay out of your way, but I'd like to be here to see the man we've been searching for when you pull him out of the water."

Agent Fought leaned back against his car, folded his arms, looked me in the eye. "Okay, but it's going to be a while. I need to get with the sheriff and his men and see what's happened up to this point."

I motioned to Jill. "We'll head on up the road and be back in a bit."

We walked up the trail in silence until we were out of earshot. "Where to now?" Jill asked.

"Let's head back up to Bradley's house and see if any of the neighbors are at home. Somebody needs to look after that coon dog, and I'd like to know if they heard anything around there Monday evening."

9

WE DROVE BACK TO Carey Lane and pulled into the driveway with the fancy brick entrance. Two doors down, a sheriff's car sat beside Bradley's house, which had been decorated with yellow and black garlands of crime scene tape.

"Somebody has a nice SUV up here," Jill said.

I swung onto the circular drive that ran in front of a large two-story brick home with white shutters. Despite being out in the boonies, some of the newer homes in the area rivaled those in Nashville's affluent suburbs. I parked behind a Cadillac Escalade. We walked up to the front door past an artful array of pink, white and purple blossoms and rang the bell.

A young woman in blue jeans and a tee shirt with an orange basketball and a Lady Vols logo opened the door. She looked tall enough to have been a player at some point in her life. She held the door as though trying to decide whether to invite us in. "Yes?" she said, smiling.

I handed her a business card. "We're Greg and Jill McKenzie from Nashville. I presume you're acquainted with your neighbor, Pierce Bradley?"

"Yes, of course. Has something happened to him?" Her smile dimmed. "I saw a sheriff's car pull in over there a little while ago."

"We're not sure what's happened, but we've been looking for him. He has some information we need. Apparently he hasn't been around his house since Monday night. Did you by chance hear anything going on over there that evening?"

She shook her head. "We watched a long movie on DVD that night, then went to bed. We wouldn't have heard anything short of a major riot."

"You must sleep like I do," Jill said. "I think the house could fall around me and I wouldn't wake up."

"That's me." She paused, looking thoughtful. "I don't think I've seen Pierce in the past few days. He stopped by Saturday to ask my husband about a new radio. John's a pilot, too."

Jill perked up. "Does he have his own plane?"

"He's a part owner with some guys from Nashville. He flies now and then with Pierce."

Sounded like another prospect if we needed more background on the late Mr. Bradley.

"You might try Martha Urey next door. They're a lot closer than we are. She looks after Pierce's dog when he's gone." She stared off to her left. "The bus is back, so she should be at home. Sorry I can't help."

"No problem," I said. "But if you think of anything else, we'd appreciate a call."

We drove next door and pulled up beside the yellow school bus. I caught the deputy giving us the eye from his car in Bradley's driveway. This house was a brick and frame ranch, much smaller than the one we had just visited.

The woman who came to the door wore jeans and a yellow shirt with the sleeves rolled up. A little older and a bit heftier than her neighbor, she had the frazzled look of someone who had just come through a trying experience. She frowned as she studied first Jill, then me.

"Are you Jackie Varner's folks?" She spoke in a hesitant voice.

Thinking of the school bus, I got the picture. I smiled. "No, Mrs. Urey. We're not related to any of your passengers. We're private investigators from Nashville." I handed her a card. "We wanted to ask a few questions about your neighbor, Pierce Bradley."

Her faced relaxed, but not into a smile. "What's going on? I was planning to go talk to that deputy. When I heard Rambo barking this morning, I went over there and he obviously hadn't been fed. Pierce always tells me when he's gonna be away."

"I think you'd better take care of the dog until it's clear what's going on," I said. "We've been looking for Bradley to get some information for a client of ours. It seems he hasn't been around since Monday night. We're wondering if you might have heard anything out of the ordinary over there that evening?"

She rubbed a hand across her cheek. "Monday night? Seems like maybe somebody was visiting Pierce that night. I don't remember hearing any racket, though. I'm not sure when he left, either."

"It was a man?"

"Sorry. Just an expression. I didn't see who it was."

'Did you notice what kind of car they were driving?"

"Hmm. I really didn't pay all that much attention to it."

Jill nodded sympathetically. "It's tough to recall things like that. Sometimes I'll try to picture the scene, like the driveway in this case, and it'll come back to me."

Martha Urey squinted her eyes as she looked over toward Bradley's house. "Wasn't a sheriff's car for sure. Seems maybe it could have been one of them little sports cars. You know, with a rakish sweep to the front end."

"Do you remember the color?"

"It was pretty dark when I saw it."

We thanked her for her help. I gave her the usual call us if you think of anything else routine. Occasionally a witness would recall more details later, particularly if they talked to somebody else about what they saw. We headed back to my Jeep.

"Sounds like a Corvette," Jill said.

I opened the door for her and stood there a moment. "Could be, but there are any number of little sports cars with rakish front ends. And don't forget, eyewitness accounts can be notoriously unreliable." That was a point most people didn't understand.

"Then why bother asking?"

"Sometimes we get lucky. What I'm saying is we need a lot more info before we can slot that little piece into the right place in the puzzle. Let's get back over to the lake and see if the investigators have arrived."

THE STRING OF VEHICLES clustered along the shoulder of the road looked like worshipers parked for Sunday morning at a country church. The sheriff's cars had been moved out to allow a more detailed search of the lakefront. A few other cars and pickup trucks added to the gaggle of vehicles. A small group of men stood around the deputy who had been posted at the opening of the trail. Word of the tragic drowning had probably spread to the nearby boat dock. I parked behind a pickup, and we walked down to the uniformed officer.

"Has the TBI truck arrived yet?" I asked.

"Just got here."

"Agent Fought told us to come on back."

He pulled out his radio and said something about "the PI and his wife." I heard Sheriff Driscoll's voice reply, "Send 'em on in."

We hiked into the woods, happy the clouds had migrated westward, blocking out the sun. The humidity made me feel like I'd forgotten to dry off after a shower. We found a large white truck parked behind the sheriff's car. Lettering on the side spelled out Tennessee Bureau of Investigation, below that "Crime Scene Investigation."

One of the techs logged us in. Wayne Fought stood a few yards away with Sheriff Driscoll, talking to a couple of the investigators. I debated whether to tell them about our visit to Martha Urey. The idea lost out in the debate. I decided it would be best to stick with our side of the bargain and stay out of the way. The small bit of info we had gleaned might make a good bargaining chip later on.

I watched as one of the techs bagged a few small items the deputies had picked up in their search around the lakefront. It looked like cigarette packs or candy wrappers. Another took photos of the entire area. Photography usually proved one of the major sources of information gained from a crime scene. My interest centered on their truck, which was a new one I hadn't encountered. Three large panels on each side lifted up to give access to all the tools of the trade. One section featured every size, shape, and type of evidence bag or container imaginable. Large metal boxes in another bore such labels as "Fingerprint," "Serology," and "Firearms." No doubt specialized kits for gathering evidence in those fields.

The driver finally cranked up his wrecker and began to pull the Jeep out of the lake. The photographer kept snapping pictures as the vehicle emerged like a submarine breaking the surface of the water. It resembled some mud-encrusted sea monster trailing tentacles of weeds. I saw a bloated body slumped against the steering wheel when the front end came up out of the water.

Fought and Driscoll walked over to the vehicle with one of the rubber-gloved techs, who moved the victim's head around for a better view.

"That's Bradley," the sheriff said. "He loved this old Jeep. Even installed seat belts in it."

"He's strapped in," said Agent Fought.

The investigator studied the head for a few moments. "The question is was he really driving? Looks like he's been struck a pretty good blow just in front of the right ear. Not the sort of injury that would likely come from a plunge into the lake."

My cell phone rang at that point and I turned away from the group to answer it.

"Greg, we need your help," said Warren Jarvis, a dire note in his voice.

"What's wrong?"

"I think I just killed a guy."

10

I STOOD THERE FOR a moment in shock, not sure I heard what I had just heard. After what we had encountered at the lake, Warren's words hit me like a thunderbolt.

"You what? Who?"

"It was an accident. I've called the police. I guess they'll send a homicide officer. Do you have any contacts there?"

"I have a good contact in Homicide, Detective Phil Adamson. He knows about that scroll business in Israel and that you helped me out over there. But what happened?"

"I'll tell you the whole story when you get here. Basically, I got back to Mr. Liggett's house a little while ago and found Kelli being accosted by the guy who tailed her across town earlier in the day. When he tried to run, I tackled him. He hit his head on a large metal umbrella stand. Before we could do anything, he was gone."

After hearing that horrifying experience, I couldn't add to his misery by telling him about Pierce Bradley. I took a deep breath. "You have Kelli as a witness. I think they'll treat it as an accident, at least initially. Jill and I are up in Trousdale County. We'll head on back right now. Hopefully we'll be there within an hour. Just be careful what you say. You might want to get a lawyer."

Despite the anxiety evident in his voice, Jarvis seemed to be in complete control. I knew he had faced many crises during his Air Force career, but I suspected few rivaled this one. Jill agonized over the possibilities all the way to Nashville. Looking at it from an investigator's standpoint, I knew there could be real problems, especially if somebody like Murder Squad Detective Mark Tremaine, my personal nemesis from the past, happened to show up. But since the person responsible for the death was known, it wouldn't be a job for the Murder Squad.

The big question we faced was could they keep the story from the newspapers, and if not, could they keep Kelli's name out of it? Maybe I could prevail on Phil Adamson to soft pedal her role in the affair.

When we got back to discussing events in Trousdale County, Jill looked downcast. "It's really sad when a young man survives all the carnage in a war zone, then comes home and has one of his fellow citizens do this to him."

This kind of case always stirred feelings of sadness and anger, but over the years I had learned to compartmentalize the anguish, step aside, and view the situation with as little emotion as possible. Jill, new at this detective business, had a long way to go.

"It's bad," I said, "but the best thing we can do for him is to find those papers he planned to give Arthur Liggett. Plus, see if we can tie them into his murder."

"Without Bradley's help, where do we start looking?"

"I need to give that some thought. I wish we could have stayed until they searched his house. Maybe they'll turn up the Marathon papers when they pick the place apart."

"But if the murder had anything to do with them, the papers probably won't be there."

I turned off Twenty-first Avenue onto Blair Boulevard and gave her a sidewise glance. "Then let's hope Bradley stashed them somewhere else. At any rate, we need to put on a full court press to find those papers before anything else breaks loose."

A Metro Fire Department ambulance pulled away from the Liggett house just as we drove up. A white Malibu, the type used by Metro homicide detectives, sat at the curb. Three cars were parked in the driveway, including Kelli's and Warren's rentals. I parked behind the Malibu, and Jill and I walked to the front door.

When I punched the chime button, Kelli promptly opened the door. She had changed into brown slacks and a light green blouse. Her hair had been put up in a swirl and nested gold rings dangled from her ears. Her eyes were dark with stress. She looked more vulnerable than we had ever seen her.

"Come on in," she said. "Detective Adamson is here."

Thank God for small favors. As we walked in, Phil rose from a chair opposite where Warren sat on the sofa, hands clasped beneath his chin. Tall and gaunt, Adamson looked like a guy with his nose out of joint. Not figuratively, but literally. It angled slightly to one side, the result of a bad encounter early in his police career. He was a sharp investigator who taught the subject for other law enforcement officers at a local community college. Phil stuck a pen in his shirt pocket and swiped a hand through thinning brown hair, turning to me with a modest grin instead of his usual dour look.

"After Colonel Jarvis told me about the connection, I figured you'd show up sooner or later." He looked over at my partner. "Hi, Jill."

She waved.

Phil and I had been friends for some time, but our relationship was more firmly cemented a few months earlier when we shared a traumatic moment with an armed and deadly felon. I returned the grin.

"I wasn't in any hurry," I lied. "I knew Metro's finest would have everything under control. How's it going?"

"If by 'it' you mean the case at hand, I've about wound up the initial phase of the investigation. The Medical Examiner's man has already been here and gone."

I looked around at Warren and Kelli, who were now seated side-by-side on the sofa. I was sure they weren't happy with that "initial phase" remark.

"Would you excuse us a moment, folks," I said. "Come on back to the kitchen, Phil."

He followed me down the hall. "You seem pretty familiar with the place."

"Jill and I were here early this afternoon." I pulled out a chair and beckoned him to join me at the table. "Matter of fact, we sat right here and talked with Kelli about her grandfather. Getting to the case at hand, how about filling me in? All I know is Warren called and said a guy was dead."

I didn't want to say any more than necessary until I learned what they had told Phil. He was smart enough to know what I had in mind.

"According to the colonel and Miz Kane, who I presume is his girlfriend, this guy comes in posing as a real estate agent wanting to list the house for sale. Said he was told Kane's grandfather, who owns the place, was in a nursing home. She accuses him of following her to the nursing home earlier, and he gets his dander up. She says he made a threatening move toward her just as the colonel walks in. She screams, the guy sees Jarvis and starts to run. Jarvis says he tried to grab the guy but knocked him off balance. The guy falls and hits his head on a big brass stand with a cupid figure holding an arrow."

I flinched at the image. It was the stand I had noticed when we first came in. "Did he hit the cupid?"

"The arrow caught him right in the temple. The paramedics say that's likely what killed him. We'll let the medical examiner say for sure."

Two deaths in three days from blows to the head was scary. I leaned my elbows on the table. "Do you know who the guy was?"

"Yeah. He was one of yours."

"What's that mean?"

"A private investigator named Harold Sharkey. Know him?"

I had never met the man, being new to the ranks, but I'd heard he was not too highly thought of by most others in the profession.

"By reputation," I said, "which isn't very good. I hear he'll take on anything, legal or otherwise."

"That's my impression. Why do you suppose he was tailing Miz Kane? I have to tell you, Greg, your friends are holding back something. Kane has been awfully evasive. I haven't been able to get much out of her at all."

I debated for a moment what to say. He could check into her background and hit a dead end, which I was sure he would. But that would only make him bore in harder on both Kelli and Colonel Jarvis.

"Can I tell you something in the utmost confidence, Phil? It mustn't go any farther than right here."

He clenched his teeth and twisted his mouth to one side. "You don't mind putting a guy on the spot, do you? You old military types and your secrets. Oh, well. If it'll help me understand what's going on here, let's have it."

"I have your word?"

"You have it."

"First, let me put in a plug for Warren Jarvis. He's a topnotch guy, Air Force Academy graduate, son of a Baptist preacher from Indianapolis. You already know he was the air attaché in Tel Aviv who provided lifesaving assistance when I sorely needed help locating Jill in Israel."

"He reminded me of that."

"Jarvis met Kelli several years ago when he was working on the project developing the F/A-22 Raptor, the Air Force's new state-of-the-art fighter plane. She suddenly left the project, vanished like an airplane disappearing into a cloud. When he tried to find where she'd gone, no one would tell him anything. The Pentagon even denied her existence. Seems she was working undercover for some agency he couldn't discover. Well, she's still working for them and recently got back from an overseas assignment. When she flew to Nashville to check on her grandfather, Jarvis was on the same plane, headed for Arnold Air Force Base."

"First time he'd seen her in years?"

"Right. He recognized her immediately. He approached her when they landed in Nashville. She denied who she was at first. But after Jarvis told her he'd been looking for her all that time, even got into the intelligence business to better his chances of finding her, she broke down and admitted he had it right."

"Sounds like a fairy tale romance."

I caught the hint of a grin. "Call it whatever you wish."

Adamson sat back in his chair, hands on his hips. "Okay, she's some kind of federal spook. As far as I can determine, she's not in any way responsible for Sharkey's death. So what's the problem?"

"The problem is if the media gets Kelli's name and plasters her picture all over the newspapers and on TV, it'll probably blow her cover and could put her at risk. She may be involved in some anti-terrorism operation, Phil. I don't think we should do anything that might put her in danger."

I wasn't sure if the patriotic pitch would help, but it was worth a try.

"You know I'll have to put her name in the report," he said.

"Just say as little as you have to about her."

"I'll see what I can do. But I still want to know the reason Sharkey tailed her and came nosing around here. Your friends claim they have no idea. I'm not so sure of that. You got any take on it?"

Now he had me in a quandary. "I'm not at all sure, but it could have something to do with a case I'm currently working."

"And that would be?"

"Sorry, Phil. The client insists on absolute confidentiality."

"And the client is probably sitting in there. Hey, partner. What happened to that quid pro quo arrangement we used to have?"

I put my hands on the table and pushed back. "Damn. This is embarrassing, Phil. It could be something entirely different, you know. Maybe somebody has an agenda involving Arthur Liggett. Hopefully, I'll be able to nail something down tomorrow on my case. If I find any connection, I'll let you know."

He gave me a chilly look. "If there isn't, then we may never know. From what I hear, Sharkey was a loner. He had a hang-up with writing things down, in case his office got tossed. We'll do it, of course, but probably won't find anything."

A scrupulous record keeper, I had no idea how you could run a PI shop any other way. The guy either had a great memory or a penchant for writing fiction.

Phil aimed his finger like the barrel of a pistol. "You realize when the newshounds see the PI angle, they're gonna jump on this like pups in a frenzy. You'd better see that Miss Kelli gets lost for a few days. We'll want them both available for further questioning, though."

I got up from the table. "Shouldn't be any problem. Jarvis is assigned to the Defense Intelligence Agency at the Pentagon. He'll have to report the details to them, and I'm sure they won't be too happy. But accidents happen."

"Yeah. You'd better hope the DA sees it that way."

11

PHIL HAD CALLED FOR a wrecker to haul Sharkey's car off to the tow-in lot. As soon as he left, I suggested Warren and Kelli get their cars away from Blair Boulevard and meet us at our office. On the way, I told Jill about my conversation with Adamson.

"Sounds like you did a pretty good job of defusing the situation," she said.

"That remains to be seen. You can be certain Phil's going to do a lot of digging. And I feel the same way he does. I'd sure as hell like to know what Harold Sharkey was up to, who he was working for."

"How about this, Greg? What if whoever was after the Marathon papers hired him to make sure Kelli was away so they could search her grandfather's house? Then he came back to see what else he could learn from her."

I nodded. "Good scenario. Of course, it assumes someone is after the papers, which we have no proof of as yet. And if they're the same people who killed Bradley, it would mean they didn't find the papers on him or at his house."

"Which means we'd still have a chance to recover them."

I reached over and patted her knee. "I like your positive attitude, babe. Let's try to keep it up when we talk to our clients."

It was well after six when we swung onto I-40, headed for Hermitage. Rush hour traffic had slowed and the only bottleneck was perennial construction between downtown and the airport. We tuned in a weather report, getting the usual August forecast for tomorrow —hot and humid, possible afternoon thunderstorms. At least for the moment the sky was being swept blue by a steady southerly breeze.

"I need to get a little flying time in during the next day or so," Jill said. "Anywhere we need to go?"

I shrugged. "I hope not." Flying wasn't my favorite mode of transportation. I used it when necessary and knew I'd have one of the best pilots in the business. Still, every time I made it back to terra firma, I vowed I'd never leave again. Maybe it all stemmed from my parents' death in an airliner crash on the way to my graduation at the University of Michigan. Maybe it's just some kind of weird hang-up. anyway, I preferred to keep my four wheels and my two feet on the ground.

By the time we pulled into the parking area, the evening crowds were beginning to pack the restaurants near our office. I unlocked the door and we headed for our desks. The answering machine light winked as though burdened with a nervous tick.

"I'll check the calls," I said.

There were two messages. I played the first one. It was a real shocker.

"Mr. McKenzie, I'd appreciate your giving me a call. This is a fellow PI., Harold Sharkey. We've never met, but I've heard good reports about you. I'm sure you'd be happy to give a little professional courtesy to another investigator. I have a question about your interest in a certain woman visiting here."

Jill looked at me with a raised eyebrow as he rattled off his phone number. "Did I just hear what I thought I did?"

I pressed the repeat button.

"How did he know about us?" she asked.

"I'd guess he came by Liggett's house while our car was parked in the driveway around noon. He checked our license number. The call was made around one-thirty."

"Did he think we would tell him what we knew about Kelli?"

"I'd say that's exactly what he thought, stupid bastard."

"Greg!"

She didn't care for my four-letter vocabulary. Seven letters, either. "Sorry, babe. But that's the most descriptive term I have for him. Though I guess I shouldn't talk ill of the dead."

"Right. But it still doesn't tell us anything about his interest in Kelli, does it?"

"No. Let's check the other message."

This one was from TBI Agent Wayne Fought. He left a cell phone number where I could reach him.

"What do you suppose he wants?" Jill asked.

"Probably for us to come in for a formal statement. I'd better give him a call before Jarvis and Kelli get here."

Fought answered on the third ring, and I identified myself.

"I need to come down to Bureau Headquarters in the morning. I want to see what the crime lab boys have come up with on that Jeep. I need you and your wife to meet me over there and give us a statement."

"Sure. What time?"

"How about eleven o'clock?"

"We'll be there. Did the wound on Bradley's head appear consistent with a blow from the walking stick in his living room?"

"I'm not at liberty to discuss the investigation at this point, Mr. McKenzie."

"Did you find anything at Bradley's house that looked like those Marathon Motors papers we mentioned?"

"No, but I can't tell you any more."

"Think about it, Agent Fought. A little discussion between us might prove quite fruitful. There's a good possibility of a tie-in with Pierce Bradley's involvement in this case we're working in Nashville. Cooperation could benefit us both."

"We'll talk about it in the morning," he said and hung up.

I had just relayed his request to Jill when Jarvis and Kelli walked in wearing solemn faces.

"Cheer up," I said, strolling over to give the colonel a pat of encouragement. "I think Phil Adamson is going to push this thing as purely an accident."

"That's not what's bothering me," he said. "I was against it, but Kelli insists if you're going to be our advocate, we should level with you."

I frowned. "What the devil does that mean?"

Kelli spoke up. "I'm the one who made the tackle that killed Mr. Sharkey, not Warren. He took the blame in an attempt to keep my name out of it."

12

THEY TOOK CHAIRS AS I perched on the edge of my desk. "Frankly," I said, "I wish you hadn't told me. I may be a personal advocate, but not a legal one. There's no client confidentiality that would stand up in a courtroom."

"I'm not concerned about that," Kelli said. Her face showed the strain of an agonizing decision. "You and Jill have put forth a lot of effort on this. I want to keep everything above board. If there is anything else you'd like from me, just say the word."

"I think I can speak for both of us," Jill said, leaning forward on her desk. "We really appreciate your feelings, and we'll let you know if anything comes up where we could use your help."

I just hoped Phil Adamson didn't ask me anything else about the episode on Blair Boulevard. I didn't want to cause our clients any more problems, but I would have to answer with the truth if questioned.

"Detective Adamson told us this Harold Sharkey character was a private investigator," Kelli said. "Is there any way to find out who he was working for?"

"No. That's something Phil wanted to know, too, but he won't likely find out." I moved around to sit at my desk. "Are you sure this couldn't have any connection with your work?"

She gave me a you've-got-to-be-kidding look. "The kind of people I have to deal with rely on their own resources. They don't hire PI's."

"Just thought I'd ask. Now, I hate to bring up more bad news, but you won't be getting a visit from Pierce Bradley."

"Why not?" Jarvis asked.

"Mr. Bradley is no longer with us."

"You mean—"

I gave a slight nod. "He's dead."

They looked at me in shock. Kelli recovered first. "How?"

I told them about the Jeep in the lake, what we had learned from Pierce Bradley's sister, our visit to Bradley's house, and the information Sheriff Driscoll had given us concerning the former A-10 pilot.

"Jeez. Sounds like any number of people could have wanted to do him in," Jarvis said.

I gave a dismissive wave of my hand. "That was my initial reaction. But there's still the issue of the missing papers. Maybe I'm grasping at straws, but my instinct says this is all tied together somehow. The Tennessee Bureau of Investigation is handling the murder case. Jill and I are meeting in the morning with Agent Wayne Fought."

Jarvis looked at me with renewed interest. "Will he help you look for the Marathon papers?"

Jill spoke without a trace of humor. "I think he'd like us to fade into the sunset."

She was right, but I thought it best to put a little more positive spin on things for our clients' benefit. "I hope we can convince him there's a link in our cases. It would sure help if we had something more tangible to go on."

I saw Jill glance up at the clock across from her desk. "I move we adjourn this discussion to a nice restaurant across the parking lot. It'll soon be eight o'clock."

"Damn." Kelli grabbed her handbag off the floor and stood. "I promised Grandpa I'd come back over there and fill him in on what we'd learned. I'm going to omit the part about Harold Sharkey."

"Good idea," I said, standing behind my desk. "Don't forget Detective Adamson's warning to stay out of sight if you want to avoid the media."

"I'll check into the motel where Warren's staying. You have my cell phone number if you need me."

"I plan to keep a low profile, too," Jarvis said. "That's what the duty officer I talked to advised. I haven't been able to reach my immediate superior yet. I think I can arrange to take a few days leave when I explain the situation."

After they left, Jill and I were gathering up our things to head home when the phone rang. I checked the Caller ID, saw the newspaper identified and let the answering machine pick up.

"Hey, Greg," said Wes Knight's voice. "I didn't expect to find you in, but give me a call when you get this message. A reporter turned in a story about an accidental death out beyond Hillsboro Village. And guess what? That woman you asked about was identified as a witness."

Jill just looked at me and shook her head.

13

AFTER A FULL DAY of dashing back and forth across the countryside, alternately baking in the sun and chilling out in the air conditioned depths, Jill begged off the promised "something good" concoction for supper. We stopped at the restaurant across the parking lot and dined on their seafood special. Before getting to the main course, I had a sudden thought and called Kelli's cell phone. She had arrived at the nursing home a few minutes earlier.

"Just so we can rule out everything else," I said, "how about asking your grandfather if he's had any major disagreements in the past, something that might prompt a retaliatory trashing like you found today."

She hesitated a moment. "Are you suggesting it could have been a spiteful act rather than the work of untidy snoopers?"

"Not likely, but possible."

"Very well. I'll ask. If I learn anything, I'll call you at home."

I snapped the phone shut and waded into a large helping of grouper with a savory sauce.

"Quite good," I said, brushing my lips with a napkin. "But not nearly as good as what you'd have fixed, I'm sure."

Jill gave me a skeptical look. "After a day of slave-driving, you're trying to butter me up, huh?"

I chuckled. "I told you some days it would be like this. Then it gets worse."

She paused in the midst of buttering a roll. "After we wind up this case, let's take a week or so off and go down to Perdido Key."

We owned a condo on the narrow neck of sand that lay just off the Gulf coast southwest of Pensacola. I hadn't been all that thrilled about the place until our best friends sent us down there to solve a murder. That was the energizing experience that had prompted Jill to suggest, and me to accept, the idea of opening a private investigation agency. The attitude adjustment had also mellowed my view of the Florida barrier islands.

"Sounds fine to me," I said. "We should be due a little R&R."

"Rest and Recuperation." She sighed. "I could use a bit of that when we get home."

"I will be at your beck and call," I said.

"We'll see about that."

It was almost nine when we arrived at our cabin in the woods, actually a large two-story log house not far from the county line. I had installed motion-triggered floodlights that bathed the outside. On the inside, a sophisticated burglar and fire alarm system warned of intruders. We'd had a couple of nasty experiences in the not-so-distant past, so I always checked the place carefully on arrival.

Finding everything in order, we went in and prepared to unwind.

"You are off duty, I presume," Jill said with mock gravity. "We have a new bottle of Riesling just dying to be opened. I'll go up and wriggle into my nightgown, then we'll pop the cork and indulge in a little pacification program."

"Yes, I'm off duty, thanks. Which means I get to watch you wriggle." I gave her a lecherous grin.

She waved me off. "Save the wriggling for later."

I started toward the room we used as a home office, calling back over my shoulder. "I believe pacification refers to peaceful submission. That'll work."

I dropped my briefcase on my desk, was about to turn and walk out when the ringing phone stopped me. It was Kelli.

"What do you have?" I asked.

"It seems my Grandpa is a bit more of a hardass than I was aware. He told Warren and me several tales of run-ins he'd had over the years. I don't know that any of them would result in the sort of thing that happened today, but who knows?"

I sat on the edge of the desk. "Run-ins with who?"

"One was the head of a medical equipment company headquartered in Nashville. Seems Grandpa nixed a multi-million-dollar deal the company had arranged with the hospital shortly before he retired. The man tried to get Grandpa fired and appears to have had him on his list ever since."

"And there's more?"

"Well, he got the Teamsters Union and the truckers association all riled up a couple of years ago when he went to the governor and state legislature complaining about some of their activities."

That brought a grin to my face. I admired the old guy's spunk. He apparently thought a lot like me. He had no intention of letting anybody run over him, ignore him or push him around.

"House trashing sounds like something the Teamsters might pursue," I said. "But they would need some current dispute to provoke it."

"Probably so. That's all I was able to come up with at the moment, though. Have you heard anything else?"

"I hate to tell you this, but you'll need to check the newspaper in the morning. There'll probably be a story about the accidental death on Blair Boulevard." I didn't want to explain how I knew, since it was an outgrowth of my inquiry into her past.

"We expected that. Hopefully it won't be too detailed."

"I'm sure Phil Adamson did his best to keep it low key. Anyway, thanks for the information, Kelli. Let's compare notes tomorrow after Jill and I meet with the TBI agent."

I hung up and found Jill standing in the doorway holding a wine bottle and two glasses.

"I thought you were off duty," she said.

I walked over, took the bottle and glasses from her, set them on my desk, threw my arms around her, and gave her a monstrous kiss.

She leaned her head back and grinned. "That was an off-duty kiss if I ever experienced one."

"You're right, babe," I said, pulling her closer. "Duty is only skin deep. We've got lots more pacifying to do."

14

THURSDAY MORNING'S PAPER carried the story of Harold Sharkey's death, but not on page one, thank the Lord. We had been saved by major coverage of problems with TennCare, the state's medical insurance program for the poor and uninsurable. Quotes from Homicide Detective Phillip Adamson indicated the fatal wound appeared to have been accidental, the result of a fall during a scuffle. Kelli was identified as a witness, but only as the granddaughter of Arthur Liggett. The reporter's attempts to reach her and Col. Warren Jarvis for comment were unsuccessful. The nursing home declined to permit an interview with the retired hospital administrator, who was described as "needing rest." According to the news story, police speculated Sharkey had gone to the Liggett home as part of an investigation, though no one had any idea what it might have involved. He appeared to have made a threatening move on Kelli Kane. The reporter came up with little background on Sharkey, except for neighbors who said he rarely socialized with anyone and came and went at all hours of the day and night.

"You made out about as well as could be expected," I told Jarvis when he called before we left for the office.

"I guess so, but I'm sure the general won't be too happy about it."

I laughed. "Making generals unhappy was something I excelled at. Of course, it doesn't do your career a lot of good, as I found out."

Getting crossed with a B-52 wing commander fairly early in my OSI days resulted in my retirement as a lieutenant colonel, instead of achieving bird colonel status like Jarvis. The wing commander later became the Air Force Inspector General, who was overseer of the OSI.

"Thanks for your help on this, Greg," Jarvis said, his voice solemn. "Without you, I'm sure things would have gone a lot differently, and we would be facing a lot more trouble."

It was the most touching thing he had said since his arrival. I was only sorry I couldn't have done more, particularly where Kelli was concerned. The newspaper story had gone easy on her, though. Hopefully, she hadn't been compromised.

"Hey, no problem," I said. "If I had been around there, I'm sure I'd have done the same thing Kelli did."

"You think so?"

"Back in my pre-Air Force days, when I was a deputy sheriff in St. Louis County, I once got in trouble for using too much physical force. Bruised a bunch of knuckles in the process, too."

His voice lightened up. "I've had a reputation for being pretty scrappy myself. But not in my early days. My dad was a stern disciplinarian and kept me on a short leash. After I left home, things changed. I learned a lot about bumping heads while playing football at the Academy."

"Let's hope you don't have to bump any more around here."

"Amen."

"I don't know what it's going to take to get to the bottom of this Marathon business, Warren, but we need to do it as soon as possible. We'll check back with you later this morning."

Jill and I headed for the office a few minutes later. As soon as I finished shifting the daily trivia about, I called the Chamber of Commerce and inquired if Craig Audain had returned. No luck there.

Jill usually answered the phone, but she was back in the supply room when it rang a little later.

"Mr. McKenzie, this is Camilla Rottman," said a cultured voice. "I'm with the Nashville Symphony League. Your firm is a valued part of our community, and I would like to come out and talk with you about becoming involved in furthering the development of Nashville's artistic excellence."

"We already contribute to the symphony, Miss, uh…is it Miss Rottman?"

"Mrs. Roger Rottman," she corrected. "I'm aware that you're a contributor, Mr. McKenzie, but with the new world class symphony hall going up, we need as much additional help as we can get."

I could hear the dollar signs ringing up like musical notes in a casino slot machine. "I think you'd better talk to my wife, Mrs. Rottman. This sounds like something in her department. Just a moment."

I pressed the hold button and turned to Jill, who was walking back to her desk. "You'd better talk to this lady, babe. It's a Mrs. Rottman with the symphony, and it sounds like she's after big bucks."

Jill picked up the phone. "Hello, Mrs. Rottman. This is Jill McKenzie. Some years back my mother was a first violinist with the symphony. What can I do for you?"

Jill was the classical music enthusiast. We attended the concerts on a mix and match basis. I was more into jazz, though I liked a good rousing piece by somebody like Tchaikovsky or Mahler. She had grown up with the classics, so we settled on a mixture of classical and pops concerts. We supported the symphony and other local arts ventures, though we stayed clear of the high society crowd that ran most of them. With her dad, Daniel Parsons, a highly successful life insurance salesman, Jill would likely have ended up in their ranks if I hadn't whisked her off to life among a different breed of jet setters. Mr. Parsons left her an extensive portfolio of investments, which she had parlayed into a tidy sum that gave us the luxury of doing pretty much whatever we wished.

While Jill chatted with Lady Camilla, I got on the other line and called Wes Knight at the newspaper. Happily, I got his voice mail.

"Hi, Wes," I said. "This is Greg McKenzie. Got your message about Kelli Kane. Also saw the story this morning. Too bad about Sharkey, though it's no great loss to the profession. I'd heard Miss Kane was in town and wondered who she was. Sorry I don't have any more info. See you around."

What I meant was I didn't have any more info for him. I hoped that would hold him off for a while. I had just gotten on my computer when Jill hung up and walked over.

"That was Camilla Rottman. You were right. She's raising money for the Schermerhorn Symphony Center and wants to drop by. I told her we were awfully busy, but we'd give her a few minutes. I've been thinking about making a donation in memory of my mother."

"Sounds fine to me." I rarely argued money with the treasurer. "When's she coming?"

"In about half an hour. I told her we had to be at a meeting at eleven."

I puzzled over the possibilities for finding some other place to be in half an hour but hadn't come up with any acceptable ideas when Mrs. Rottman arrived. She walked in looking regal, attired in a stylish pink suit with matching high heels and purse. The sultry August morning hadn't left the slightest blemish on her attractive, tanned face. A small woman with silky blonde hair, she had the look of many hours spent on the golf course or tennis courts. The gold earrings that showed when she swept her hair back could have been carved out of a bullion bar.

She grasped my hand and squeezed it warmly. "Mr. McKenzie, how nice to meet you."

Up close, faint crinkles around the pale blue eyes told me she was somewhat older than I had first thought, though all that makeup made it difficult to tell just how much.

"Nice to meet you, Mrs. Rottman." I finally managed to retrieve my hand and turned to my partner. "This is my wife, Jill."

Jill shook her hand and showed an equally sweet smile, though I had doubts of its total sincerity. She didn't care for people "who put on airs," as she called it.

Mrs. Rottman took a seat and looked around at the office, which I'll admit provided little to impress anyone. "If you don't mind my asking, what do private investigators investigate?"

"We do work for attorneys, insurance companies, private individuals," I said. "We're called on to find people who've disappeared, track down heirs, do basic background investigations."

"I read something in the newspaper about the murder of a private investigator. Is that something you'd get involved in?"

"That's a job for the police, Mrs. Rottman," Jill said. "If we encounter something involving a crime like that, we promptly turn it over to law enforcement officers. As a matter of fact, that's what we'll be doing in a little while when we leave here."

Our visitor looked around, eyes widened. "That sounds exciting."

I smiled. "Exciting is not a term we normally use. Most of what we do you'd probably call boring."

"You're just being modest."

"I haven't been accused of that lately," I said.

"But I've seen detectives on TV——"

"Welcome to the real world, Mrs. Rottman. Being an investigator involves a lot of routine leg work, asking questions, digging around with the computer."

Jill had reached her limit with the small talk. "I'm interested in donating to the symphony hall in memory of my mother. Tell me a little about how the gifts are handled."

Mrs. Rottman spread out a copy of the plans and talked about different areas of the project, what was available for memorial contributions. When she had finished her presentation, Jill surprised her— and me—with the announcement that McKenzie Investigations would pledge $25,000 toward the new symphony hall.

After a quick elevation of her eyebrows, Mrs. Rottman resumed her carefully controlled demeanor. "That is very generous of you, Mrs. McKenzie. On behalf of the symphony, I want to thank both of you for this gift. I would like to invite you to a small party my husband and I are hosting tomorrow evening for new contributors. I hope we can count on you to join us."

Jill glanced at me. I wasn't one for schmoozing with the upper crust, but she deserved recognition for her civic-mindedness. "Unless something unforeseen crops up with the case we're working on, I see no reason why we can't make it," I said.

Mrs. Rottman smiled broadly. "Excellent. We look forward to seeing you."

After showing her to the door, I walked back to Jill's desk. "That was a very generous thing for you to do, babe. I'm proud of you."

She gave me a muted smile. "If you'd known my mother, how much she loved the symphony, you'd realize this was just a small token of what she would have done."

Jill was only fifteen when her mother died. It was a traumatic time in her life. After that, her father became overly protective, which was the main reason he and I had never been too chummy. She showed her independence by defying him until he gave in and accepted our intent to marry. I had long ago learned, particularly when she got into the air charter business, that she would let nothing stand in the way of achieving whatever goals she set for herself.

I also knew she wanted to get to the bottom of this Marathon Motors case every bit as much as I did. She put the focus back on it when she asked, "Isn't it about time we headed on over to the TBI Headquarters?"

15

HOUSED IN A MODERN brick building only a few years old, the TBI Headquarters occupied a secluded spot in the Inglewood suburb. Though it could be seen from Ellington Parkway, a major route between downtown Nashville and Madison on the northeastern edge of the county, Tennessee's version of the FBI required a circuitous approach. Jill and I drove past the Tennessee Highway Patrol station, curved around a hill and turned into the large parking lot beyond an unmanned gate.

Three stylized antennas stood in line, reaching skyward like church spires, as if to lead visitors toward the front entrance. The building had three-story wings on either side, with an atrium in the center. We walked past the glass-walled entrance and stopped at a large window fronted by a counter. A uniformed officer sat at a computer behind it.

I spoke through the small opening above a curved slot in the counter. "Greg and Jill McKenzie to see Agent Wayne Fought."

"Is he expecting you?"

"Yes."

"Could I see your identification, please?"

I dropped our PI licenses into the slot.

"Answer the phone on the counter when it rings," he said.

We retrieved our licenses, scooped up the visitor badges and moved over to the phone to wait.

"Do you suppose he's tied up in a meeting?" Jill asked after a few minutes.

"I imagine he's checking with the lab boys on the evidence they brought in yesterday."

When the phone finally rang, I answered it.

"Sorry to keep you waiting," Agent Fought said. "I'll be right down."

A couple of minutes later, he appeared in the corridor beyond a bullet-proof glass wall to the right of the officer's station. He opened the door and beckoned to us.

"Come on in. Do you have any weapons?"

We both shook our heads. "I never carry unless I'm expecting trouble," I said with a hint of a smile. "This looks like a pretty secure place."

"You said you'd been here before. You know the drill."

I did. All the employees wore badges hung around their necks. Every office had a small box beside the door with a series of lights. Flashing the badge in front of the box triggered the door to unlock, if the badge permitted entry to that area.

Fought turned to Jill as we entered. "Would you prefer to take the elevator or the stairs?"

"We'll walk," she said. "Greg needs the exercise."

That brought a grin as he directed us to the open metal stairway, which took us to the second floor. Here the center atrium was open to the curved roof. Banquet type tables lined the area, which was used for large meetings or social functions. He led us to a door on the left that led into the Criminal Intelligence Division, which included special agents like Fought who investigated political crimes and assisted local law enforcement agencies.

After walking down a gray-walled corridor carpeted in blue, we entered a room with a large conference table. The agent ushered us to chairs at one end and set a recorder in front of us. He explained that he would normally take separate statements, but since we were professional investigators and had been together the whole time in question, it would be simpler and just as effective to let us collaborate. He went through the usual routine of giving the date, time, location, who was present.

He began with a general statement, then asked, "How did you

become involved in a search for Pierce Bradley?"

We described the Marathon Motors papers and how Bradley had contacted Arthur Liggett, promising to bring them to him at the nursing home. When I came to the part about the cell phone found on Carey Lane, Fought leaned forward.

"Do you still have it?"

I reached in my pocket, pulled the phone out and laid it on the table in front of him. "It was handled by several people before I got it," I said, playing down any forensic value. "My theory is that he may have been conscious enough to throw it out when they were driving him away from his house. He hoped somebody would find it and start looking for him."

That's what happened, though it did him little good since he was already submerged in the lake at that point.

Fought put the recorder on pause. "I'll ask the medical examiner if that's possible. We wondered about the empty cell phone scabbard hooked to his belt."

"Have you gotten a report on the cause of death?" Jill asked.

"Only a preliminary one. Blunt object trauma could be the cause, although they're looking into the possibility of drowning." He took the recorder off pause. "What happened when you went to Bradley's house looking for him?"

I described our fruitless visit on Tuesday night, then told him about my call to Bradley's sister Wednesday morning and our return to Walnut Grove that afternoon. After repeating the information I had given him verbally beside the lake, I followed up with our questioning of Bradley's neighbor, Jackie Varner.

"When was this?" he asked, brow furrowed.

"While we were killing time yesterday, waiting on your crime scene investigators."

"And she thought the visitors drove a small sports car with a rakish sweep to the front end?"

"That's right. I can't say how reliable that observation was, but at least it's a place to start."

He paused a moment before saying, "Is that your complete statement?"

I looked around at Jill, who nodded. "Yes," I said.

He switched off the recorder and leaned back in his chair. "Thanks for coming in. I'll let you know if we need anything else from you."

"There's one other point I didn't want to mention on the tape, because it's pure speculation at the moment," I said. "Our client was tailed yesterday by a man we think had an interest in the missing papers in Bradley's possession. That adds to our belief that this murder may have had something to do with our case."

"Mr. McKenzie, I spoke at length with Sheriff Driscoll yesterday about Pierce Bradley's background. We have several areas of interest to look into."

I didn't like the dismissive way he moved his hands. "The sheriff gave us similar information," I said, "specifically Mrs. Cook and two men he'd had altercations with."

"Yes, and the circumstances of the crime—nighttime, a secluded location likely known only to someone familiar with the area—tell me the person we're looking for is a local."

I couldn't argue that point, but the circumstances also indicated an accomplice had been involved. An accomplice who could be local, or from anywhere.

"Have you had a chance to question any of them yet?"

Fought eyed me like a biology teacher contemplating a frog. "I'm not sure how far I should go with you, McKenzie." With the formalities over, he had dropped the "Mr." tag.

"We're quite willing to share anything we have," I said, leaving off the implicit question of why can't you do the same?

"Sheriff Driscoll filled me in on your background. I know several guys at Metro. I talked to the lead investigator in that Fed Chairman murder case. He gave you a glowing recommendation, said I could trust you."

He referred to Phil Adamson. After our talk yesterday afternoon, I hadn't been so sure he would still feel that way.

"On the other hand," Fought continued, "another source said you were really bad news. I should avoid you like a night shift on New Year's Eve."

"You must have talked to Detective Tremaine or one of his buddies. I made some remarks about him a couple of years ago I shouldn't have. They were made in private but showed up on page one of the morning newspaper. It was a miscommunication that got blown all out of proportion."

"Tell you what. You bring me some solid evidence tying Bradley's murder to your Marathon auto case, I'll put our full resources on the trail of your missing papers."

"Fair enough," I said, though at the moment it sounded like an invitation to climb Mount Everest and bring back a snowball. "You haven't told us who you've talked to so far."

He gave a sigh of resignation. "I went with Sheriff Driscoll to Patricia Cook's house last night to inform her of her brother's death. She appeared genuinely shocked, broke into tears. I agreed I'd try to hold off any further questions until after the funeral."

"When will that be?" Jill asked.

"Not until the ME turns the body loose."

I leaned an elbow on the table and thought about the murder scene. "Have you come up with anything from the Jeep?"

He considered that for a moment, then made a decision in our favor. "They're working on it now in Forensics. Come on. We'll go down and take a look."

The right side of the building housed TBI's extensive crime lab. We walked down to the ground floor where three vehicle bays equipped with suction devices provided the techs with a place to thoroughly examine anything on wheels. A tractor-trailer cab sat in the largest bay. We found two guys going over Bradley's Jeep with their version of a fine-toothed comb. Evidence bags sat around for placing trace evidence they collected.

"What have you got, Larry?" Fought asked a burly man with a large black mustache.

"Not a lot that will likely do us any good. Two days underwater doesn't leave much to go on. Any exposed fingerprints are gone. We found a few papers in what passes for a glove box that weren't soaked through. Apparently these old military vehicles weren't equipped with glove boxes, but somebody had fashioned one that closed pretty tightly. We'll send them up to the fingerprint folks."

"The water probably washed away any fibers, too," Fought said.

"There's plenty of mud and silt. And a couple of small items that were wedged in beside the seat. A matchbook, for one. Also, we found a piece of stainless steel tubing on the floor behind the front seat. I'll send it upstairs to see what they can make of it."

"Okay, thanks. I'll check back later."

Agent Fought escorted us back to the main entrance. On the way, I asked about the two Trousdale County men who had been involved in fights with Pierce Bradley.

"They're on my list to question. The sheriff provided names and addresses."

He didn't volunteer anything further, and I didn't ask. I knew I could get it from the sheriff.

I shook his hand as we reached the front door. "I hope you turn up something soon. We'll get back to you the minute we track down any kind of link."

He smiled and nodded to Jill. "Nice meeting both of you."

Out in the parking lot, she looked around, shading her eyes from the sun. "He seemed like a nice enough man, after he finally came around. Don't forget to thank Phil Adamson for that."

"Yeah. I wish I had something to give Phil in return."

"Like what?"

"Like what Harold Sharkey was after when he knocked on Kelli's door."

I wished even harder when we got back to the office and found a message to call our favorite homicide detective.

16

"HI, PHIL," I SAID when he answered. "Thanks for giving me good marks with TBI Agent Fought." "You meet with him?"

"Just got back. He was willing to give us a little slack thanks to you. But he wants a solid tie-in with my case before he'll really cooperate."

"Can't blame him there. One of the other boys in Homicide told me he'd worked with Fought on a case. Said he was a no-nonsense investigator. A lot of talent. I think he has a criminal justice degree and worked for a few years with the Knoxville PD."

"He seemed pretty competent to us. But Agent Fought wasn't the reason for your call, was it?"

"No. I thought I'd warn you not to get too excited when you hear your friend's been called into the DA's office."

"Warren Jarvis?" That didn't sound good. "What's up?"

"I did some checking on the colonel, and the military seems to think very highly of him. However, the assistant DA handling the case wants to talk to him. He's one of these cocky young lawyers, thinks he can dig stuff out of people they won't give to cops. I told him we hadn't come up with any idea of what Sharkey was doing there."

I decided it was time to level with Phil. I owed him that. "I had a message on the answering machine from yesterday afternoon about one-thirty. Harold Sharkey called to ask in effect what I was doing at Arthur Liggett's house. Apparently he came by while my Jeep was parked out front. The idiot talked like he expected me to tell him."

"Interesting." Phil's voice had an edge to it. "So he thought you'd tell him more than you told me, huh?"

That hit more like a jab with a hypodermic needle than a subtle pinprick. "Okay, I get the point. Confession is good for the soul, right? I don't think the client would mind my telling you our case involves Arthur Liggett."

I told him briefly about the Marathon Motors papers and Pierce Bradley's apparent murder. I added that Agent Fought remained to be convinced of any connection between the two.

"So you're thinking Sharkey was looking for the papers?"

"That's my guess, but I don't have any proof."

"And you'd really like the identity of his employer."

"I'd lick your boots for it, buddy."

"Well, your tongue's in no danger. We checked Sharkey's office and came up with a blank. Not even any doodles on the desk calendar. If this guy wrote anything down, he burned it before he left the place."

I thought of the possibility someone connected with our case had tossed the office before the cops, but the people who searched Bradley's and Kelli's places had hardly been that subtle.

"What a character," I said. "I wonder how he managed to hang onto his PI license?"

"I can't help you there. We don't issue PI licenses."

"I know. Well, thanks anyway for the heads-up on Colonel Jarvis. I'll get back to you if we learn anything of interest."

When I told Jill about the plan to call Jarvis into the assistant DA's office, she slapped her hand on the desk as if trying to kill a fly. "Why don't they quit playing their little boys' games?"

"Warren is a big boy. I'm sure he can take care of himself." I really wasn't so sure, but I hoped he could.

"We promised to call them when we got back from the TBI," she said. "Let's see if they want to get together now."

She picked up her phone and dialed. I heard her say, "Kelli, this is Jill. Would you like us to meet you somewhere, or do you want to come over here? . . . Okay, we'll be looking for you."

As soon as she hung up, Jill went into hospitality mode. Ever the consummate hostess, she had to serve food whenever mealtime lurked anywhere in the vicinity. "I'll go over to the little café up the street. They have a darling tray with all kinds of sandwich fixings. I'll be right back."

She hurried out the door, leaving me to wonder if my talents as an investigator would impress clients more than her mastery of the culinary arts. I didn't have long to ponder the image before the phone rang.

"Mr. McKenzie, this is Martha Urey," said a voice I recalled from Trousdale County. "You asked me to call if I remembered anything else about last Monday night."

"Right. What did you come up with?"

"Well, I was driving through town this morning after I finished my bus route, and I saw a car that struck me as just like the one in Pierce Bradley's driveway."

"Are you sure?"

"As sure as anything. It was parked at the store, a little red car."

My attention sharpened like the point on the pencil I held. "What store was that, Mrs. Urey?"

"Cumberland Farm Supplies."

I thanked her, remembering Sheriff Driscoll's account of Bradley's fight over a bill he didn't think his father owed the farm supply store.

17

WARREN JARVIS DRAINED his glass and set it on the corner of my desk, where we had indulged in small talk while devouring a tasty array of sandwich fare. "That tea was delicious, Jill," he said. "I don't believe I've ever had anything quite like it."

I finished off mine, too. "It's her own secret formula. We call it fruit tea. She pours in a mixture of pineapple and orange juice, plus a dollop of Marachino cherry flavored syrup."

Kelli smiled. "If it isn't too secret, I'd like the formula."

"I can give you an idea, but I don't measure the stuff," Jill said. "I just put in what looks like the right amount. Say, I guess you two are dying to hear about our visit to the TBI. Why don't you bring them up to date, Greg?"

I gave them a brief account of what we had learned, and didn't learn, during our meeting with Agent Wayne Fought. "The bottom line is, until we can come up with some reliable link to the Bradley murder, the TBI couldn't care less about the missing Marathon Motors papers."

"So where does that leave us?" Jarvis asked. "What's the next move?"

Jill got up and started gathering the remains from lunch. I leaned back in my chair and tried to look more useful than ornamental. "I'm going to contact Sheriff Driscoll and see if he's picked up any loose ends that might be helpful. I got a call from a lady we interviewed up there yesterday that gives me something to offer him."

"I thought it was a TBI case now," Kelli said.

"True. But the sheriff will still be a major player. Also, he seems to think quite highly of me, even if Agent Fought doesn't."

Jill walked over and stood behind my chair, kneading the muscles at the back of my neck. She knows when I've reached an impasse and need a little boost to get back in the groove. She also knows how to needle me into doing something I'm reluctant to do.

She gave my shoulders a vigorous squeeze. "Did you ask Warren if he had heard from Phil Adamson today?"

I reached up and grasped one of her hands. I looked the colonel in the eye. "You may have a problem, Warren, though I hope not. I talked to Phil a little while before you got here. He said the assistant DA handling the Sharkey case wants you to come in and talk to him."

Jarvis had been sitting with his hands together. He began nervously twisting his Academy ring. "What on earth for? Does he think I did this deliberately? That would be murder."

"If it comes down to that, I'll tell them the truth," Kelli said.

I raised a calming hand. "Let's wait and see what he wants. Phil said it's a young hotshot lawyer. He's probably just flexing his wings. I had problems with a few guys like that when I worked for the DA."

That was before my widely publicized problem with Murder Squad Detective Tremaine, which wound up getting me fired by the District Attorney.

"Just look confident and answer his questions calmly," Jill said, always ready with motherly advice. She'd have made a good mama, I'm sure. We had tried, but the doctor finally said no way.

"Should I turn myself in?" Warren asked.

"No," I said. "If they want you, they'll call. They know where you're staying. Did you work out taking some leave time?"

"Yeah. I've got a week. I hope you can come up with some answers by then."

He didn't hope it half as much as I did. This case was rapidly turning into a big time frustration. I wanted to recover those papers for Kelli and Warren's sake, but the affair had also become a personal challenge. As soon as they left, I turned to Jill.

"I'm going to call Sheriff Driscoll. Then let's sit down and go over all our notes. There's got to be something in there we haven't honed in on."

When I got Driscoll on the line, I described our visit with Pierce Bradley's neighbor, Martha Urey, and her call about seeing the "little red car."

"In front of Cumberland Farm Supplies?"

"That's right. Is the guy Bradley had the fight with still manager there?"

"Hell, yes," the sheriff said. "His name's Malcolm Parker. But I never saw him driving any little red car. I'll check him out. I don't know if Wayne Fought's contacted him yet."

"Who was the other man you mentioned? The one who tinkered around with Bradley's airplane?"

"Kid named Casey Olson. He's in his early twenties. Local boy. His dad served in Vietnam near the end of the war, then worked on a tobacco farm until he moved into Hartsville. Casey is a troublemaker. We never caught him in anything more serious than drunk and disorderly, but he's always hanging around in the wrong places. I gave his name to Wayne, too."

"By the way, Fought told me he went with you to inform Patricia Cook about her brother's death."

"Yeah. She took it pretty hard. I mentioned something about your missing Marathon Motors papers, but she was probably too distraught to pick up on it."

"Thanks anyway. Say, I'd appreciate it if you'd let me know what you find out about Parker."

"Sure. I'll give you a call."

I gave him both office and cell numbers, then relayed what I'd learned to Jill as I jotted down a few notes for the record. She printed out the case file from the computer and laid it on my desk.

"Pull up your chair," I said, "and let's wade in."

I took a sheet of paper and sketched out a chart with headings for each day this week. We made shorthand listings of everything we had ferreted out, from Pierce Bradley's rage on leaving his sister's house Monday up to Martha Urey's report this morning of the "little red car."

"Okay," I said, "what pops out at you? Where are the gaps?"

"The first thing is we haven't established who else knew about the papers before they disappeared."

"Right. Craig Audain at the Chamber hasn't checked in yet. Make a note on your list."

"We still don't have any details on what happened back in 1914 that apparently brought this on." Jill held a long yellow pencil and tapped it against her cheek.

"It might be a good idea for you to dig a little deeper into the library's files. Maybe look through the newspapers from that year."

Jill looked up with a thoughtful frown. "Don't forget, Kelli hasn't brought us copies of those letters from her great-great-grandmother, either."

I made check marks on the chart beside items we had discussed. "That still leaves the possible murder suspects in Trousdale County. Let's see what we can get out of the sheriff or Agent Fought before we go tooling up there again."

Jill glanced at her watch. "It's almost two o'clock. Where do you want to start?"

"I'll check on Audain. You can ask Kelli about the letters."

When I called the Chamber, I recognized the voice of the young blonde with the peek-a-boo hairstyle. "This is Greg McKenzie," I said, "the worry-wart PI Do you have any news yet on the whereabouts of Craig Audain?"

"Oh, hi, Mr. McKenzie. Not really, though I've heard a rumor that he'll be back this weekend. Let me give you his home number. The office won't be open."

I jotted down the number and thanked her. If we hadn't made any progress by Saturday or Sunday, I'd keep his line hot until I got him. I looked around at Jill, who was just hanging up her phone.

"Kelli apologized profusely," she said. "She promised to make copies this afternoon and get them to us. Warren had a message at the motel to call the District Attorney's office."

If it were me, I'd tell the young jerk to get real and spend his time on something productive. Fortunately, Warren wasn't me. "I hope he gives a convincing performance," I said.

Jill leaned back in her chair and folded her arms. "I guess that leaves us with the library option. They have plenty of microfilm readers. We can both go at it."

I was about to reply when the phone rang.

"Hello, Greg, this is Terry Tremont," said the staccato voice of a hard-charging attorney with Tremont, Tisley and Tarwater, our best lawyer clients. We called them the Three Tees.

"How's it going, Terry?"

"Great. For us, that is. We have a client who's got a bit of a problem, though. I'd like your help with it."

"Sure. What do you need?"

"We're trying to settle an estate with a sizeable piece of property involved. It was bequeathed to two brothers. One is our client, Nate Yancey, who runs a local trucking company. He has no idea where his brother might be located. We need you to find him."

"We should be able to do that. Interestingly, we're involved in another case where we ran into a similar situation."

"Two brothers?"

"This is a brother and sister combination. Only they were very much in evidence and mad as hell at each other. Couldn't agree on selling the place."

"That sometimes happens. Hopefully these two will agree if we can get them together."

"Is this something you need yesterday?"

He laughed. "There's no great rush, but I'd like to get it resolved without too much delay. Drop by the office when you're down this way and I'll give you the details."

"Jill and I are heading into town in a few minutes. I'll catch you shortly."

I hung up the phone and looked around to find Jill with a big question mark on her face. "I presume that was the Three Tees?"

"Yeah. Terry Tremont wants us to track down a missing heir."

"So you're going to shunt me off to the stacks while you schmooz it up in the lawyers' office, drink coffee or have a glass of wine." The tone said she was only half serious.

"Terry's a Scotch drinker."

"Aha! All the more incriminating."

I rubbed my chin thoughtfully. "Tell you what, babe, you go ahead and get started with the microfilm and I'll bring you a box of Turtles." Her favorite chocolates. She couldn't resist them.

"Now we add bribery to the charges."

I gave up. She could always get the last word.

18

I FOUND JILL AT ONE OF the Nashville Room microfilm readers scrolling through 1914 newspaper files. She had been there by herself for almost an hour. I hated to get close enough to blow my breath on her, but it wouldn't have been neighborly to refuse a client's offer of a Scotch and soda. I reached over her shoulder and held out a red-striped box of chocolates.

"Thank you, Mr. McKenzie," she said, looking up with a grin.

That "Mr." tag meant I was back in her good graces. If I were in the doghouse, it would have been "Colonel."

She laid the box beside the reader and pushed the control to focus on a large advertisement. "It's hard to keep from stopping on these old clothing ads. You wouldn't believe the prices. What did you accomplish?"

"I got the info on the man we're looking for. Terry wanted to talk, of course, so I spent some time cementing client relationships."

She gave me a beady eye. "Did the cement have plenty of ice in it?"

"Okay, super-sleuth. No putting anything over on you. What have you found about Marathon Motors?"

"Not much as yet. I finally figured out the paper had a Sunday feature on automotive news. I've been reading through those. So far things sound like they're going great. New dealers, new distributors. The man who was sales manager got involved in a separate company that took over as national sales agent for Marathon. I'm afraid it's going to take several hours to go through all of these files."

I looked at the microfilm boxes she had stacked beside the machine. "Without any kind of date to go by, we're strictly shooting in the dark, babe. Let's hold off until we see what Kelli's great-great-grandma can tell us."

WE GOT ON THE ROAD in the early stages of rush hour. The downtown streets hadn't slowed to crawl mode yet. We had just reached the I-40 on-ramp when the cell phone rang. Jill answered it. Kelli asked our location and what we wanted to do about getting the letter copies.

"Are you at your motel?" Jill asked. And, after a pause, "We'll just come by there."

They were staying near the airport, which was on our way to Hermitage. Before we got that far, one of those pesky scattered thundershowers blew into our path. A few monstrous raindrops pelted our windshield, mutating into what my dad always called a gully-washer.

"Slow down, dear," Jill said in an urgent voice.

"I was about to anyway." I gave my usual excuse. I sometimes chided her that I didn't drive nearly as fast as she flew in her Cessna.

"I don't want to end up in a creek like the plunge Pierce Bradley took into that lake."

"Which reminds me, I should probably call Wayne Fought and see if the Medical Examiner has made a ruling."

"You think he'd tell you?"

"Why not, as long as I tell him what a great job he's doing."

Rain blew across the hood at a sharp angle as I pulled up to the motel, a three-story brick structure with a covered entrance. Jill hurried inside, and I moved back out into the deluge, looking for the nearest parking place. We kept a couple of small, collapsible umbrellas in the Jeep, but those wind gusts made them of doubtful use. I parked, jumped out, and ran for cover.

I found Jill waiting in the lobby. We took the elevator up to the third floor and looked for Room 317. Kelli opened the door when we knocked.

"Sorry about the rain," she said as I followed Jill in. "I should have brought this out to the car and you wouldn't have had to park."

"Don't worry about it. I like playing duck." I glanced at the water splotches on my tan knit shirt. Though I don't play the game, I like what they call golf shirts because they have a pocket for my pen and small note pad.

Warren stood near the window beside a round table. "Come on in and have a seat. You might as well wait till this blows over. Shouldn't take long."

He wore a tie and his jacket hung on the back of a chair. "Have you had your audience with the junior prosecutor?" I asked.

He shrugged. "It wasn't as bad as I'd feared. I explained in fairly graphic detail our version of what happened, and he seemed to accept it."

"I'm sure he wanted to know what the PI was after."

"Yes. I told him we had no idea unless it somehow involved the missing Marathon Motors papers."

I took the chair across the table from Jarvis. Jill sat at a small desk and Kelli perched on the queen-size bed.

"How did he take that?"

"Actually, he got real interested. Seems he's an antique car buff. He was familiar with the Marathon, said he'd been over and looked at a couple of them at the old building they're remodeling."

"That probably helped your case."

"Right. I think maybe I'm off the hook."

"That's a relief."

Jarvis's eyes had a new twinkle. "My boss at the Pentagon said the same thing when I called him."

"Have you two come up with anything new today?" Kelli asked.

I told her about Audain's pending return and Jill's digging at the library. "We're looking for more info on the situation at Marathon in 1914. I hope your letter stash can shed some light on it."

"They do. My great-great-grandma gave a lot of details on what happened at the company both before and after Sydney's death."

"Good. We'll take them home and——"

My cell phone rang, interrupting things as usual. It was Sheriff Driscoll.

"Did you check out Malcolm Parker?" I asked.

"Yeah. He's got an airtight alibi for Monday night. That little car wasn't his, anyway. I talked to him shortly after you called, but we've been damned busy the last couple of hours." He sounded harried.

"What happened?"

"We've got ourselves another body."

The little phone seemed to get heavier. "Who?"

"Casey Olson. Some kids hiking along the river came across his car at the edge of the woods. It was off Highway 141 down in Puryear's Bend."

"Was he in the car?"

"No. The body was found in the underbrush nearby. Shot in the head and back and arm."

"Sounds like whoever did it wanted to make sure he was dead."

Jill, Kelli and Warren stared at me with puzzled looks.

"Yeah. That shot in the back makes it look like he was trying to get away," Driscoll said.

"Any idea when it happened?"

"I don't get enough killings around here to make a good guess, but the TBI boys say it looks like maybe two or three days."

"Is Agent Fought investigating this one, too?" I asked.

"He and his crew are still at the scene. The main reason I called is I thought you'd like to know about Olson's car."

"What about it?"

"It's a 1990 red Corvette."

19

MY AUDIENCE BARELY moved a muscle as I repeated Sheriff Driscoll's story. When I got to the part about the red car, Jill's eyes flashed like a pair of headlights suddenly switched on.

"I knew it," she almost shouted. "He must have been at Bradley's house Monday night."

"You may be right," I said. "But if so, somebody else had to have been with him."

Kelli folded her arms and cocked her head. "Sounds like co-conspirators who had a falling out."

I glanced through the window, where the sky had begun to brighten and the rain had stopped. "You may be right, too, Kelli. But we're no closer to establishing a link between those murders and the missing papers."

"Do you still believe there's a connection?" Warren asked.

For no good reason, the question rankled me. I pushed up from the table and stood there, hands on my hips, staring out the window, hoping for a ray of sunshine to penetrate the confusion. It failed to arrive. All of a sudden I felt tired, more tired than I had any cause to be. Was I getting too jaded for this business? I wondered. For a moment I considered giving back their retainer and saying sorry but I want the hell out. Whether it was pride or loyalty or a pure streak of stubbornness, I couldn't do it. I looked back at Warren.

"My instincts say yes, there is a connection. I've always been a firm believer in the intuitive process. I think what it really amounts to is perception. We gather a bunch of information from lots of different sources. It churns around somewhere deep in our brains and gets distilled into something useful by the subconscious. But right now it doesn't seem to mean shit."

"Greg!" Jill had a shocked look on her face. "We don't need that language, and just what are you talking about?"

I kicked the table leg out of frustration, damned near injuring my toe. "This case is getting under my skin, babe. Everything we've learned so far leads absolutely nowhere. In 1914, some money went missing and a man died. Now some papers that might solve the mystery of the money are missing, and two men have died. Is that a link? Where is it headed? What's going on?"

Jill picked up the large envelope Kelli had put the letter copies in. "If you'll pardon us, folks, Greg and I need to get home and see if something in these letters won't steer our intuitions onto the right path. Let's go, Greg."

I APOLOGIZED ON THE way, and by the time we reached the friendly confines of our weathered log walls, Jill had talked me into viewing the situation from a different perspective.

"You've always been a man who believed in action," she said. "Let's get busy doing something instead of mulling over what isn't happening."

She decided we needed a good dose of "brain food" to beef up our deductive abilities before tackling the letters. She brought a couple of generous servings of salmon ("high in omega-3 fatty acids," she said) from the freezer, sprinkled spicy looking stuff on them and shoved them into the oven to bake. To accompany the fish, she prepared corn and string beans with slivered almonds. A salad of romaine lettuce, red cabbage, carrots, tomatoes, and radishes topped off the menu.

After that tasty—and healthful, she assured me—meal, we sat at the dining room table and spread out the sheets of neat though faded handwriting. I started with 1914. Jill worked downward from 1919.

"This is a refreshing exercise," I said. "People don't know how to write letters like this anymore."

"So true. This lady didn't mind pouring out her soul."

After I had studied several of them, one particular letter caught my attention.

"Listen to this, babe," I said, then read:

"Dearest Sister,

"I was happy to hear that Elmer's gout has improved. I wish I could say the same for the situation here, but I fear it is getting no better. It seems to have become worse than any physical affliction I have ever encountered. After hearing disturbing rumors from another Marathon wife, I finally prevailed on Sydney to confide in me. He swore me to secrecy, that I would talk to no one but him about it. Since writing is not talking, and since you are so many hundreds of miles away, I see no problem in relating this to you.

"Sydney said the national sales representative keeps making glowing reports about all the cars being sold and new deals made. But the cash coming into the company fails to reflect such success. He said bills to suppliers are being paid late and the workers frequently don't get all of their pay. Sydney says this isn't good for morale and has resulted in poor workmanship in many cases.

"Sydney has talked to the Treasurer about all of this, but the man insists there is no problem, everything will be all right. It is just a temporary condition, he says, but Sydney is quite worried and is determined to find out what is causing the problem.

"Tell everyone we are in good health and hope to see you in a few months.

"Your loving sister, Grace."

I could always count on Jill to catch little idiosyncrasies in people's behavior, and she came up with one right away.

"Have you noticed she never uses his boss's name? It's like she has a deep-seated antipathy toward him."

"You're right," I said. "In one letter she wrote something like, 'I cannot abide the man. He has no moral compass.'"

Jill sorted through several sheets in her stack. "Here's one that pretty much sums up the final chapter. It was written five years after Sydney Liggett disappeared."

"What does she say?"

"She refers to her son's recent wedding, then says, 'I know I should be happy about Henry's marriage, but the enclosed newspaper story crushed all my hopes for seeing Sydney again.' Kelli copied the old clipping, which must have been yellowed and faded."

Jill summarized the story. In the fall of 1919, a hunting party in Dickson County, about forty miles west of Nashville, ran across a dilapidated barn on a farm unused since being tied up in an estate controversy for several years. The land was located near the original highway between Nashville and Memphis. One of the hunters looked inside and saw a car. When he investigated further, he discovered a human skeleton on the front seat. The car was a Marathon. A check of the license plate showed it belonged to Sydney Liggett.

Liggett's body was identified by what was left of his clothing, and papers in his wasllet. Finding no obvious signs of foul play, the county coroner ruled it death by dehydration or starvation. After consulting old news reports of the disappearance, he reasoned that Liggett had pulled his car into the barn to hide. His fear of being detected caused him to stay there too long to survive in the extreme summer heat. Apparently the weather that year matched what we were experiencing now. The coroner also reported evidence of animals around the car, possibly feasting on the remains. Although no money or papers were found, the local sheriff speculated they could have been carried off by animals.

"Mrs. Liggett objected to this line of reasoning but got nowhere with her protest," Jill said, glancing back at the letter. "By that time, Marathon Motor Works had gone out of business and the case was considered closed."

She looked up at me, her eyes narrowed. "Sydney Liggett was railroaded."

"Sure sounds like it. The coroner probably wasn't a doctor, more likely an undertaker. All he had was a bag of bones. Without any knowledge of forensics, he'd have had no clue if it was a natural death or homicide."

She placed the letter back onto the pile. "And without those papers, we've got no chance of proving it was murder."

20

I PICKED UP FRIDAY'S newspaper from the driveway as we returned from our morning walk. I pulled it out of its plastic bag, a useless precaution with the rain only appearing these days in afternoon deluges, and checked the front page. Gasoline prices were going up, as usual. TennCare, the state's version of Medicaid with added benefits for the uninsurable, garnered more headlines. The latest news from Iraq and a drug-related double murder finished off the morning's top stories.

"Casey Olson didn't make page one," I said as Jill and I rounded the driveway where our house popped into view like a secluded mountain cabin. Except the only thing around that remotely resembled a mountain was the small knoll that it sat on.

"How about the inside pages?"

I stuck the paper under my arm. "Hard to walk and read an unfolded newspaper, babe. I'll check it when we get to the house."

As we came through the door, I grabbed a towel I had left on a chair and began wiping my face. My Titans ball cap felt soaked around the sweatband. Friday was destined to be another scorcher.

Jill started up the stairs toward our bedroom. "I'm getting my shower," she called back.

I felt like I'd already had mine. Walking into the kitchen, I spread the newspaper out on the table. The story occupied a choice spot at the top of page onhe of the local section. The headline read: "Second murder reported in Trousdale County." The account offered little we didn't already know, except for some background on Olson, listed as age twenty-four. He was identified as a maintenance worker at the Samran plant in Lafayette, a small town about fifteen miles north of

Hartsville in Macon County. The company made high-tech hospital gurneys. Olson's background showed destructive tendencies—he had competed often as a demolition derby driver.

After showers and breakfasting on instant oatmeal and fat free muffins, we headed to the office. I had just settled down at my desk when Phil Adamson called.

"Was your pal summoned to the DA's office yesterday?" he asked.

"He was, and apparently got along famously with your young prosecutor."

I told him about Warren's fortunate mention of Marathon, which struck a positive chord with the antique car buff.

"Well, I hope he's still in a good mood when I report the latest development," Phil said.

I leaned back and shook my head. "And that would be?"

"We got an anonymous tip this morning, no doubt brought on by that news story, that we should dig a little deeper into Warren Jarvis's past. The guy even gave us the date for an article in a Las Vegas newspaper."

I tried to recall what Jarvis had told me about his career. Then it hit me. "He was stationed at Nellis Air Force Base outside Vegas years ago. What was the story about?"

"According to the paper, *Captain* Jarvis was with a bunch of hot-shot fighter pilots at a bar one night when a guy starts making snide remarks. They got into a scuffle and Jarvis shoves the guy, who falls and hits his head on the corner of a table. He went into a coma and died a couple of days later."

Cops get very uncomfortable when they find a pattern of activity. I knew what Phil was thinking. Did Jarvis make a practice of overreacting in a violent manner? Had he used more force than necessary to stop Harold Sharkey? The big problem was that Jarvis hadn't even touched the PI.

"Did you check on the outcome of the case?" I asked. "Was Warren Jarvis charged with anything?"

"The newspaper didn't say. I've contacted the Vegas PD for more info. They haven't gotten back to me."

I felt a pang of conscience that told me I should do something to help my friend out of this mire. "Were you able to ID the guy who called in the tip?"

"No. He used a pay phone. You know how many anonymous tips we get."

I did. And I knew Phil wasn't concerned about who had called, just was there any truth to the tip. Unfortunately, there had been. I was concerned, however. Either it was a friend of Harold Sharkey looking for revenge, or someone out to make trouble for Warren. I'd just have to wait and hope for the best.

When I told Jill what had happened, she sat there and rubbed her forehead, then looked up. "One more reason we need to find some answers to this Marathon business as quickly as possible."

I decided to try Agent Fought again, see if I could pry any new insights out of him. When I reached him on his cell phone, he tossed me a fast one.

"Did you find a link to my case?"

I couldn't bluff my way out of that. I decided to try candor. "No, I'm afraid not. But it isn't for lack of effort. Things just don't seem to be meshing for us. I guess you know how that goes."

"Been there, done that."

"I understand from Sheriff Driscoll that you have another body to deal with. Does it look like Casey Olson's murder is tied in with Bradley's?"

"Fits your red car tip, doesn't it?"

"Right. But there are too many little red cars around."

"I've seen my share. The crime lab boys are analyzing mud from Olson's car to see if it matches the soil at the lakeside. They have some other trace evidence they're looking at, also."

"Have they come up with anything regarding that piece of stainless steel tubing you found in the Jeep?"

"Not its origin, but the ME says it was probably used for a blow to the back of Bradley's head to make sure he was out of it before they drove his Jeep into the water."

"Does that mean they've turned to drowning as the real cause of death?"

"Right. The doc said the lungs and sinuses contained bits of debris, indicating he was still breathing when he entered the water."

I cringed at the picture that conjured up. Drowning must be one of the most unpleasant ways to go. Drowning was a new twist, and I made a note on my legal pad. "Has the ME completed his autopsy report?"

"Not yet, but he's released the body. Bradley's sister is planning a funeral for tomorrow morning."

That was definitely an event we would attend. "Getting back to Casey Olson, has the autopsy produced anything interesting there?"

"I'm not sure what you consider interesting, but we have a nine millimeter bullet. We'd like to know whose gun fired it."

"Do you have any theories on that?"

"Not that I'm prepared to say." I heard another voice in the background, then Fought spoke hurriedly. "I've got somebody waiting for me. I have to go. Let me know if you come up with anything."

It had the ring of *don't call until you have something for me.* Fought didn't sound overly interested in talking about the case, except for a few obvious pieces of evidence. At least he wasn't shutting us out cold.

"Don't forget our party tonight at the Rottman's." Jill looked across as I sat there doodling with my pencil. "I haven't decided what I'll wear. Something a bit dressy but not flashy."

As much as I hated it, I knew I'd have to dress up. "Will my business suit do?"

"Sure. This won't be a formal affair. Just be your usual charming self and you'll be the hit of the party."

"Oh, boy. It's getting deep in here. As you have been known to say, babe, flattery will get you everywhere."

She gave me her beta-eating-its-neighbor smile. "I'm counting on it."

"One thing we haven't done," I said, "is check out the place where it all started."

"Where what started?"

"The Marathon murders. We haven't been to Marathon Village to see where they found the papers. Maybe there's something around the place that will give us a lead."

21

YOU COULD GET TO Twelfth Avenue and Clinton Street much easier back when touring cars were at their prime. Just travel out Charlotte Avenue from the State Capitol, turn right at Twelfth, go north a few blocks and there you were. But modern engineers came up with a design they called the Inner Loop, a multi-lane monstrosity that channeled three interstate highways around downtown Nashville. Besides altering street patterns, its path split neighborhoods apart. A public housing project north of Charlotte became so rundown the city finally abandoned it. The section around Clinton was part industrial, part residential. It had become a high crime area and a hangout for drunks and homeless men. A railroad line ran past it to the north.

We found the Marathon Motor Works buildings refurbished into decent looking brick structures. The two-story, block-long factory stood on the north side of Clinton Street. The administration building, with three floors, sat across from the west end of the plant. Its large square entrance had been restored to the original glass façade, faced by a geometric design of metal rods. A glass door in the center opened onto a lobby floored with tile laid early in the last century. Not surprisingly, the walls and stairways showed considerable wear and tear. Taking into account the shape it must have been in a few years ago, the place looked quaint but attractive.

Blow-ups of old Marathon ads, some from the *Saturday Evening Post*, lined the walls, along with copies of documents dealing with the car's history. We entered the office on the left, where a dark-haired woman in a casual looking tan shirt stood behind a long wooden counter.

"Can I help you?" she asked.

"We're Greg and Jill McKenzie," I said. I gave her a business card and told her we were looking into the old sheaf of papers that had been found in the building.

She started to smile but caught herself. Her look turned somber. "Mr. Bradley told me about that. I was shocked to hear what happened to him. Wasn't that awful?"

"It was," I agreed. "We think there's a possibility those papers had something to do with his death."

"Really?" Her eyes widened. "That's scary. What could be in there that would make somebody do something like that?"

"That's what we'd like to find out."

"Did Mr. Bradley tell you what the papers were about?" Jill asked.

She looked thoughtful. "Just that they were dated back in 1914 and mentioned some man's name. He said he was going to see if he could find a living relative."

We were in a large area that opened onto a conference room on one side and what appeared to be an office around the corner. "Is Mike Geary in?" I asked. "We'd like to take a look at where those papers were found."

"I'm sorry, Mike's in Jackson today. He bought a building down there where they first worked on the Marathon. I know he'd want to talk to you. When he found out about those papers, he said he'd like to get them back for the archives. He's compiled a lot of historical stuff on Marathon."

"If we can locate the documents, I'm sure we can get copies for him."

Jill had been looking at a photograph on the counter. "Are these yours?" She pointed to the photo, which showed the woman holding two small children.

The woman nodded, smiling. "That's Billy and Brenda. Oh, pardon me for not introducing myself. I'm Shannon Ivey, Mike's girl Friday. If you'd like, I'd be glad to show you where the carpenter was working when he found those papers he gave Pierce."

"That would be great," I said. "Jill brought our camera. Would it be okay if she shot some pictures?"

A tall woman, Shannon Ivey had a voice that carried and a laugh that reverberated. "Hey, shoot anything you like. Mike is turning this place into a Marathon museum. He's got a couple of restored cars in the back."

She came out from behind the counter and led us toward the front of the building, then around to an area that was still being renovated. A ladder stood in one corner, a power saw beside it. One wall was bare to the brick, which must have measured almost two feet in thickness. Weathered oak paneling gave a vintage look to another section.

She pointed to an area that had been stripped of its paneling. "This is where he found them."

Examining the wall up close, I saw two small holes in the mortar.

Mrs. Ivey noted my interest. "I think he said there were nails in the wall there that held up the papers."

Jill had her camera out and took a few shots of the area.

"Is the carpenter who found them still on the job?" I asked.

"No. I think they moved him to another project. Things have been slow this week without Mr. Bradley."

I thanked her for her help, and we started out.

"Would it be okay for Mike to call you sometime about those papers?" she asked. "I'm sure it would tickle him to death to get his hands on something like that."

"Sure. No problem," I said. "In fact, tell him to call when he gets back. I'd like to find out what he's turned up in digging around among all that old Marathon memorabilia."

SINCE WE DIDN'T KNOW what kind of fare we might get at the Rottman's tonight, I suggested we try a nice Italian restaurant for lunch. One with a reputation for great cannelloni or manicotti. But Jill was in a torture mood and insisted on stopping at a place that specialized in salads. When we got back to the office, I called Warren.

"Have you heard anything else from the assistant DA?" I asked.

"No. Should I have?"

I told him about my conversation with Detective Adamson. He was livid.

"Who the hell would bring up something like that? It was years ago, and nothing ever came of it. The authorities in Vegas ruled it purely an accident. I'd like to get my hands on whoever tried to stir that up."

"Calm down," I said. "If that's all it amounted to, I imagine Adamson will let it slide."

"Maybe so, but it's damned disgusting. Who could have made that call?"

"It could have been a friend of Sharkey's, though I'm not aware that he had many friends."

Jarvis paused for a moment. "I don't know anyone around Nashville, so I have no idea what else it could have been about."

I didn't, either, though in the back of my mind I couldn't dismiss the Marathon angle. "What have you and Kelli been up to today?"

"She's been over to see her grandfather. Look, Greg, she's an action-oriented person. I hope you can come up with some ideas on what she can do to help. She gets out and runs like a sprinter to work off some of that pent-up energy."

I told him what we had learned from Agent Fought and about our visit to Marathon Village. "We're going up to Trousdale County in the morning for Pierce Bradley's funeral. We'll probe around for some new leads while we're there. Maybe we can come up with something to keep Kelli busy."

"I hope so. She's going to wear out the soles on her running shoes. I don't know how much longer I can hold her down here. She's like a rocket waiting for ignition. Thank goodness you sound better than when you left us yesterday."

"Sorry for that little performance," I said. "Kelli isn't the only one suffering from acute frustration."

"I know it's been rough, but we really appreciate all you and Jill have done."

"Thanks. And don't worry, we're not giving up. I'm hopeful we'll come up with some new leads in Trousdale County tomorrow."

Jill had been listening to the conversation from her desk. She looked across with a gentle gaze. "Why don't we concentrate on tracking down the Three Tees' missing heir and let the Marathon buggy idle for a bit?"

I swung my chair around and gripped the armrests. "I'm not happy with my performance, babe. I should have done more."

"Come on, Greg. We're in this together."

"True."

"I have faith in you."

"Thanks." I forced a smile. "Let's track down Mr. Yancey."

The search turned out to be so simple it would result in one of our smaller bills to the lawyers. Since Terry Tremont had provided the missing brother's social security number, we used our on-line resources, made a couple of phone calls and soon located Norris Yancey in Wenatchee, a town of about 30,000 on the Columbia River almost in the center of Washington State. I called Terry to give him the information.

"Hey, you guys are great," he said. "Nate will be here in about an hour. Any chance you could come by and give him the details? The client is always more impressed when it comes from the horse's mouth."

I wasn't sure I cared for the metaphor. Since we were billing on an hourly rate, however, I didn't mind reporting in person what could have been given on the phone.

"That'll work," I said. "We can come by your office before heading home. Got to get ready for a party at Roger and Camilla Rottman's, something Jill got us into with a symphony donation."

"You're traveling in high society there, buddy."

"That's what I was afraid of. I don't even know the people."

"Roger is one of those that helped give Nashville the reputation of a son-in-law town. You know, guys who came to Vanderbilt, married young debs and got cushy jobs with papa's company. Camilla was a Hedrick."

"As in Hedrick Industries?"

"You got it. Anyway, see you in about an hour."

When I told Jill what Terry had said, she looked down at her nails and ran a hand through her hair. I could almost hear the wheels turning in her head, playing a message that said: *you should have gotten your hair done today.*

"I ought to have known that about Camilla," she said. "I think Dad sold some insurance to Mr. Hedrick years ago, back when the company was a lot smaller. Now it's an international behemoth."

I leaned back in my chair and clasped my hands behind my head. "I'll bet the Rottmans put up enough cash to have something named for them at the new symphony hall."

"Probably. But knowing you, I don't expect you to be intimidated."

She was right there. One of my basic tenets had always been never let anybody intimidate you. And I stuck by it, though sometimes it meant suffering the consequences, as with the general at Minot AFB who busted the rung out of my career ladder.

LOCATED IN A HIGH RISE office building downtown, Tremont, Tisley and Tarwater occupied a corner suite with a panoramic view of Nashville's northern and eastern environs. The hills that circle the city and play havoc with weather forecasters were somewhat obscured by typical summer afternoon cumulus buildups. A frumpish woman with round spectacles and graying hair ushered us into the senior partner's office, which resembled a living room more than an office. It included a plush white sofa and chairs arranged around a dark wooden coffee table. The "desk" was a small table at one side of the room.

Terry met us with hand outstretched in greeting, the cuffs of his white shirt turned back. A bear of a man in his mid-forties with eyes crinkled at the corners by frequent laughter, he seemed perfectly sized for the spacious office. I had learned to appreciate his style. He took nothing for granted but everything in stride.

"Hi, Mrs. McKenzie . . . Greg." He shook hands with both of us like priming a pump, a sparkle of humor in the twist of his lips. "Have a seat. Nate Yancey should be here any minute."

"What a lovely office," Jill said. It was her first visit. She gazed around at the green plants and blooming flowers.

Terry took one of the chairs as we sat on the sofa. "I like to feel at home when I'm working."

"Well, you've surely succeeded."

Before I could add a comment, the secretary re-appeared with a gangling, black-haired man who showed a broad grin as he walked in.

"You must be the private eyes," he said, looking from me to Jill. "Terry says you found my brother."

After Terry made the formal introductions, Nate Yancey joined us in one of the plush chairs.

"We found your brother Norris in Wenatchee, Washington," I said. "He seems to be happily engaged as an installer for a cable company out there."

"The hell you say. That boy used to tinker around with radios. I guess he's moved up to television. Last I heard of him, must have been at least ten years ago, he was somewhere in Texas."

"You haven't had a letter or anything since?" I asked.

"Nope. I don't think he knows how to write or use a telephone. I'm surprised my dad didn't cut him out of the will. Dad turned the business over to me a while back, but he kept hoping to hear something from Norris. Guess we should've hired you sooner."

Terry shifted a clipboard on his knee, where he had been jotting notes. "Nate runs Big Red Express. You can't miss those red trucks."

Jill grinned. "I think I've encountered a few of them."

"Hope they didn't do anything wild," Yancey said. He stared at her for a moment, his brow furrowed. "Did you know you guys were in a dangerous profession? I saw where a local PI got killed the other day at the home of an old nut named Liggett. I know all about that man."

That perked me up. "How did you know him?"

"He got really steamed at the truckers a couple of years ago. Claimed trucks were running him off the interstate, all kinds of stuff. He even went to the governor, tried to stir things up in the legislature. I just ignored him, but some of the others weren't so willing to take it lying down."

I saw Jill cut her eyes toward me. Maybe that idea about the house trashing on Blair Boulevard being revenge by truckers or Teamsters wasn't so far-fetched after all. But why now?

22

A TRIBUTE TO ROGER Rottman's ability to marry well, our destination lay on a tree-lined street of opulent mansions in Belle Meade, Nashville's ritziest suburb. We drove through an elaborate stone entrance, up a circular driveway, into a large parking area that fronted a stone mansion resembling something out of nineteenth century England. My Jeep Grand Cherokee seemed hardly grand between a sleek Lincoln and a high-powered Mercedes.

"What a beautiful Georgian house," Jill said in a hushed voice.

I had only a vague notion of Georgian architecture. Whatever it was, it certainly looked imposing. Four large white columns held up what I would have called the front porch roof, though Jill promptly set me straight on that.

"Look at that impressive pediment. Its triangular design is repeated in the gables."

"Thanks for that architectural enlightenment," I said.

The retreating sun bore down at a sharp angle, filtering narrow shafts of light through the trees, as we started for the entrance, a large white door flanked by narrow glass panels and topped by an arched window. It rested beneath a wooden balcony that could have been designed for a latter-day Juliet. Smaller room wings on either side joined the main part of the house.

I gave a self-conscious tug at my tie and pressed the button beside the door. Our arrival had been noted, as the door opened seconds later to reveal a man about my height, though heavier. He had a jowly face, graying hair, and glasses that enhanced a benign smile.

"Come in," he said. "I'm Roger Rottman. I recognize you. You're Greg McKenzie."

My eyebrows lifted. "How did you know that?"

"When Camilla told me who was coming, I thought I recalled the name. I looked it up and found you played a prominent role in tracking down Dr. Elliott Bernstein's murderer."

I waved a dismissing hand. "I wasn't much help to the poor chairman, I'm afraid, but it sure gave me a load of publicity."

He turned to Jill. "I believe you had a hand in that, too, Mrs. McKenzie."

She nodded, tight-lipped. It had been better than four months ago, but she still bore some lingering fallout from the experience.

I smiled. "Fortunately for us, there are plenty of other evil-doers around to keep us busy."

"That's good . . . or is it? Anyway, let me show you into the drawing room where the rest of guests have gathered."

He led us past the broad entryway, where a curving staircase wound upward. Colorful area rugs covered the gleaming hardwood floor here and there. We entered a large room lighted by a crystal chandelier. A table bearing an attractive array of finger foods sat near a bar where a white-jacketed young man dispensed drinks. Several round tables with chairs had been placed about the room, though no one seemed interested in sitting at the moment.

Camilla Rottman turned as we came in. She broke into a big smile and hurried over, her blonde tresses just touching bare shoulders that glowed bronze in the light from the chandelier. She wore a slinky, low-cut black dress that barely contained her ample bosom. Those pale blue eyes looked sultry. Taking Jill and me by the hand, she led us over to a group of six people.

"I want you to meet Greg and Jill McKenzie," she said with a little more vigor than I thought necessary.

She went around the group, introducing two married couples and two singles. I recognized the names of a lawyer and a prominent heart surgeon. The unmarrieds were thirty-ish, the others not a lot younger than Jill and I. When the bartender came over to ask what we would like to drink, the chatter returned to its previous level. The doctor made a comment to Jill, and she began telling him about our wanderings after retirement, before settling in Nashville.

Camilla brought my drink with a gleam in her eye. "I love a man who drinks Scotch. Shows he's made of the right stuff."

I suspected she had been hitting the stuff long before our arrival. "I guess it comes from my Scottish heritage," I said. "I had a chance to spend a little time in Scotland during my Air Force career."

Her smile appeared glued on. "I believe you were a colonel?"

"Lieutenant colonel."

"I'm not too well versed in military matters, but it sounds impressive. I never had much contact with the military. My grandfather was a pilot, killed in World War II, so I never knew him. Roger missed Vietnam, of course. He was in Vanderbilt at the time. My father served in the Army in World War II, but he never talked much about it."

"Was he in combat?"

She shook her head, letting the blonde hair sweep about her shoulders. "He was a finance officer in the Medical Corps. He's always been good with dollar signs."

If he lived anything like his daughter, he had to be. "I presume your dad's retired?"

"In name only. Actually, he serves as chairman of the board of Hedrick Industries. Roger is president."

Camilla left to greet the last of the guests, and I moved over to Jill's side. She linked her arm in mine.

"Dr. Wallace was just telling me about his service in the Navy," she said.

A slim man with long fingers and strong hands, he seemed like the right type for a surgeon. "I never made it past lieutenant," he said with a chuckle. "I just didn't fit in with the military psyche."

I grinned. "A lot of people thought I didn't fit in too well, either."

"Greg had a bad habit of pressing forward on an investigation," Jill said, "regardless of whose toes got trampled in the process."

The doctor reached over to pat my shoulder. "Good for you."

Camilla came back with the last couple, the head of a large accounting firm and his wife, a woman with a girlish face and a body that showed obesity was alive and well.

"Now that we're all here, everybody help yourselves to the buffet," Camilla said. She began ushering us toward the table.

I followed Jill around, filling my plate with canapés, Swedish meatballs, shrimp, cheese chunks, and mini kabobs. We sat at a table with Dr. Wallace and his wife and were soon joined by Camilla Rottman, who took the chair next to me. Her husband sat with another group of guests.

"Frank, I trust you know Greg is a former Air Force investigator," Camilla said.

"Oh, yes," said the doctor. "And he and his wife now run their own detective agency."

"Isn't it exciting?" Camilla turned to me, eyes fluttering. "Roger said you were an OSI agent. That sounds like some kind of spy."

"Sorry," I said with a laugh. "OSI is the Office of Special Investigations. I had a few undercover assignments, but mostly I did gumshoe work. Like pounding the pavement looking for witnesses. Not much of it was the sort of thing you read about in detective novels or see on TV."

She nudged me with her shoulder. "You're just being modest. Tell us what goes on behind the scenes in one of your fascinating murder investigations."

I caught Jill putting a hand to her mouth and giving a slight shake of her head. Most of my cases hadn't been all that enthralling, though some had their captivating aspects. What the hell, I thought. If flyboys like Warren Jarvis could wow audiences with their war stories, why couldn't I?

"Well, I worked a case down in Texas one time that involved a bit of intrigue," I said. "Most homicides these days are drug related, but this one was a family affair. The agent assigned to the base had been sent out on another mission, so they flew me down in a T-Bird to handle it. That's a T-33, a two-seat jet trainer."

I didn't bother to explain how I kept my eyes closed and sweated the entire flight, which was mercifully short thanks to the T-Bird's speed. I didn't look at Jill, knowing she was inwardly laughing her head off at my nail-biting plight that day.

"I was taken to the scene as soon as I arrived. It seems a pilot taking off early that morning had spotted something odd in a lake next to the golf course, which sat to one side of the base."

"Had somebody run his golf cart in the drink?" asked Dr. Wallace.

"Good guess. The security police had pulled it out and found a body behind the wheel."

"The plot thickens," Camilla said, eyes glowing.

"The victim was a young sergeant from the motor pool. When I questioned his co-workers, I learned he had recently married, but things were not moving smoothly. They said his wife was off visiting a friend in San Antonio. She had been notified and was on her way back to the base."

"So she obviously wasn't the murderer," Camilla said.

"When you've been in this business a while, you learn not to jump to obvious conclusions," I said.

Camilla turned to the bartender. "Phillip, another round for everyone. Greg has us thirsting for more."

Jill and Mrs. Wallace declined, but the doctor and I accepted. We would let the wives drive home. Camilla grabbed a fresh one.

"What was the cause of death?" Dr. Wallace asked.

"The medical examiner ruled it a severe blow to the back of the head with a blunt instrument, probably something metallic."

Camilla took a generous sip of her drink. "So the mechanic did it?"

"Patience," I said, grinning. "In questioning acquaintances, I learned the wife had broken up with another airman not long before she married the sergeant. This guy belonged to the weather detachment. When I interviewed him, he obviously lied about where he'd been the night before. Then I discovered his best friend was in charge of maintenance on the golf carts. We took a wrench from the mechanic's tool kit, and the medical examiner matched it to the wound on the sergeant's head."

"Forensic pathologists can do some amazing things," Dr. Wallace said.

Camilla gave me a questioning look. "Was it the friend?"

"When I confronted the friend with the ME's findings, and threatened to charge him with murder, he confessed. There were probably dozens of wrenches like his on the base, but he didn't know we couldn't link his specifically to the case. He admitted he had lured the sergeant to the golf course in the middle of the night and provided the wrench to the jilted lover. He claimed he had no idea his buddy would deliver such a sharp blow. Said he was horrified when it happened. 'I could have killed him for getting me into this' was his comment." I chuckled. "He might have gotten away with it if he had."

"Was the wife innocent?" Mrs. Wallace asked.

"No. The weather guy admitted she begged him to do something so they could get back together. He sent her off to San Antonio to avoid suspicion. We charged him with murder and the wife and friend with being accessories."

Camilla looked around the table with the smug air of a queen viewing her court. "So all was again right with the world."

"Would that it were so," Jill said.

I nodded. "The same old problems keep cropping up again and again. I don't envy the job of homicide detectives these days."

As I looked at Camilla, her mood shifted suddenly from carefree to concerned. She stood, eyes fixed on the doorway. "Please pardon me," she said in a flinty voice I hadn't heard before. "I have a little motherly business to take care of."

She walked quickly toward a stocky young man standing in the doorway. He was dressed in jeans and a tee shirt that read: "I only came for the beer."

23

OUR TABLE COMPANIONS looked around as Camilla Rottman strode toward the door, grabbed the young man by the arm, talked to him a couple of minutes, a stern look on her face, then steered him into the foyer, out of sight.

"That's her son, Kirk," Mrs. Wallace said. "He doesn't live here, but I think he's been a frequent visitor of late."

Dr. Wallace changed the subject in what seemed reluctance to pursue any discussion of his friend's son. "Do you play golf, Greg?"

"Sorry," I said, "but I never found the time to get into sports. I guess I'm a failure at learning to appreciate leisure pursuits. Reading is my main hobby."

"It's a good one. But I've been looking for a golfing partner with a low handicap, somebody who can help me get some of my money back from Roger."

"He must be pretty good."

"He plays like a pro."

Mrs. Wallace looked at Jill. "What do you do for leisure?"

"Just trying to keep Greg out of trouble keeps me busy."

That brought a round of laughter, though I suspected Jill hadn't meant it all in jest.

"Actually, I have friends at church I do things with occasionally," Jill said. "And, of course, I enjoy attending symphony concerts. Greg sometimes watches the Titans on TV, but I can't get him interested in going to a game."

"Cavorting in a crowd of fifty-thousand-plus people doesn't do much for me," I said. "I'm not a crowd person."

Dr. Wallace pushed his empty glass aside and leaned on the table. "You'll have to join us sometime in the friendly confines of the Hedrick Industries club suite at the stadium. I'm sure Roger would be happy to have you enjoy a game with us."

"I appreciate the offer."

I'd seen pictures of the glassed-in boxes nestled high in the stadium but had never been inside one. I glanced about for Roger, finally spotting him near the door. He looked somewhat deflated as his wife gave him what seemed to be an angry lecture. I turned away for a moment. When I looked again, I saw Camilla heading our way, the smile plastered back in place. She stopped beside our table.

"To quote the Bard, 'All's well that ends well.' Greg, you're the airplane pro. Come let me show you something you should find fascinating."

I cut my eyes toward Jill, who I knew was fighting to contain herself at that "airplane pro" remark. Camilla reached for my arm as though to help me up. I suspected it indicated a refusal to accept "no" as an answer.

She led me over to a large stone fireplace across the room, where a section of wall displayed framed photographs. She pointed to one of a man in coveralls standing beside a squat, single-engine airplane that sat low on the ramp. It had a long, greenhouse type canopy. The pilot held a leather helmet and goggles.

"That's my grandfather back in the thirties," Camilla said. "He was in the 105th Observation Squadron of the Tennessee Air National Guard."

I was sure I had seen an aircraft like that, probably at the Air Museum in Dayton. "What kind of plane is it?"

"You'll find it on the picture caption."

I looked closer. It read: "Captain Randall Hedrick with his O-47 at Berry Field, Nashville, May 30, 1938."

I had to admit, I found it quite interesting. "You said he was killed in World War II?"

Camilla linked her arm in mine as she stared at the photo. "He flew in China with the Flying Tigers, Claire Chennault's American

Volunteer Group of former Army and Navy pilots. My grandfather joined the group a few months before Pearl Harbor. The Japanese shot him down not long after the U.S. entered the war."

She seemed pretty well versed for a woman who professed to know little about the military. I had a feeling she knew a lot more about a lot of things than she cared to admit. I looked around at some of the other photos. I pointed to a picture of two men with rifles, a large wild boar at their feet. Menacing tusks curled out of its mouth. "Somebody likes to hunt. Who are they?"

"The younger one on the left is Randall. The other one is my great-grandfather, Samuel Hedrick. He was named after Samuel Adams, the hero of the Revolution who started the Boston Tea Party. Samuel Hedrick started the company back during World War I."

The mansion and all the trappings of wealth began to come into focus. Hedrick Industries had a long, and no doubt lucrative, history.

"I suspect Randall was in the prime of life when he was killed," I said. "Wars are filled with that kind of tragedy."

Camilla glanced up at me, then away with a look I couldn't fathom. "I'm afraid tragedy has become rather commonplace in our day. Like that tragic turn of events you told about in your Texas murder case."

"True. It's really a shame when an innocent guy gets his life taken for no good reason. We're involved in a case now where a man was apparently killed because he had something somebody else wanted. And he really didn't know the significance of what he had."

"Is that the case you and your wife were going to the police about after I was in your office yesterday?"

"You're pretty sharp," I said. "You should have been a detective."

She turned until I felt her breast nuzzle against my arm. "I'll bet you could teach me how to be one."

Camilla ranked as an attractive, well-endowed woman, but she was beginning to meddle in my comfort zone. I had an attractive, shapely wife with whom I had been quite happy for nearly forty years, and I was not about to get involved with a rich woman who believed she could buy anything she wanted. I slipped my arm away from Camilla's and nudged her in the direction of our table. "I think we'd better rescue the doctor and his wife. Jill is the real pilot in the family. She's probably boring them to death with her tales about flying."

I lied. Jill would never mention her exploits as a commercial pilot unless somebody brought it up. I found it a good excuse, however, to steer our tipsy hostess back to a safe harbor.

Dr. Wallace pushed his chair away from the table as we walked up. "The camaraderie has been great, and we've really enjoyed the party, Camilla. But I need to get home and take care of some things before bedtime."

"Don't wake me up when you leave in the morning," his wife said. She added for our benefit, "Frank has an obscenely early tee time. I prefer sleeping late on Saturdays."

Camilla looked downcast. "Surely you don't have to leave us so early."

He stood and pushed his chair under the table. "I'm afraid so. Greg, Jill, it was certainly a pleasure meeting you."

Jill and I stood for the farewell formalities, after which I turned to Camilla. "This is a good time for us to bow out as well. We have some commitments tomorrow, including a funeral up in Trousdale County."

"Not a relative, I hope."

"Actually, we never met the man," Jill said. "But he was involved in a case we're investigating."

Camilla gave us one of her most congenial smiles. "I hope you'll come back soon when you can spend more time. It's been a delight meeting you and getting to know you better." The last part was accompanied by a glance toward me.

We stopped to thank our host, who appeared to have imbibed somewhat less than his wife. As we started out the door, Jill whispered in my ear.

"While the doctor was gone to the bathroom, his wife gave me the scoop on Roger and Camilla's wayward son."

24

JILL AGREED TO DRIVE home. She looked around after I got into the passenger seat. "I'm surprised you were so willing to leave, Colonel McKenzie. You seemed to be having a great time in there."

I wasn't sure if she was being serious or facetious. "Just following instructions, ma'am. You told me to be my usual charming self and I'd be the hit of the party."

"I don't know about the party, but you sure made a hit with Camilla."

I chuckled. "Do I detect a hint of jealousy, babe?"

She knitted her brows. "You were too busy to see me making goo-goo eyes at the doctor."

"Seriously, the lady had spent way too much time at the bar. She was toying with me. I think I did a neat job of cutting her off at the pass. You mentioned learning something about her son."

I must have defused her momentary displeasure, as Jill calmly related the story of young Kirk Rottman, of whom Mrs. Wallace could find little to extol.

"Kirk is in his late twenties," Jill said. "He was a rebellious kid, got expelled from two colleges. His parents pulled some strings to get him out of a DUI charge and another related to marijuana. They gave him a job with HI, as the company is called, and he soon got a girl in the office pregnant. They finally exiled him to a company plant, threatened to disinherit him and throw him to the wolves if he didn't shape up."

"He sounds like only a step up from some street punks I've run into. They get caught up in an endless cycle of what they call partying. Ggambling, drinking, prostitutes and drugs. They spend money like mad. When it runs out, they get into trouble trying to raise more cash."

"I don't imagine young Rottman had that problem."

"No. He probably bummed cash or borrowed from his parents. But they finally got tired of doling out the cash and gave him an ultimatum——work or hit the road."

"I'm sure the boy's antics gave his mother a lot of grief," Jill said. "I feel sorry for her."

"You didn't sound like that a few minutes ago."

She gave me a look. "It was just that she made such a spectacle of herself fawning over you, but she obviously has problems."

"Well, I hope she keeps them to herself. I'd prefer not to have to listen to them."

BACK HOME IN HERMITAGE, we found the answering machine winking like a creature with one bleary red eye. Warren Jarvis had left a message to call him. I had turned off my cell phone at the Rottmans' and forgot to switch it on again.

"Sorry we missed your call, Warren," I said when I got him on the line. "Anything new?"

"Kelli's missing."

I sat there for a moment, unsure what to make of it. "You mean you don't know where she is."

"I don't. And for me, that means she's missing."

"When did you last see her?"

"The middle of the afternoon. She spent the morning with her grandfather, then came back here and we ate lunch. She seemed a little distant, preoccupied. When I asked about Mr. Liggett, she said her talk with him gave her an idea." He sounded both worried and annoyed.

"What kind of idea?"

"She didn't say, just that she needed to find a Wal-Mart and she'd be back around three."

I was beginning to get the picture of a covert operator preparing to step back into the shadows. "Did you see her at three?"

"I think so."

"What does that mean?"

"I was in the lobby getting a cup of coffee when I looked up and saw this woman walking toward the door. I thought it was Kelli. I was about to say something when I realized the hair color was wrong."

"What color?"

"Red. She wore faded jeans, a dark blue shirt, a ball cap and sunglasses. I was about to turn away when I saw her step into a cab and realized the black bag she carried was Kelli's."

Just as I suspected. "What kind of bag?"

"Like a carry-on. I have a key to her room, so I went up and checked. Her bag was gone."

"I don't imagine she left a note."

"No. But something else was missing, too."

"Like what?"

"We had talked a long time last night. She told me a little of the type of work she told me a little about the undercover work she been involved in. And she showed me a small case with make-up and such she used for disguises. It was gone."

I felt sorry for him, but all I could offer was a bit of solace. "Warren, it's going to be difficult to tie down someone who's accustomed to living that kind of life. At least until she's ready to give it up."

"She told me how much she had enjoyed being with me the past few days. She sounded very sincere. She said she had resisted getting close to anyone since her husband's death, but I had changed her outlook. I'm not one to talk about such things, but we made love last night, and it was something special. I want to help her, Greg, but how can I? What's she doing?"

"I'd say she's looking for the Marathon papers just as we are."

"Where?"

"I have no idea. I don't know what we could do beside talk to Mr. Liggett and try to find out what sparked this sudden decision to head off on her own."

"We can't do that until tomorrow."

"True. And not until after Pierce Bradley's funeral up in Hartsville. We need to head that way early in the morning."

"I'll drop by and see Mr. Liggett."

When I repeated the story for Jill, she didn't appear too concerned. "More power to her if she can find what we haven't been able to."

"I just hope she doesn't get blindsided by whoever is behind all the mayhem up in Trousdale County."

25

WE SPOTTED WAYNE Fought, dressed in his Sunday best, as soon as we entered the funeral home, a long, single-story yellow brick building on the main highway. I had donned a suit and tie, also——two days in a row, and in the middle of August. Ugh! I felt sure he had come for the same reason we did. In a murder case, who showed up for the funeral could sometimes tell a lot.

Fought frowned when he saw Jill and me. I decided to ignore him for the moment and walked over to a doorway marked "Chapel," where a guest book sat on a small table with Pierce Bradley's name on a placard above it.

"Shall we sign in?" Jill asked.

"Why not? We need to be sociable."

She wrote our names and the office address. We entered the chapel and looked around. It was already half filled with a mixture of people dressed in everything from suits and dresses to tee shirts and overalls. One crusty looking fellow wore tomato-red galluses. Sheriff Driscoll stood in the back, his uniform freshly pressed, talking with a lanky teenage girl with stringy blonde hair and braces on her teeth. Her full face seemed a mismatch for her slim body. We waited a couple of minutes until he looked around and saw us. When he waved, we walked over.

"I didn't expect to see you two, but glad you're here," Driscoll said. "Mr. and Mrs. McKenzie, this is Marcie Cook. She's Pierce's niece. "

I shook her outstretched hand. "Patricia Cook's daughter?"

"That's my mom," she said, smiling. "You folks aren't from around here."

"We're from Nashville," Jill said.

The sheriff nodded. "They're private detectives. Pierce had some papers for a client of theirs, but we haven't found them yet."

A lanky girl with stringy blonde hair and braces on her teeth, Marcie narrowed her eyes. "Must have been about a building or airplanes. That's about all Uncle Pierce ever talked about."

"The papers were about a man named Liggett who worked for Marathon Motors in Nashville, many, many years ago," I said.

"Did they sell Jeeps? That's what Uncle Pierce was in when they found him."

"No. They sold a car called a Marathon. It was way back, even before I was born."

"Who would want that stuff now?"

"Mr. Liggett's family for one, and probably some other people." I turned to Driscoll. "Has anything new been turned up on Casey Olson?"

"Nothing I know of. I haven't had a chance to talk with Wayne this morning. I think they're having Casey's funeral on Tuesday, if the docs in Nashville get finished over the weekend. Marcie, you'd better go get with your mom and dad. It's about time for the service to get underway."

When the girl walked toward the doorway, the sheriff lowered his voice. "Didn't want to say anything around her. She's nosier than a billy goat. Wayne told me last night they matched the mud on Olson's Corvette with that around the lake. And they solved the mystery of the stainless steel pipe. It came from an IV stand they hook to gurneys at the Samran plant. Looks pretty certain Casey was one of the killers."

"When I talked to Fought yesterday morning, he said they had taken a nine-millimeter bullet from Olson."

"Yeah. It got too dark on the TBI team Thursday to locate any cartridge cases. The lights didn't help. I sent a couple of my boys out there yesterday morning. They went at it on hands and knees until they came up with a nine-millimeter casing. I had one of them take it to the TBI lab in Nashville."

Jill kept her eyes moving, checking out the crowd, while I spoke to the sheriff. "Did they come up with any footprints, anything that might give a clue to the guy who fired the shots?"

"The sun had baked the area pretty good. There were some beaten down weeds where he probably walked in or out, but nothing good enough to get a shoe impression."

With the room beginning to fill, we left the sheriff and moved into the next to last row of seats. I gazed around the room before sitting down. The only person I recognized was the old farmer we had talked with at the convenience store Tuesday evening. He wore the same garb we'd seen that night.

"Spot anybody you know?" I asked Jill.

"Nobody but our farmer friend. Who did you expect?"

"Maybe the Lone Ranger. We could use a good silver bullet at this point in the game."

She rumpled her brow and turned toward the center aisle as a group headed toward the front of the chapel. I saw Marcie Cook holding hands with a woman who had the same thin build and stringy hair. She reminded me of the Wicked Witch of the West without her pointed hat.

"I'd say that's Patricia Cook," I whispered. "She sounded more like Aunt Bea on the telephone."

"And the big guy beside her must be the banker."

After they took their seats down front, the service began. It was mercifully brief. The preacher quoted some scripture, spoke a bit about Bradley and his family, and introduced one of the pilot's Air Force buddies from the Gulf War. The former colleague described a few of Bradley's exploits, and told how he had helped save lives of other soldiers and airmen. As the service ended, his sniffling sister followed the casket out to the parking area, and we looked around for Wayne Fought.

We found him outside watching people head for their cars. When he seemed to lose interest and started walking away, I hailed him.

He turned, glanced at us and stopped. "I saw you two come in. Did you find anything of interest?"

"Not much. The only new person we met was Marcie Cook,

Patricia's daughter. Sheriff Driscoll says she's as nosy as a billy goat."

He gave me a half-hearted smile. "I'll make sure she's not around when I talk to her mother."

"The sheriff also told us he sent you a nine-millimeter cartridge case from the Olson crime scene. Have your lab folks determined the make of the gun, anything on manufacture of the cartridges?"

The agent gave me a wary eye and folded his arms. "You know, McKenzie, you ask too many questions for an outsider."

Jill smiled. "I thought we were all in this together, Agent Fought, trying to find out why this man was killed and, hopefully, who did it?"

He took a deep breath and shoved his hands in his pockets. I suspected he felt uncomfortable trying to stiff a woman who may have reminded him of his mother. "Markings on the bullet indicated it was fired from a Beretta."

"Interesting," I said. I carried a government-issue Beretta on active duty and still owned a smaller version. "What about the ammo manufacturer?"

"They've been contacted, but it'll take a while to research the lot and what stores received them."

If we had a suspect, a lot of shoe leather could be expended calling on retailers that sold the cartridges, hoping to find somebody who could ID our man. But at present, we had no suspect.

"Are you going to the cemetery?" I asked.

He looked around at the cars lining up behind the hearse. "Yeah, and I'd better get moving. See you around."

With that he hustled off toward his unmarked car, leaving us to wonder who owned the Beretta that fired those three shots into Casey Olson.

26

INSTEAD OF GOING TO the graveside, Jill and I pursued another line of investigation we had decided on earlier. The first thing I did was get rid of my coat and tie. We drove to the edge of Hartsville, which was just far enough to warm up my Jeep, and found the small white frame where Jeff Olson, Casey's father, lived. The place was a prime candidate for a paint job. The small front porch accommodated a wooden swing, suspended from the ceiling by chains, and a rocking chair with a faded yellow cushion. A cocker spaniel came sniffing around as we approached the porch.

The door stood halfway open. From what we could see of the inside, the house looked dark as a cave. The whir of a floor fan sounded through the screen. Although a layer of clouds had kept the heat at bay more than in recent days, the temperature had slipped well into the eighties. I knocked and waited. A man with a full gray beard appeared after a couple of minutes. Considering when Casey's father had served in Vietnam, this man looked much older than he should have.

"Mr. Olson?" I asked. "Casey Olson's father?"

"Yeah."

"We're Greg and Jill McKenzie from Nashville. We're private investigators looking into the circumstances surrounding your son's death."

His eyes narrowed. "I've already talked to the cops."

"I know you have, but we're doing an independent investigation. We'd like to ask a few questions, if you don't mind."

"What you want to know?"

I smiled. "It would be more comfortable for all of us if we came inside or sat out here on the porch. Which would you prefer?"

He frowned, making it clear he preferred neither, but opened the door and came out. Jill and I moved to the swing, while Olson took the rocker.

"Did Casey live with you?" I asked.

"He stayed here some."

"Does that mean he also had another home?"

"He had a girlfriend. Sometimes he stayed at her place."

That gave us another subject to interview, though I realized she might be even more reluctant to talk. I could always use my secret weapon—Jill. She had a real knack for pulling information out of women. Looking out in the front yard where a large maple tree stood still as death, I began to push my foot against the floor, attempting to create a little breeze.

Jeff Olson stared across at the dog as it chewed at fleas on its brown coat.

"Did your son bring his girlfriend around here very often, Mr. Olson?"

"Not when his Ma was here. Mazie couldn't stand the girl.."

I was sure that little fact would give Jill some ideas. "Did you have a chance to talk to Casey on Monday?"

His eyes blinked, and he looked down at his rough, weathered hands. "Not much."

"Did he say anything that might have indicated he was having trouble with somebody?"

"Casey was always having trouble with somebody."

"Anybody in particular?"

"I don't know."

"Did he mention where he was going that night?"

"I didn't pry into his affairs, and he never said much." Olson rubbed a hand across his chin. It sounded like sandpaper.

"Can you tell us anything about his close friends?"

"Some was stock car drivers. And I guess he had some from that Samran plant where he worked."

"How about some names?"

He took out a large handkerchief and swiped it across his forehead. "You ask a lot of the same fool questions as that state cop. Why don't y'all get together and save both of us some breath?"

"I'm sure it gets a little old," I said, trying to show a bit of sympathy, "but sometimes a fellow will remember things he didn't think of the first time he was questioned. Do you have any idea who would want to do this to your son?"

He shook his head, heavy brows pinched. "It don't make no sense to me. The boy was a little wild at times, but he never done any real harm to nobody I know of. It just don't make no sense."

When we left him sitting on the porch, his eyes were closed. His head rested on one hand. About all we had managed to get out of him was a name and an employer for the girlfriend.

MICKEY EVANS WORKED as a waitress at a small café in Hartsville. It was run by a large woman with frizzy brown hair and the gentleness of a grizzly bear, according to Jeff Olson's description. The place was wedged between a grocery and a real estate office. The cash register, a genuine antique machine, had keys you pressed to make a ca-ching sound. The clock above it showed eleven when Jill and I walked in.

"You must be the proprietress," I said to the woman who approached us wearing a flowery dress that covered her like a tent.

"Most folks just call me Big Mama. Two for lunch?"

"Not yet. Right now we're looking for Mickey Evans. Is she working today?"

Big Mama gave a grunt that sounded more like a growl, which fit the grizzly description. "Girl ain't been in since they found Casey Olson's body. Said she'd be in today at three. We'll see."

"We'd like to talk to her. Do you have her address?"

"You a preacher or something? You don't look like police."

I guess I looked too old to fit her image of a cop. I handed her a business card. "We're private investigators." Recalling Jeff Olson's last comment, I added, "Trying to make some sense out of this."

Big Mama snorted. "Well, if you can make any, I sure wish you'd tell me about it. Trousdale County don't have one murder a year, much less two in one week. That's the sort of thing you folks probably have in Nashville all the time, but it just don't happen around here."

She gave us directions to where Mickey Evans lived on the lower floor of an old house that had been split into apartments. It sat on a hill that looked down toward the town, a small, sparsely populated chunk of rural Middle Tennessee that made a valiant struggle to create its niche in the fast-moving world of the twenty-first century. We had earlier noted such enhancements as the Tennessee Technology Center at Hartsville, a small school that trained young people for jobs in offices and factories like Samran, where Casey had worked.

Discussing what might lie ahead, we decided if the young waitress showed any reluctance, I would make some excuse to move on and leave the questioning to Jill.

A small yellow Ford sat in the rutted driveway, which needed a new layer of gravel. On the right side of the house, an outside stairway led to the second floor apartment. We got out of the Jeep and walked to the front door across a wooden porch painted dark gray. The air smelled of freshly-mowed grass. I used the brass knocker to rap with a metallic clanking sound.

A girl about Jill's height opened the door just wide enough to poke her face out. She had short brown hair and a plain though pleasant face, highlighted by sad brown eyes behind thin metal-framed glasses. She gave us a blank stare. "Yes?"

"Mickey Evans?" I asked.

She nodded.

"We're Greg and Jill McKenzie, private investigators from Nashville. We have been asked to look into some aspects of Casey Olson's death. It would be a great help if you could answer a few questions."

Her look hardened. "You think he killed that Bradley man, don't you? That's what they're saying. Casey wouldn't of done that."

"That's part of the case that we're not concerned about," Jill said. "We're only interested in finding who killed Casey."

Mickey hesitated a moment. "I don't know."

I took a step back. "I need to get into town to pick up some things. Why don't I just leave Jill here and you two can chat."

"That'll be fine," Jill said before Mickey could reply.

I turned and headed toward the car. As I slid into the driver's seat, I heard Jill say, "I know this has been a rough time for you, dear. I've been through something like this of my own. I can sympathize with you."

I glanced up, key poised at the ignition, as Mickey Evans swung the door open wider and Jill stepped inside.

27

WITH TIME TO KILL, I decided to check out the area where Casey Olson's car and body were found. I stopped by the sheriff's office and got instructions to follow Church Street, or Highway 141, south of Hartsville and across the Cumberland River. I drove leisurely past vintage churches, an odd lot of small businesses, and several nondescript homes on the south side of town. When I spotted a historical marker near a sign pointing to the Battle of Hartsville Park, I pulled in to see what it was about. Since the Japanese hadn't made it this far in World War II, the battle had to have taken place during the Civil War. I'm not much of a student of that period in our history, but a couple of friends from our Sunday School class were rabid Civil War buffs. This would give me an opportunity to surprise them with a bit of unexpected battle lore tomorrow morning.

The World War II analogy turned out to be not all that far-fetched. The battle took place on December 7, 1862, seventy-nine years to the day before Pearl Harbor. According to the marker:

"After marching 24 miles in four inches of snow and crossing the icy Cumberland River, Colonel John Hunt Morgan and 1,300 men attacked the Federal 39th Brigade under the command of Colonel Absalom B. Moore. Although greatly outnumbered, Morgan succeeded in capturing 1,800 prisoners and recrossing the Cumberland before Federal reinforcements arrived from Castalian Springs. Federal losses were 2,096 while Confederate losses totaled 139."

I found the park just off the highway behind a building that housed ambulances. Maps and descriptions showed how the Rebels had approached Hartsville along the same route we had taken Wednesday afternoon. The battle had been fought in this area, with a Confederate artillery battery firing from across the river near where Olson was found.

Back in the car, I crossed a concrete span over the Cumberland and located the dirt trail leading off to the spot where Olson must have been lured to his death. Realizing a party of tired, half-frozen Rebel soldiers had fired cannons in this area nearly a century and a half ago, I wondered if any Confederate ghosts had lingered about Monday night when someone fired three shots into Casey Olson. If so, they weren't talking.

I saw tire marks where the wrecker had pulled the Corvette out from a cluster of trees. If there had been another car around, its tracks had likely been washed away by the storm that came through Wednesday afternoon. I knew there was no need to search for possible clues. The sheriff's deputies had combed the area on hands and knees around where the body was found at the left of the Corvette. When I checked along the line of trees off to the right, however, I noticed what appeared to be a path leading toward the river.

I followed the path, too rough to reveal any footprints, through a dense stand of oak and hickory until it emerged at the riverbank. Rocks stacked on the bluff suggested someone had used them to prop up a fishing pole. Looking down at the brownish water that swirled noisily along the bank, I had a sudden thought. This would make an ideal spot for someone to toss a 9mm Beretta where it would never be found.

On my return to the clearing, I examined every bush and every limb a person might have brushed against in the dark. He would have needed a flashlight to find his way, but the narrow beam likely left him at the mercy of small obstacles. I had to admit the recent rain had no doubt dislodged any evidence of that sort. All my searching produced was a crumpled cigarette pack. I didn't recognize the red and blue colors on the wrapper but picked it up with a tissue I had brought along just in case. I took it to the car and stuck it in the glove box.

When I got back to Mickey Evans' apartment, the front door stood open. She sat on the living room sofa, legs curled beneath her. Now that I could see her, I noticed she wore short shorts and a skimpy halter. Jill sat in a chair facing the sofa. Mickey jumped up and came to open the screen as soon as she spotted me.

"You two look comfortable," I said. "How's it going?"

"Your wife has been real helpful," Mickey said in a soft, hopeful voice. "She's showed me how to get a better handle on things. I, you know, needed something like that. I don't have anybody to turn to around here. My mother lives in South Carolina, and . . . well, we haven't talked in ages."

Mother McKenzie had evidently worked her magic. I looked across at her. "It'll soon be one o'clock, babe. We'd better get back and check in with Warren Jarvis."

Jill got up and hugged Mickey. "I'm sure things will work out for you," she said. "Don't get discouraged. You have my card. If you hear of anything that might help our investigation, or if you just want to hear a friendly voice, give me a call. And be careful who you talk to around here."

She waved at the girl as we got in the car.

"It looks like you two hit it off pretty well," I said. I turned onto the street that would take us back into town.

"She's a confused little girl. She came here a few years ago with her father, while she was still in high school. After graduation, she went to work in a grocery store where her dad was manager. He got arrested for taking money from the till and wound up in prison. They fired her, though she hadn't done anything wrong."

"Guilt by association," I said.

"That's about it. She's been working as a waitress for the past year."

"How did Casey come into the picture?"

"They met at Big Mama's place. Mickey's been going with him for around six months. She admits she let him stay at her apartment a lot but, denies she slept with him."

She must have felt burdened with some small-town scruples. "Did she tell you anything about his friends?"

"Some race car people, like his dad said. And lately, he'd been real chummy with a guy he knew at Samran. I believe she said it was his supervisor, someone called Kayjay."

"Is that a name or just initials?"

"I asked. She thought it was a nickname. He had been to Mickey's house, but she didn't particularly like him. The last time she saw Casey was on Sunday, so she doesn't know who he might have been with on the day of the murder."

I turned off Main Street, headed for the restaurant. "What else did she tell you about Casey?"

"He was an occasional pot smoker, though he didn't smoke regular cigarettes. She said he drank too much and liked to gamble. She hated that he was using marijuana and tried to get him to leave the stuff alone. She told me something interesting on that score. Casey had bragged about his connection with a supplier who knew of a bigtime local source. Mickey thought they were growing plants in a cave."

"Is that what you had in mind with that be careful who you talk to?"

"Right. I knew it had the potential to get her into a lot of trouble."

"If the wrong people heard her, that's for sure."

I pulled into the lot in front of Big Mama's restaurant and parked.

Jill turned to me with a troubled look. "I hope I did the right thing. I didn't mean for her not to be forthright with Agent Fought or the sheriff."

"I imagine she got the correct message."

"Do you think she could really be in any trouble?"

"Over the marijuana business? I was just wondering, could that be what Sheriff Driscoll referred to when he talked about an operation where Pierce Bradley could have spooked somebody with his low-level flying?"

"You're not suggesting that could have something to do with Bradley's murder?"

"Not at all. I just hope that idea doesn't resonate with the sheriff or Wayne Fought. We don't need any more complications to sidetrack our case."

We got out and went into the restaurant, where the front windows glowed with a halo effect, the result of blinds closed to ward off the afternoon sun. The halo hadn't touched Big Mama, who led us grim-faced to a table in the back.

"Did you find Miss Mickey?" she asked in a gruff voice.

I reached out to take a menu from her. "Right where you said she'd be."

"The poor girl has been through a rough time," Jill said. "I tried to cheer her up."

"She needs to get her tail in here and get back to work," Big Mama said. "I'm short-handed. She don't need to mope over that Olson boy. He wasn't worth frettin' over. Among other things, I think he hung out with dopers."

"Do you know any of his friends?" I asked.

"Only one he ever brought in here was a young guy he said was his boss. He worked at the Samran plant."

"When was this?"

"A week ago maybe."

"Must be the Kayjay Mickey mentioned," Jill said after Big Mama left with our order.

"Yeah. We need to find him and see what he knows. The plant probably won't be open until Monday, though."

A slim red-headed waitress brought our sandwiches a few minutes later, and I had just started on mine when the cell phone rang. I put the sandwich down and answered it.

"Have you been talking to the newspapers?" Agent Fought asked in an angry voice.

"No. I avoid the press like the Asian Flu. Why do you ask?"

"I just got cornered by a reporter in Hartsville who knew more details than she should have."

"A newspaper reporter?"

"Right. All the way down from Boston."

"The hell you say. Boston?"

"Bean Town."

"Who does she work for?"

"Would you believe *The Christian Science Monitor*? Why the hell would they send a reporter down here on a story like this?"

"There must be some intriguing angle to this case we hadn't considered."

"Well, there's one you damned sure did consider. She asked about your Marathon Motors affair."

28

I CALLED WARREN JARVIS after getting Fought off the phone. "I found out where where Kelli is," I said. "Or at least where she was."

"Where?"

"Here in Hartsville. She posed as a newspaper reporter and interviewed TBI Agent Fought."

I told him about the call I'd just had.

"You're sure it was Kelli?"

"Who else? She claimed to be a *Christian Science Monitor* reporter and knew about the missing Marathon papers. Have you been talking to the *Monitor*?"

"I've never even read a copy of it."

"I haven't seen one in years, but it's a well-respected newspaper. Anyway, I asked Fought what the reporter looked like. I backed into it so he wouldn't start wondering about my questions. I asked first if she was at the funeral home or the cemetery."

"Was she?"

"He saw her at the cemetery and asked around, but nobody knew who she was. She cornered him later when he was leaving a restaurant after having lunch with Sheriff Driscoll."

"How did she look?"

"Like Kelli in size and shape, but she had auburn hair and lots of makeup."

"Damn." I let him mull that over for a moment. Then he gave a short grunt and said, "Maybe I should head on up that way."

"You won't find her unless she wants you to. I'd suggest you stick around and listen for your cell phone. If she needs help, I'm sure she'll call."

I finished my thought for Jill after snapping the cover shut on the phone. "And I have serious doubts that she'll call."

"What do you think she's up to?" Jill asked.

"I wish I knew. Her big advantage over us is that she doesn't have any constraints on who she talks to and how she approaches them. We have to play it legally and reasonably fair to protect our licenses."

Jill suddenly turned to me with a frown. "You haven't told me where you went while I was talking to Mickey Evans. You must have been sniffing around somewhere."

I told her about my visit to the Casey Olson murder scene and my hapless forensic foray, which produced only a single piece of unlikely evidence.

"What did you do with it?"

"I put it in the glove box. We'll take a closer look when we get back, but it's unlikely to have any fingerprints. Particularly considering the weather since Monday night."

"And it's probably a popular brand that won't lead you to anybody."

"More than likely." But I never rule out any possibility, which is why I picked it up.

WE DROVE STRAIGHT BACK to Nashville and stopped by the office before going home. I looked up the number I'd gotten for the Chamber of Commerce guy, Craig Audain. Getting his wife on the phone, I explained what I was after.

"I'm sorry, Mr. McKenzie," she said. "Craig called a little while ago and said he wouldn't get back until very late tonight. I'll ask him to call you in the morning."

"I'd appreciate it," I said, leaving both phone numbers. I was beginning to feel like a big fat telephone put on permanent hold.

Jill got up from her desk and retrieved her handbag. "If you're not in any hurry, I think I'll go by the craft shop down the street. I'm getting tired of that flower arrangement on the buffet."

Flower arrangements didn't do a lot for me. I could take them or leave them. I was happy to relinquish any interest in home decorating to Jill's capable hands. She hadn't been gone but a few minutes when the phone rang.

"Greg," said the cooing voice of Camilla Rottman, "I wondered if you might be there today."

"We just got back from Trousdale County and stopped by the office on our way home."

"Is your wife there?"

"No, she just walked up to a nearby craft shop. I'll be happy to have her call."

"That won't be necessary. You're the one I wanted to talk to."

I didn't like the sound of that but let it slide. "What can I do for you, Mrs. Rottman."

"It's Camilla, you silly man. I need your help."

"What sort of help?"

"I have a problem that requires some detection."

"Actually, we try to avoid detecting on weekends."

She gave a warbling laugh. "But you'd do it for me."

"What's the problem?"

"You need to come by here and let me explain things. Could you do it this afternoon?"

"I'll have to check with Jill when she gets back. I don't think we have anything pressing." Despite my reluctance to risk becoming one of her minions, taking on a client in her rarified circle of acquaintances couldn't be bad for future business.

"Quite frankly, Greg, this is a situation that requires a man working solo. I need you to come alone."

Was she for real? I wondered. I had encountered a few women with suspect pasts who set up questionable scenarios to try and trap a red-blooded American male. But I was a lot younger in those days. I had received no hints about Camilla's past. More compelling, I was on the downhill side of sixty-five.

"I'll see what I can work out," I said. "It's nearly three o'clock. I doubt I could make it before four."

"That will be fine. And, Greg, please don't mention anything about this to your wife. It's highly confidential."

She hung up before I could say anything else. She was really putting me under the gun. Did I stonewall Jill and make up some excuse? Or did I ignore Camilla's wishes and tell Jill the whole story? Damn!

Being an old hand at taking risks that not always appeared worth the possible consequences, I agonized a bit over how to handle it. Failing to come up with anything better, I decided to leave Jill a note saying something had come up I needed to check into. I would fill her in on the details when I got back.

When the phone rang again, I debated whether to answer it. Enough was enough. Then I saw Warren's motel number on the caller ID.

"I'm going stir crazy over here," he said. "This sitting around waiting and staring at the phone is about to drive me batty."

"Would you like me to drop by and chat a bit?"

"I don't want to put you out if you have plans, Greg, but I'd be grateful for the company."

Put me out? It gave me an excuse to head toward Belle Meade, and I wouldn't have to lie to Jill.

"I'm waiting for Jill to get back to the office," I said. "I'll drop her off at home. Then I have a little mission to accomplish, and I'll see you shortly."

When Jill came in toting a large flower arrangement with fall colors, I told her about my conversation with Jarvis. "He'd like for me to drop by and talk to him a bit. Says he's about to go batty staring at the phone."

"You're probably just what he needs, dear. I have some things to do at home. Just drop me off and I'll get to work."

I rationalized that I was not lying to her, just omitting part of the truth. If I told her about this now, she might say to hell with Camilla, stay out of that vixen's path. But it could be an opening to some good business down the road. When I got a handle on the situation, I'd be able to tell Jill the rest of the story.

29

WHEN I ARRIVED AT THE Rottman mansion, I found a lone red Jaguar sitting in the parking area in front. I remembered seeing it Thursday when I escorted Camilla to our office door. Other cars could be garaged at the rear of the house, of course. And there was always the possibility of servants around. It sounded plausible, but I suspected no one would be here but the queen of the realm.

I had left my jacket and tie at home, changing into a short-sleeve white shirt. I walked to the door, rang the bell and waited. After a minute or so, I rang again. I was about to turn around and leave when the door swung open just enough to highlight Camilla with her customary smile, dressed in a short, luxurious terry cloth robe open to reveal a two-piece yellow bathing suit. If it wasn't a bikini, it was the first cousin to one. Her legs glowed bronze in the sunlight. She wore yellow flip-flops that matched the swim suit. I tried not to concentrate on the rest of her.

"Oh, hello, Greg. You're a little early. Sorry to take so long, but I was out in the pool. We have a bell back there that alerts us when someone arrives or I might have missed you." She opened the door wide and beckoned me to enter.

The story sounded reasonable, and she appeared sober. I stepped inside, nodding my head in the direction I had come. "I hope the water was cooler than the air out there."

"It's heating up. Sometimes I think we should float cakes of ice in the pool."

She walked toward the drawing room, her tanned legs glistening where she hadn't dried off. "We could sit out by the pool, but it's a lot cooler in here."

Under the circumstances, I wasn't too sure about that.

It looked like a different room from last night, except for the bar. The tables and folding chairs were gone. Sofas and plush chairs had been arranged in cozy groups, including one that faced the fireplace. Camilla headed for it. She pulled off the robe, folded it and placed it on the sofa.

"The suit isn't dry yet, so I'd better sit this way." She dropped carefully onto the robe. She patted the cushion beside her. "Sit over here where we can talk."

I took the other end of the sofa. "Jill and I enjoyed the party last night, Camilla. Thanks for inviting us."

"I'm glad to hear it. I just love parties." With a sudden swing of her legs, she jumped up, kicking off the flip-flops. "And I'm being a terrible hostess. Let's see, you like Scotch and soda." She headed for the bar.

"Just a Sprite for me," I said. "Maybe it's a holdover from the military, but I never drink while on duty."

Her brow furrowed. "This is duty?"

I laughed. "I guess I should say while I'm at work. Detecting is my job, Camilla."

She brought two glasses over and handed one to me. I was sure hers didn't contain anything so plebeian as Sprite. Then she plopped down right beside me on the sofa.

I gave her one of my what-the-hell-are-you-doing looks and said, "What about the wet swim suit?"

She giggled. "If the sofa gets wet, I'll buy a new one. Now, where were we?"

I set my glass on the small end table and folded my arms as her hip pressed against mine. I felt my face turning warm and sweat beginning to dampen my shirt. "I think I was about to ask what kind of detecting it was you wanted me to do."

She turned up her glass to take a swallow and spilled some of the drink down her chest. "Oooo! That's cold." She reached a thumb down to pull out the halter and almost dislodged a tanned breast that had obviously been bared out in the sun.

I hadn't seen a show like this since I took in a New Orleans strip joint with some OSI buddies fifteen years ago. Talk about provocation. I knew better. I should never have agreed to come out here.

"Camilla," I said, "I'm not sure what you have in mind, but I'm pretty damned sure my wife wouldn't approve of it."

"Oh, Greg. I'm sorry." She feigned an innocent look. "Am I embarrassing you? All I had in mind was to enjoy the company of a fascinating man . . . while on duty. I was quite impressed by you last night. I thought it would be helpful to get a little better acquainted before we talk about the detecting task I have for you."

I had stared down some tough felons during my law enforcement career, and I thought I had encountered just about every variety of calculating female known to man. But I realized now I was playing in a totally new ballgame. The old rules no longer applied. With Camilla Rottman, I was playing out of my league.

I glanced at her shapely torso and at the sensuous lips turned up in a puckish grin. I noted that Lady Camilla, up close with the makeup washed away, showed lines in her face that said she was not the spring chicken she sought to portray. She'd had plenty of years to polish her act to a fine point. Bottom line, considering that copper-colored skin and the sensuous way she moved, I suspected she could be as dangerous as the copperhead snakes that writhed about our backwoods.

"You want to get a little better acquainted? Here's my pedigree," I said. "I'm the son of a master brewer with Anheuser-Busch in St. Louis. My mother was a high school English teacher. When I joined the Air Force, I was pursuing a military career like my Scottish ancestors had followed since the seventeen hundreds."

Camilla's eyes glowed. "How intriguing."

"Maybe. But no generals. My grandfather, Staff Sergeant Alexander McKenzie, fought in the Boer War and in World War I with the First Battalion, Argyll and Sutherland Highlanders Regiment. He was forced to retire after complications from wounds he received in France. He immigrated to America when my dad was a teenager."

"I'll bet he was highly decorated."

I shrugged. "He had some medals. I found them in a drawer after my dad died. My dad, incidentally, was an Army cook in World War II. Now, what about you?"

She had almost finished her drink. She pulled one leg up, tucked it under her and turned to face me. "I told you last night about my great-grandfather, Samuel Hedrick, who started the company during World War I to provide medical supplies to the Army. And my grandfather, Randall, the Flying Tiger. My father, Stone Hedrick, built HI into what it is today. They say I take after him more than my mother, a quiet woman who preferred to avoid the limelight."

"I'd have to say I don't exactly picture you that way." I had begun to feel self-conscious sitting with my arms folded. I shifted around, laying an arm on the back of the sofa.

She took the last swallow of her drink and grinned. "You're right. Nobody has ever accused me of being shy or retiring. After high school, I went to Vassar. It was strictly a girl's school back then. I studied in France and came back home to Nashville in the early seventies. Roger was a young engineer with HI when we met. I suppose I'm the antithesis of my husband. He's a whiz with facts and numbers, but he has a problem with the hard decisions. As a member of the board, I have to keep him in line. Anyway, after marriage I got involved with the symphony, the Junior League, that sort of thing. And here I am." She got up and looked toward my glass. "Wouldn't you like something more stimulating than Sprite?"

I shook my head. "I don't believe I could take any more stimulation than you."

She let out a burst of laughter, leaned over and kissed me on the cheek. "You darling man. What a compliment."

I checked my watch as she busied herself at the bar. Nearly four-thirty. I needed to get out of here and head for Warren's motel.

"Where's Roger today?" I asked as she came back with her drink.

Her lip curled for a moment. When her face softened into its usual smile, her voice had cooled. "Roger takes off occasionally with one of his old Vanderbilt cronies. They're supposedly fishing at a lodge up on Center Hill Lake."

I realized I had asked the wrong question when she slid up against me, closer than ever. Despite all the bravado, she appeared to be suffering from the neglected spouse syndrome. I shifted to my businesslike voice.

"I appreciate the hospitality, Camilla, but I have an appointment with another client shortly. How about clueing me in on this detecting job you have in mind?"

Her expression turned serious. "This is highly confidential, Greg. It must go no further than you."

"We never reveal a client's identity and only discuss aspects of a case necessary to the investigation."

"Very well. What I want you to do is find out who Roger is sleeping with. It must be done—"

I held up my hands to stop her. "We don't handle domestic relations cases. Sorry, but that's something Jill and I decided from the start."

She stiffened, eyes blazing. "You refuse to help me?"

"Camilla, I work as an investigator because it's what I'm good at and something I love to do. I take cases where I can feel good about the results I achieve, where it's obvious an injustice has been done and I might be able to right the wrong. I don't feel good about taking sides between a husband and a wife."

Her chest rose and fell with rapid breaths. "That's a flimsy pretext, a plain old cop-out."

"Call it whatever you will. It's a firm policy from which McKenzie Investigations does not deviate." I got up from the sofa. "I'm sorry if you're having problems, Camilla, but no, I can't help you."

She didn't move, but her face turned crimson. "You're going to regret this, Colonel McKenzie."

I was already regretting it, but not for the possibility of something she might do. "I'll show myself out, Camilla. Good-bye."

I turned and strode quickly to the front door. I left without looking back.

30

U NTIL HE OPENED THE door for me, Jarvis had been sitting in front of the TV where a baseball game was in progress. The muted sound left only the rumble of the air conditioner to make the room resemble something other than a hollow shell. Warren gave me a vacant, out-to-lunch look at first, then he shook his head.

"I still haven't heard a word, Greg. Come on in."

I knew my own expression wasn't much of an improvement over his. "Everybody's got troubles," I said.

"What's happened to you?"

I sat in the room's other chair and told him about my visit with Camilla.

He shook his head. "Jesus. She must be some piece of work."

"Well put. But now I've got to go confess to Jill."

"You think that's necessary?"

"I do. I've always been up front with her, and I don't intend to change at this late date."

"Sometimes, some things are better left unsaid. I don't feel any compulsion to relate all of my past female encounters to Kelli."

"That's a bit different. You aren't married and haven't been living with her for the better part of forty years."

He clicked off the TV. "You've got a point there. Still, I'm not sure confession is always good for the soul. It could undermine the underpinning of a relationship."

"That's a chance I'll have to take, Warren."

He gave me an I-surrender look. "You're a determined man.

Have you come up with any new ideas from your trip to Hartsville?"

I told him about our adventures at the funeral, about Jill's visit with Mickey Evans, and my trip to the Battle of Hartsville area.

"I once studied a couple of Civil War campaigns," Warren said. "Interesting stuff from a military standpoint, but not a lot of help to a fighter pilot. I did learn, however, that aerial balloons were first used for surveillance and gathering intelligence during the Civil War."

"Really? I'll bet my Rebel classmates didn't know about that."

"Both the North and South used them. The Union came up with the idea first. They sent up a tethered hydrogen-filled balloon in 1861 near Arlington, Virginia. It spied on Confederate troops at Falls Church, three miles away. The observations were telegraphed back to the ground, resulting in the first case of guns being accurately aimed and fired without being able to see the target."

"Thanks. I'll try that one on my buddies in the morning."

Warren looked thoughtful. "You said something about finding a cigarette pack. What can that tell you?"

"Maybe nothing. Probably not much. It's in the car. I haven't really examined it."

Warren got up, walked over to the window and looked out. After a moment, he turned. "Why don't you go get it and let's take a look. Would sure as hell beat standing around here waiting for a phone that won't ring."

I went out to the Jeep and retrieved the crumpled cigarette pack, still wrapped in the tissue and locked in the glove box. I'm always concerned about chain of custody when I come across potential evidence. Back in Warren's room, I laid it on the table, straightening it out with another tissue, careful to do as little tampering as possible. The pack was white with a partial red background, a blue design on the left side of the front. Letters spelling "DALLAS lights" were reversed out of the color in white.

"Never heard of that one," Warren said.

"Neither have I." I turned it over, and we looked at the back.

Warren scratched his stubble of beard. "I'll be damned. They're made in Russia."

He was right. The small print indicated packaging in St. Petersburg, Russia. No question it was a rare thing to be found on a riverbank in rural Trousdale County, Tennessee. The chances of its being tossed there by some redneck fisherman were about as good as the chances I'd be invited to join the Murder Squad at the Metro Nashville Police Department. So who had dropped it there? The killer?

As I felt of the package, I realized a cigarette had been left inside it. The end could contain DNA if the smoker had put it in his mouth, then returned it to the pack. But that was an extremely long shot.

I pulled out my cell phone. "I need to call Agent Fought. This might possibly be a real break."

Instead of a voice, I got Fought's voice mail. I left a message asking him to call me about a potentially important piece of evidence I had turned up. Next I called Jill and told her about the cigarette pack.

"Where could they buy something like that?" she asked.

"That's a question Fought needs to answer. Or we could. We'd have to go through the phone book and start calling tobacco stores."

"Should I give it a try?"

"Let's hold off until we hear from Fought. He can devote a lot more manpower to the job. I won't be here much longer, babe. Then I'll head on home."

Warren leaned back against the windowsill. He toyed with the TV remote. "I can't get interested in a baseball game or anything else for worrying about Kelli."

"Have you tried her cell phone?"

"Numerous times. It just switches to voice mail."

"Why don't you come on over to the house? Give you somebody to talk to. If you stay around here, you'll drown yourself at the bar and feel lousy in the morning."

"I hate to impose on you."

"Impose, hell. Jill and I would be delighted to have you. Come on. You can follow me out there, and I won't have to give a bunch of confusing directions."

"Confusing directions are part of the Air Force way, pal."

I laughed and headed for the door.

I kept an eye on the mirror to make sure I didn't lose Warren along the way, but my thoughts rarely wandered from worrying about how Jill would take my little indiscretion. It kept looming larger the closer I got to home. When I called to alert her that Warren was coming over, I decided the confrontation might be blunted a bit with our friend on hand.

Jill met us at the door and welcomed Warren with a hug. "I've been scouring around the kitchen to find something to fix for supper," she said, as if she didn't stock the makings of most any delectable dish you could name.

"Don't go to any trouble for me," Warren said. "I can do with peanut butter and jelly."

"Not around here," I said.

Jill scurried toward the kitchen to finish what soon took shape as grilled chicken breasts with a blueberry sauce, sliced carrots, tomatoes and zucchini and a salad of chopped endive with ripe olives and almond slivers. Just a little something she whipped up on the spur of the moment.

When we sat down to eat, Jill smiled at Warren's compliments. "It was nothing. Now tell me what you two geniuses came up with regarding our troublesome case."

I took a deep breath. "First, I think we'd better talk about a new troublesome development."

"What . . . ." She stopped, apparently after gauging my dire expression.

"I did something I shouldn't have done, and I apologize sincerely for it."

She sat still, gripping her fork. "Go on."

"After you left the office to go to the craft store, I got a call from Camilla Rottman. She talked about how much she appreciated our coming to the party, then she gave me a story about needing help with a 'detecting task,' as she called it. Could somebody come over this afternoon. When I told her I'd check with you, she claimed the matter was extremely confidential and could only be investigated by a man working alone. I should come by myself and say nothing about it to you."

By now Jill's lips were tightly compressed, her eyes shifted from bright to stormy.

I struggled on. "I know I shouldn't have done it the way I did. I rationalized that I wasn't lying by telling you I was going to see Warren. I just didn't tell you the whole story. I thought if I followed her instructions, it might lead to some good business among her friends with fat billfolds."

"What did Dr. Trent say about moneygrubbing in his sermon last Sunday?"

Boy, my wife really knows how to zing a guy. I winced. "I'll try to listen more closely tomorrow. Anyway, I found Camilla at home alone, just out of the pool, dressed in a skimpy swim suit."

I described the scene and everything that happened, down to my reaction when Camilla tugged on her bra and my abrupt departure after she made her little threat.

"And that's it?" Jill said in a cool voice.

I held up my hand like a witness at the bar. "That is the whole and complete story, so help me God. Warren can tell you it's the same account I gave him."

He nodded.

Jill stared at me for a few moments, twitching her lips. Her face remained as solemn as a judge pronouncing sentence, but her voice softened as she spoke. "I'd like to have seen you sitting there sweating. Serves you right."

"Agreed," I said. "Am I forgiven?"

"I'll have to take that under advisement. You had better eat before your food gets any colder."

Colder than that look you're giving me, I wondered?

31

J ILL REMAINED COOL but outwardly calm through dinner. Afterward, she carried things into the kitchen to load the dishwasher, while Warren and I adjourned to the living room. When we were seated, he leaned toward me and spoke in a low voice.

"You're a brave man, Gunga Din."

I worked up a semblance of a grin. "Thanks."

"You sounded pretty convincing. Maybe she'll accept it and move on."

"I hope so. We've had our ups and downs, but we've always managed to work things out."

When the phone rang, I answered one on a table by the sofa. I recognized the voice of Casey Olson's girlfriend. She asked for Jill.

"It's for you, babe," I called out. "Mickey Evans."

I hung up after she answered in the kitchen.

"Is that the girl from Hartsville?" Warren asked.

"Right. Jill told her to call if she ran across anything that might be helpful in our investigation."

"I wish she could tell us something helpful about Kelli."

He got his wish when Jill came in a few minutes later, grinning. "Mickey talked to a lady newspaper reporter at the restaurant."

"Kelli?" Warren almost jumped out of his chair.

"No doubt. She said she was writing a story about the two murders. Said her editor in Boston was interested because an AP story said the county hadn't had a murder in several years."

I leaned forward, elbows on my knees. "What did Kelli ask about?"

"A lot of the same stuff I did. Mickey told her about Casey's friends. She seemed particularly interested in the guy called Kayjay from Samran. Mickey didn't tell her anything about the marijuana business."

"Did Kelli mention anything about where she was staying?" Warren asked.

"No. And I don't remember seeing any motels around Hartsville. Do you, Greg?"

"The closest one is probably in Lafayette. That's where the Samran plant is located."

"I'm going up there." Warren rapped a fist against his palm.

I held out my hands in a gesture of caution. "I wouldn't advise it tonight. You go nosing around in that area, and if she's there, you'd probably blow her cover. I suspect she'd be as unhappy with you as Jill is with me."

I checked out of the corner of my eye and saw her raise her eyebrows in a gesture that appeared to border on a grin. I took that as progress.

"Why don't we all sashay up that way tomorrow after church," Jill said. "Isn't it time we talked to Patricia Cook?"

I agreed. Warren calmed down and decided to go along with our suggestion. After he left for his motel, Jill and I moved to the reclining love seat that faced the TV and turned on the early evening news. I reached over to take her hand, pleased that I found no resistance. Then the phone rang. I answered it.

"Hi, Greg," Wayne Fought said. "What's this about a piece of potentially important evidence?"

I told him how I had found the Russian cigarette pack near the riverbank. "Casey Olson's girlfriend told Jill that he didn't smoke anything but pot."

"When did you talk to her?"

"While you were at the cemetery this morning."

He digested that, then asked, "And the pack has a cigarette inside?"

"Right. I haven't taken it out, so I don't know what shape it's in."

"It's possible you may have something. We found a cigarette butt outside Bradley's front door, but he didn't smoke, either. The lab guys analyzed it and said it didn't resemble any brand they were familiar with. If it matches your Russian cigarette, we may be onto something."

"Another thing," I said, "the path led right to the riverbank. It would be an ideal place to toss a Beretta in the water."

"Could you drop that cigarette pack by TBI Headquarters tomorrow? I'll tell them to get right on it. If there's a match, it might be worth sending a diver down to check beneath that ledge."

"Okay if I take it over after church?"

"No problem." He laughed. "Somehow I didn't take you for a congregant."

"My wife had to twist my arm to get me there, but I kind of like it now. Let me know what you come up with. We had already thought about calling some tobacco shops around Nashville."

"If we get a match, I'll take care of that. Thanks a lot. I'll keep in touch."

I hung up the phone and turned to Jill. "I think we may have made a convert."

"To Gethsemane United Methodist Church?"

"No. To McKenzie Investigations. I'll leave the proselytizing to you."

"So I had to twist your arm, huh?"

I put my arm around her shoulder. "I can't think of anybody I'd rather have twisting my arm, babe."

She looked into my eyes with an expression that nearly tore my heart out. "Not even Camilla?"

"Especially Camilla," I said and pulled her toward me.

We were still sitting there five minutes later when the phone rang again. I answered it.

"Mr. McKenzie?"

"Yes."

"This is Dr. Frank Wallace. I met you last night at the Rottman's party."

"Right. We enjoyed visiting with you, Doctor. How are things going?" I covered the mouthpiece and whispered "Dr. Wallace" to Jill.

"Actually, things aren't going too well," he said.

"What's the problem?"

"Frankly, the problem is Camilla. She's accused Roger of some things that simply aren't true. She told him she had called you over today to talk about it."

"She's right about that. Did she also tell him that I declined to take part in her little investigation?"

"No. You told her that?"

"I certainly did. She wanted me to find out who he'd been sleeping with. I told her that McKenzie Investigations does not get involved in domestic cases. We made a firm decision against that when we started this business."

After a long pause, he said, "That is interesting."

"She told me he claimed he had gone fishing with one of his old Vanderbilt buddies. Was that you?"

"Yes. And that's exactly where he was. I have a cabin on Center Hill Lake. There were four of us guys there."

I had tilted the phone so Jill could listen in. "I feel for him. I got the impression she can be one ruthless character." I decided against using the "B" word, a term I felt more appropriate.

"Don't be too hard on her. But, yes, she is capable of being rather overbearing. She and her son are both unpredictable at times."

"You're talking about the one we saw last night?"

"Yes. He's had his problems."

"I understand they included gambling and drugs, both expensive hobbies."

"I imagine you've dealt with people in that category."

Jill mouthed, "Too many."

"They perennially borrow money and never pay it back," I said. "When they get on the downside, they'll do anything to get more cash."

"I guess it's pay up or shut up in that economy."

"Right. The saying on the street is 'money talks and bullshit walks.'"

Jill frowned, but Dr. Wallace chuckled.

"Mr. Kirk Rottman needs to grow up. He can act terribly juvenile when he's in one of his moods."

"Is there a medical term for that?"

He laughed. "I think it's covered by that old medical adage

doctors use when they have no rational explanation."

"And that would be?"

"Whatever happens, happens."

32

OUR PASTOR, DR. PETER Trent, avoided the moneygrubbing theme Sunday morning, but he needled me not-so-gently with a sermon calling for greater understanding of those with whom we disagree. It reminded me again of the problems I'd had with Jill's dad before he died. Neither of us seemed able to accept the legitimacy of the other's point of view. Jill called it hardheadedness, which I suppose is preferable to something like pigheadedness.

During the coffee and gabbing session in our Sunday School classroom, I cornered John Jernigan, an accountant who retired from United States Tobacco Company before it changed its name to U.S. Smokeless Tobacco. They called him "Snuffy" in earlier days, but I knew he didn't like that nickname. The side of the company's plant facing downtown Nashville was emblazoned with "BRUTON'S SNUFF." Jernigan was one of our resident Civil War buffs.

"Hey, John," I greeted him, "guess where I was yesterday."

A tall, husky man with a head as slick and brown as a dried gourd, he had a sly grin and alert eyes that reminded me of Telly Savalas as Kojak. "I'd guess you were hiding behind a tall hedge somewhere eavesdropping on the bad guys."

"Well, that, too. But I was referring to the Battle of Hartsville. I didn't notice much around there to see, but they had a big plaque with a description of what happened all around the area."

"What were you doing up there?"

"We're working a case with some Hartsville implications."

John topped off his coffee cup. "Wouldn't you know, I've been to Gettysburg and Manassas and Vicksburg and Fort Donelson and I don't know how many other sites, but I've never visited one that's practically under my nose."

"Well, there wasn't really much to attract your attention. What interested me was the location of the Confederate artillery battery. They apparently fired from near where a guy was murdered last week."

"Hmm. Seems I read something about those Trousdale County murders. And you're involved in that?"

"Only peripherally."

He chuckled. "Better wear your Kevlar vest around there."

Jill walked up to tell us we'd better find our seats and get ready for the morning's lesson.

WE PICKED UP WARREN at his motel shortly after eleven, headed out to the TBI office to drop off the Dallas Lights pack, and stopped at one of our favorite seafood restaurants in the Rivergate area. We always attended the early service at church, which improves your odds of getting a table quickly for Sunday lunch, or dinner as it's called in the South.

After the waitress left with our order—we all chose the mahi mahi—Warren looked across at us with a smile. "I'm glad to see all appears well with you two."

"We had a little heart-to-heart last night," Jill said. "I don't expect Greg to have any more lapses in judgment like that."

I donned my most penitent look. I'm sure it would have gone over well in a confessional booth. That it was sincere seemed beside the point. If you don't have the right look, you're doomed.

"I will never trust another woman," I said. "Other than my wife."

She narrowed her eyes. "Don't overdo it."

"What do you propose doing when we get to Hartsville, Greg?" Warren asked, no doubt sensing the previous subject was best sidestepped.

"Actually, I thought we might drive up to Lafayette first. Maybe take a look at the Samran plant. If there's anybody around the place, we can try to identify this Kayjay person. We could also drop by the motels and ask if the *Christian Science Monitor* reporter is staying there.

Hopefully we can get the name Kelli's using."

"Good idea. I just wish she'd get in contact and let me know she's okay."

"Sorry, Warren. When you're working undercover, you make as little contact with the outside world as possible. You never know when somebody might overhear something or trace your calls."

"Even with a cell phone?"

"There are ways of tracing cell phone calls and getting the numbers, and not just by sneaking a peak during an unguarded moment."

"Do you think Kelli is following up on the Kayjay lead?" Jill asked.

"I wouldn't be surprised. Of course, we have no idea if the guy could be involved with the murders. At the least he should be able to shed more light on Casey Olson."

Jill looked across at Warren. "Have you ever encountered anything like this before?"

"Heavens no. Murder is out of my league."

"I'll bet you had some murderous experiences in Tel Aviv," I said.

He dipped his head in acknowledgment. "We had our share of mayhem, no doubt. I listened to a lot of tales from Israeli pilots that would curdle your blood."

"Do you see any way out of the current impasse between the Arabs and Jews?" Jill asked.

"I wish I did. There are a lot of people on both sides willing to put away old grudges, but far too many refuse any compromise. They're riveted to historic attitudes that have been drilled into them from birth."

The arrival of our food left little interest in other than small talk. After paying the bill, we headed out to my Jeep and started the trek to Lafayette—with the accent on the "fay"—in Macon County. I had checked the internet last night and found a couple of motels along the highway into town. We traveled up U.S. 31E to Westmoreland, then east on Highway 52. We stopped at a neat little motel on the outskirts of Lafayette. It might have been an update of a relic from an earlier day. A room wing in front and another going off to the rear were brick, the office entrance faced with stone beneath a canopy.

After suggesting we not overwhelm the clerk, I headed in alone.

I found a short, white-haired woman standing behind the front counter, which was open on one end. No walled-in cage or glass-enclosure. Evidently they didn't feel the need for such security around here. A small but homey lobby sat off to the right, behind it a hallway with a cabinet containing a microwave and coffee maker.

"Can I help you?" the clerk asked, smiling. "We were full last night, but we have some rooms now."

"I don't need a room, thanks. I'm looking for a woman reporter for the *Christian Science Monitor*. I wondered if she might be staying here?"

"You must be talking about that nice red-headed woman. She said she was a reporter, but I didn't know what newspaper she worked for."

I smiled. "That's probably her. What's her name?"

She looked down at her desk. "I know her name is Quinn. Let's see, here it is. Julia Quinn. That who you're looking for?"

"Yeah. You wouldn't happen to know if she's in her room, would you?"

"She hasn't been around the office lately. I can call her room if you want me to."

"I'd appreciate it."

I waited while she picked up the phone and dialed, gazing about as it rang.

"Sorry, no answer. You want to leave her a message?"

"No. That's okay. I'll try her again later."

I walked out to the car and reported what I'd found.

Warren slumped back in the seat, his expression a mixed bag, but mostly frustration. "At least we know she's still around. Maybe I should wait here, while you two go on to Hartsville."

"Correction," I said. "We know she's been here. If the situation warranted, she would simply skip out."

"Damn!"

"I know how you feel, buddy. Our best bet is to do whatever we can to track down those Marathon papers so Kelli can cut the charade and resurface."

I drove on into Lafayette, which wasn't all that different from Hartsville, and turned south on Highway 10. We drove a few miles with high wooded hills on either side. After the terrain began to flatten out, we saw a modern factory building with large American and Tennessee flags flying out front. A prominent sign mounted on an artistic stone base said "Samran, Inc.——a subsidiary of Hedrick Industries."

33

J ILL RESTED HER CHIN on her hand. "Now isn't that interesting." I stopped at the main driveway into the property and sat there for a few moments, staring at the sign, wondering what, if any, significance this might have for our case.

"Interesting, indeed," I said.

A few cars sat in a fenced-in parking area behind a locked gate.

"Might as well try the front entrance, see if anybody's home," I said.

I pulled onto an oval drive and parked in a Visitor slot. When I got to the entrance, I found the door locked. There was no bell or any visible means of communication. Staring through the glass, I detected no activity.

I got back in the car and turned to Jill. "If we need to contact Hedrick Industries about anything, I suggest you give Roger Rottman a call."

She smiled. "Probably not a bad idea. Shall we head on to Hartsville and find Pierce Bradley's sister?"

"Yes, ma'am."

Jill sat quietly for several minutes as we drove through more wooded areas and farmland with lots of slopes. It recalled those old tales of cows with short legs on one side grazing on the hills. She finally voiced her thoughts. "A lot of companies won't voluntarily give out information on employees."

"True," I said.

"What if I went in there tomorrow and claimed to be a close

relative of Casey, maybe talk to a secretary, tell her he had told me some nice things about his boss, Kayjay. I'd like to know how to get in touch with him. Maybe she would give me a name and phone number."

Looking in the mirror, I saw Warren shake his head. "You're a devious lady, Jill."

"Devious is how PI's operate," I said. "We have to figure out how to get information out of people who don't want to give it up. Good plan, babe. Let's try it."

When we got to Highway 25, we drove into Hartsville and turned onto the street where Patricia and A. B. Cook lived. Upscale homes that appeared to be fairly new lined the street. I asked Jill for the number, which I found on a mailbox in front of a long red brick ranch that appeared to be on two levels, following the contour of the lot. I parked in the driveway. The three of us got out and walked toward the front door.

The afternoon sun drilled down like a red-hot auger. I had forgotten to bring my Titans cap along, and my scalp felt ready to sizzle. It was something my dermatologist frequently railed against, but you do whatever it takes.

We stood on a small covered porch that offered token shelter from the heat. I rang the bell several times.

"Maybe they're eating out after church," Jill said.

I checked my watch. "It's after two-thirty. They must be slow eaters."

"Could be eating with friends," Warren suggested.

"Or visiting with relatives," I said. "Why don't we drop by the sheriff's office and see if Driscoll's around. Maybe he knows something. I think I'll leave a note."

I wrote a brief message on the back of a business card about our investigation of some missing papers from Marathon Motor Works that had been in her brother's possession. After sticking it in the door, I drove over to Main Street and pulled in at the low brick building that housed the sheriff's office and jail. Driscoll's patrol car was parked outside.

He came through the door as I got out of my Jeep. He stopped and stared, a quizzical look on his face. "What the hell are you doing up here today, McKenzie?"

"Hi, Sheriff." I gave him my best grin. "Just following up loose ends. We stopped by to visit with Patricia Cook but didn't find anybody home."

"Oh. Okay." He seemed a bit relieved by my answer, but I had no idea why. "They're taking a couple of days off to get their nerves settled down. Pat and Pierce had their troubles, but his death seems to have really knocked the props out from under her. He was the only close relative she had."

"Did they go out of town?"

"To visit A. B.'s brother in Lebanon. They'll probably be back tomorrow or Tuesday. Wayne tells me you picked up something my boys missed."

I didn't want to cause any problems. I shrugged. "Don't blame them. It wasn't in the area where the cartridge case was found."

"Well, they need to broaden their minds, and their area of interest. Think more like investigators. Maybe I ought to have you come up and give 'em a lecture."

"Don't know how much I could teach the guys, but I'm always available."

The sheriff pushed back his cap and swiped a hand across his brow. "I just might take you up on that sometime. Where you headed now?"

"Back to Nashville, I guess. We're just out for a Sunday drive."

He grinned. "Sure you are."

"See you," I said.

As I started to turn back toward the car, his urgent voice stopped me. "It might be a good idea to stay away from here tomorrow."

I looked around, puzzled. "Why?"

"That's all I can say. But you wouldn't want to get caught in a multi-agency trap. And forget I said that."

Jill looked up as I slipped into the driver's seat. "What now?"

I tapped my hand on the steering wheel. I decided not to mention the sheriff's warning. I hadn't worked out in my mind what was going on.

"It's almost three o'clock and I haven't heard from Craig Audain," I said. "Let's head for home and I'll see if I can run him down."

Warren leaned forward, almost lunged. "What about Kelli?"

"Why don't you call the motel and ask for her room? If she's there, we can head back in that direction."

He threw up his hands. "I don't know the number."

I pulled a card from my pocket and handed it to him. "I got this off the counter while talking to the clerk."

"Thanks."

I started the car and turned toward the main highway while he called the motel. After a couple of minutes, he handed the card to me.

"No answer. Just take me over there and I'll wait."

"And what if she doesn't show up?" Jill asked. "You'll be stuck up here with no clothes, no transportation, no hope of accomplishing anything."

He heaved a deep sigh. "Yeah, I guess you're right. But if I don't figure out something to do soon, I'm going to start coming unglued."

"I'll dig out my glue pot as soon as we get back." I hoped a little frivolity might brighten his mood. From the look I got, it was levity wasted.

WE DROPPED WARREN off at his motel around four-thirty.

"Let's keep in touch," I said. "If you hear anything from Kelli, call us right away. We'll let you know any new developments we uncover."

"I know you're both going above and beyond the call," Warren said. "I can't overemphasize how much I appreciate it."

"Don't give it a thought," Jill said. "After what you did for us in Israel, you're still way ahead on the ledger."

As we drove to the office, I told Jill about Sheriff Driscoll's warning. We were almost there when Agent Fought called.

"Have you heard from the lab techs?" I asked.

"Yeah. It's definitely a match."

"That makes it pretty certain the guy who whacked Casey Olson was involved in Pierce Bradley's murder. Did they find any DNA?"

"No. But I agree with you on the subject's involvement. Unfortunately, I'm going to have to put things on hold for a day. There's a big operation going on in my territory tomorrow that I need to monitor."

"Must be why Sheriff Driscoll wanted me to stay out of the way tomorrow."

That set him off. "What the hell did he say?"

"Nothing really. He merely suggested I stay out of Trousdale County tomorrow, that something big was going down." I made it more vague than the sheriff's version.

"Damn him. All we need is a leak at this stage."

"Well it won't come from me," I said. "And I'll stay clear of the place. Will you be able to get a diver in the river up there?"

"I've already talked to my supervisor. He's taking care of it."

I told Jill the gist of our conversation as we walked into the office. She gave me the old raised eyebrow. "So it looks like we'll be tracking down where the Dallas Lights were bought."

"If it's going to be done anytime soon, babe, it'll be up to us."

First, I dialed the home phone for Craig Audain, the Chamber of Commerce man.

"Hasn't he called you yet?" his wife asked in disbelief.

"Not yet. Is he there?"

I heard her yell his name. A few moments later, he came on the line.

"I humbly apologize, Mr. McKenzie. I slept late this morning, and I was still half asleep when my wife told me about your call. I didn't get home until nearly three A.M., but that's no excuse. I simply forgot. Just what was it you wanted to know?"

I reminded him of Pierce Bradley's call regarding the papers found at Marathon Village. "Who did you call to find out that Sydney Liggett's grandson was Arthur Liggett?"

"Gee. Let me think a minute. I believe I started out with Irving Glastonbury. He's a retired lawyer. You may know him. I remembered he was an antique car nut, so I called and asked if he knew anything about the folks who ran Marathon Motors. He referred me to Allen Vickers, whose great-grandfather had been president of the company at one time."

I paused after jotting down the names. "Did you tell these men how the papers were found and that they indicated Sydney Liggett intended to turn them over to the district attorney?"

"Not with Irving, but I believe I did go into some detail with Allen Vickers."

"What business is he in?"

"Vickers runs a software company that creates computer programs for clinics and hospitals. He said he'd do some checking around. He called back later the same day with Arthur Liggett's name. Said I could find him at the Safe Harbor Nursing Home."

"Do you know who Vickers talked to?"

"He didn't say."

34

WE HAD INVESTED SO much hope in Craig Audain that his call left us virtually speechless. After I repeated "he didn't say" for Jill, we sat at our desks like a pair of zombies. Several minutes later, I pulled my phone book out of the drawer and thumbed through the V's. I found AllenVickers' listing in Brentwood, an upscale suburb that straddled the county line along I-65 to the south.

I punched in the number and waited. After four rings, an answering machine picked up. "You've reached the Vickers. Sorry we can't take your call, but if—"

I slammed the phone down. "Nobody home."

"This case is plagued with a conspiracy of silence," Jill said, propping her elbows on the desk.

I switched to the yellow pages and flipped the phone book open. "Dammit, I for one refuse to sit here and take it."

I looked up tobacco products and picked out a store that sounded like something other than a discount cigarette retailer. I got a grumpy-voiced man who listened to my problem and grunted.

"I doubt you'll find anybody around here who handles them," he said. "A lot of those importers don't import anymore, so you're looking for a needle in a haystack."

When I repeated that glum forecast for Jill, she closed her eyes and rubbed her forehead. After a moment, she looked up with an enlightened smile. "I wonder if John Jernigan could steer us in the right direction. Didn't he work for a tobacco company?"

"Yes, but they made snuff, not cigarettes. Still, he's a confirmed smoker. He might have some contacts in the business."

I turned back to the phone book and looked up John Jernigan's number. A few moments later, I heard his familiar "Jernigan here."

"John, I'm delighted to hear your voice, you old rascal. This is Greg."

"What's up? Have you been prowling around some old battlefields again?"

"No, but I've been battling with a very troublesome case we're investigating. I hoped you might be able to help me out."

"I'll certainly be happy to try."

"Ever hear of a cigarette brand called Dallas Lights?"

"Is that something the Cowboys' cheerleaders smoke?"

I laughed. "If they have a name like Chekov or Tchaikovsky, maybe."

"It can't be Russian."

"Sure is. Any idea who around Nashville might carry a Russian cigarette brand like that?"

"I'd start with The Compleat Tobacconist," he said, spelling it out. "They're on West End just beyond Vanderbilt. They have a wide selection of products, both domestic and imported. Talk to a fellow named Ridley. Tell him I sent you."

I riffled through the phone book again and called the tobacco shop. A man answered with an accent that might have been Russian, for all I knew.

"Is Ridley there?" I asked.

"He has not returned from supper. Maybe thirty minutes."

I hung up and swung my chair around to face Jill. "We're off to West End, babe. Hopefully, Ridley is our man."

We found the traffic flow on I-40 heading into town moderate, likely laced with people headed home from a day at the lake or some venue farther to the east. We took the Inner Loop around to Broadway, drove up the hill past automobile row and swung onto West End when it split off to the right. The restaurants seemed to be doing a good business, the sidewalks populated with strollers of all sizes, shapes and ethnicities, thanks to a couple of hours of daylight left.

We found The Compleat Tobacconist in a row of shops that

catered to the Vanderbilt University crowd. I parked in a space not too distant, and we walked over to the store. The smell of tobacco slammed me as soon as we entered, overpowering my olfactory apparatus. I decided this probably wasn't the best place to linger. At Jill's persistent prodding, I had kicked the smoking habit for the second time—the first didn't take too well after I became immersed in the quest to find her, which wound up requiring Warren Jarvis's intervention.

Cigars, cigarettes, pipes, most any kind of device you'd need for smoking, and tobacco of all sorts filled every case, shelf and counter that could be wedged into the small shop. A white-haired man as thin as a pipe stem stood behind the counter, sleeves rolled up on his blue dress shirt, a red tie hanging loose from its unbuttoned collar.

"Would you be Ridley?" I asked.

"I not only would be, I am." His furrowed brow accented a thin smile.

I introduced Jill and myself. I told him John Jernigan had sent us.

"A good man, John. Haven't seen him for a while. What did he send you in for?"

"He said you could probably tell us if there was any place in Nashville where we could find Dallas Lights."

He reached up to a shelf behind him, pulled out a red and blue package and set it on the counter. "Sir, you have just found the place."

"The saints be praised," Jill said. "We finally scored a hit."

Seeing Ridley's perplexed look, I explained that we were looking for customers who used the Russian cigarettes.

"I'm afraid you can count them on the fingers of one hand. We started ordering them at the insistence of a good customer who had picked them up on a business trip to Moscow. I don't think anybody else has bought any for a while."

"Interesting," I said. "Who was that?"

"His name is Williams. He goes by Shelby, but as I recall it isn't his real name. He's an international sales rep. Travels all over the world."

"Who does he travel for?"

"That big medical equipment company, Hedrick Industries."

35

WHEN WE ENTERED the office, the phone was ringing with great excitement. At least that's the way it seemed to me, having succumbed to a pent-up feeling of anticipation over the possibility that one of the hooks we had cast would finally pull in a catch. I found Warren on the other end of the line.

"I just got off the phone with the clerk at the motel in La-fayette." He gave it the local pronunciation, then chuckled. "I still wonder what the Marquis would have thought of the way that sounds. Of course, he had enough other names to choke a horse, so it probably wouldn't have mattered."

"What did the clerk say?" I asked.

"Julia Quinn called to check on her messages."

"Did she leave any for you?"

"I had told the clerk to ask her to call Colonel Jarvis. She left me a weird message."

"Does that mean cryptic?"

"Sure as hell is to me."

"What did she say?"

"She said she rode a mule to find where she needed to go. She hoped to have a full report of her journey on Colonel McKenzie's desk in the morning. What the devil do you make of that?"

I rearranged the clutter on my desk as I considered her message. "Sounds like she's onto something. A mule is a drug courier. Could be the marijuana contact Mickey Evans told us about. He's led her to somebody key to the investigation. I just hope she's being real careful."

"I'm sure she carries a weapon, but you never know what you might run into."

"Right. This guy has already killed twice. He'd do it again in an instant."

When I finished the conversation and repeated Kelli's message, Jill posed an intriguing question.

"How do you suppose she plans on getting her report to your desk?"

"If it isn't hand-delivered, it would have to come by fax or email."

"Does she know our email address?"

"It's on our business card."

She leaned back in her chair and looked me straight in the eye, as any good PI would do when searching for an unequivocal answer. "Do you plan to call Shelby Williams and check him out, maybe see if he's been supplying Dallas Lights to any of his friends?"

I rubbed my chin in a gesture of futility. "I'd like to. But do you have any idea how many pages of Williamses there are in the phone book? It's almost as bad as Jones or Smith. And we know Shelby isn't his real name."

"So how do we find him?"

"We'll try him in the morning at Hedrick Industries. If that doesn't work, you'd better be thinking up a good excuse to call Roger Rottman."

WE CHECKED THE FAX machine and email on arriving at the office Monday morning but found nothing from Kelli. I didn't like the implications. Had something happened to keep her from sending a report? Maybe we'd get something later.

Jill and I had discussed today's major police operation in Trousdale County after we got home last night. One possibility was the investigation Sheriff Driscoll had alluded to earlier while talking about Pierce Bradley's "aerial spying." If Kelli had gotten involved on the fringes of the drug crowd, I hoped she didn't wind up getting snared in the law enforcement trap being sprung today.

"Want to draw straws on Allen Vickers and Shelby Williams?" Jill asked.

I gave her my "pull-eeeze!" look. "You know I always get the short end."

"Oh, and who winds up with the squints from sitting in front of a microfilm reader?"

"Okay." I decided to be conciliatory. "Let's not be arbitrary. I'll take Vickers, you take Williams."

She grinned. "I like a man who declines to be wishy-washy. Anyway, that means you'll have to do the detective work. I know where to call Williams. You'll have to find the name of Allen Vickers' software company."

She was right, but it didn't take me long to come up with the firm's name and phone number. With my usual luck, though, Vickers was in a meeting. His secretary assured me the meeting shouldn't last long. She promised to have him call as soon as he came out.

Jill fared a little better. She quickly tracked down Shelby Williams. He said he had given packs of the cigarettes to several friends as a novelty thing. He was reluctant to talk about it after learning we needed the information for a case we were investigating. He said he had just returned Friday from a two-week trip to Europe and was late for a meeting. He would be leaving town again tomorrow. Jill finally convinced him that we merely wanted to ask the people a few innocuous questions. He agreed to jot down some names and call them in before the day was out.

"If he got back from a two-week trip Friday, that certainly eliminates him as a suspect," Jill said.

"We may have to check him out after we see the other names."

A few minutes later, I got a call from Mike Geary, the owner and developer of Marathon Village.

"Good morning, Mr. Geary," I said. "You have a really interesting place over there. Did Shannon Ivey tell you what we were after?"

"Yeah. She said you came over and looked at where Pierce Bradley's man found those papers. I'd've gotten back to you sooner, but I have another project under way down in Jackson. Been tied up on it. You found those papers yet?"

"No, they've disappeared."

"That sounds mighty ominous. Shannon said you think Bradley

may have been murdered over those old documents."

"That's our theory, but the police haven't bought it yet."

"Why would anybody kill over some ninety-year-old papers?"

"If we had the papers, we might find the answer. According to what Bradley told Mr. Liggett on the telephone, a note attached to the documents indicated his grandfather, Sydney Liggett, planned to turn them over to the District Attorney."

"Sydney was assistant treasurer of the company."

Jill came over and perched on the side of my desk. I motioned to her to pick up on her extension.

"I'm bringing my wife in on the conversation, Mr. Geary," I said. "Her name is Jill and she's my partner in the agency."

"Hi, Mr. Geary," she said. "Glad to hear from you."

"A pleasure," he said.

Picking up on his previous comment, I asked, "Do you know who Sydney Liggett's boss was?"

"Sure. The secretary-treasurer, Sam Hedrick. He got involved in the company while it was still successful, before things started going downhill."

That nearly took my breath.

"Was he one of the owners?"

"He was a stockholder. I don't know how much money he had in the company. Probably not a lot, from what I've read. He'd been something of a playboy, had gone through most of his family's money by that time."

"From what we've heard, he was the one who accused Sydney Liggett of embezzling funds."

"Yeah. They had a lot of problems that came out in the bankruptcy case. There were accusations of company officers selling cars out the back door, the money not on the books. The guy who designed the cars and served as general manager until they canned him charged they priced the cars at a loss. It was a big mess. After they brought Hedrick in as secretary-treasurer, it became apparent he knew nothing about manufacturing cars. They named a new president to keep an eye on Hedrick's business habits, but this guy knew nothing about the auto industry, either."

"Sounds like the blind leading the blind," Jill said.

"That's for sure. One of Nashville's leading investment people later said there was no one in charge, and no one connected with the operation knew anything about making cars. They had a good thing going at first but made several basic errors."

"Such as?"

"Instead of concentrating on only two models at first, like Henry Ford did, they tried to compete at three different price levels and several different styles. Everybody, except a few that got out early, lost their shirts when Marathon went under."

"Was Sam Hedrick one of them?"

"He sure was."

I thanked Geary and told him we'd keep in touch. After we hung up the phones, Jill looked across at me.

"Where do you suppose Sam Hedrick got the money to start Hedrick Industries a few years later?" she asked.

I tapped my fingers on the desk as what we had just learned ran through my mind. "I have a hunch those missing papers could hold the clue."

36

WARREN JARVIS CALLED around nine, his voice tight as a guitar string, to see what if anything we had heard from Kelli.

"Nothing," I said. "No email. No fax. No phone call."

"I don't like it, Greg."

"Neither do I, but I'm not sure what we can do about it."

"Well, I've waited long enough. I'm going up there. I intend to camp out at that motel and wait until she shows up or calls."

"I don't blame you. Just let us know of anything you learn."

A short time later, I got the promised call from Allen Vickers. He was a pleasant sounding man but spoke in the hurried voice of a busy executive.

After identifying himself, he asked, "What does McKenzie Investigations want with me?"

"Irving Glastonbury told me he had talked to you, probably a couple of weeks ago, looking for a living relative of Sydney Liggett, who was assistant treasurer of Marathon Motors."

"He sure did. I told him about Arthur Liggett. Are you related?"

"No, but a client of ours is. I wondered who told you about Arthur?" I sat back and waited for another disappointing reply but got a surprise instead.

"He wasn't all that difficult to find. I called a couple of people I knew who were related to some of the Marathon folks. Stone Hedrick's grandfather was secretary-treasurer when the company closed. He knew right away who I was looking for."

"Did you tell him about the papers that were found over at the old Marathon office building?"

"Yeah. He seemed real interested in that. Of course, I told him I didn't really know anything other than what Irving had said, about the note regarding the District Attorney. Do you have any more information on that?"

"No. The papers are missing, and we're currently looking for them."

"Well, good luck. I know some folks got burned. Fortunately, my great-grandfather was one of those who cashed in his chips before things went sour."

I hung up the phone and put a big exclamation point after the notes I had taken. Jill peeked over my shoulder.

"Stone Hedrick? Camilla's father?"

I looked up. "None other. More and more signs are pointing toward Hedrick Industries."

Jill patted the heel of her hand against her forehead. "It just dawned on me where the Samran plant name came from. Sam for the founder and Ran for his son, Randy."

"Good one. I think you're right."

"Should we go up there and let me do my thing with the office people, see if I can find out who the mysterious Kayjay is?"

I spun my chair around. "The sheriff doesn't want us up there, but as long as we stay out of his way, I don't see any problem."

"Sheriff Driscoll doesn't have any say in Macon County anyway."

"You're right as usual, babe. Before we do anything else, it might be fruitful to drop by and see Arthur Liggett. I'll bet Stone Hedrick is the man he told Kelli and Warren about. The one who tried to get him fired."

We arrived at the Safe Harbor Nursing Home around ten-thirty. Liggett's room had just been cleaned. He sat in his recliner, dressed in a fresh shirt and tie, watching the latest financial news on CNBC. I noticed the gray mustache had been trimmed. He looked up when we knocked and walked in.

"Good morning, Mr. Liggett," Jill said. She walked over to pat his arm, which he had stretched out to grip the chair.

"Well, I'm happy to see you two detectives. What have you done with my granddaughter? I haven't heard from her in a couple of days."

"I think she's doing a little checking of her own up in Hartsville and Lafayette," I said. I gave his large, unsteady hand a vigorous shake.

"Tell her not to forget her old granddad."

"I'm sure she wouldn't do that," Jill said.

"Mr. Liggett, you told Kelli about having trouble with a man who tried to get you fired over an equipment order you had cancelled," I said. "Might that have been Stone Hedrick, the chairman of Hedrick Industries?"

He frowned and twitched his mustache. "You're darned right it was Hedrick. The man is only interested in making a buck. Doesn't matter if his equipment is the right thing for your hospital or not. I'm sure he would have happily swatted me like a fly."

I followed Jill's eyes over to the window, where a fly buzzed about the curtain. I felt certain Arthur Liggett was not exaggerating his problems with Hedrick. "Were you aware that his grandfather was your grandfather's boss at Marathon Motors?"

His jaw sagged and his eyes widened. "I had no idea. Do you think he had something to do with those papers disappearing?"

"We think it's a good possibility. If we can nail something down, we'll go to the police."

Liggett's eyes glared with a determined look. "You bring that man down, Mr. McKenzie. Put him behind bars."

As we walked out to the car, Jill shielded her eyes from the sun and gave me an anxious look. "Mr. Hedrick and Mr. Liggett sound like archenemies, don't they?"

"There's certainly no love lost. But I have trouble translating that into murder."

"Could Stone Hedrick know what's in those papers?"

"I suppose it's possible. He took over the business from his grandfather, so he was associated with Sam for several years."

I suggested we head home before starting out to Macon County. I didn't like the way things were shaping up in this case. There had been too much violence already, and we seemed to be closing in on a possible solution. In case we should encounter any more trouble, I wanted to be ready. I intended to pick up my Glock 27 and an ankle holster and let Jill get her little .38 revolver, which she carried in a purse with a special pocket. The Glock was a recent acquisition, ideal for a hot weather weapon. Barely six inches long, the .40 caliber pistol fit neatly beneath my trouser leg and could be accessed quickly in a pinch.

We decided to save time by grabbing a sandwich while we were at home. My watch showed well after noon by the time we started back around Old Hickory Boulevard toward Madison. We began the familiar trek up I-65 and Vietnam Veterans Parkway. Traffic remained a hassle until we passed Gallatin. After that the roads became less traveled. The brilliant August sun seemed to set fire to every shiny object along the highway as we sped past gently swaying cornfields and sweeping green pastures dotted with cows, white, black, brown and spotted.

We saw Warren's rental car in front of the motel in Lafayette. Shortly, we turned south on Highway 10 toward the Samran plant. It was near mid-afternoon when we rolled in there. Monstrous cumulonimbus clouds—a term I had learned from Jill—stretched skyward as their gray and white shoulders rose in the process of nurturing their stormy offspring. I parked in the visitor lot and let down the windows while Jill went in.

Happily, the cloud formations blocked the sun. Unhappily, rather than cooling the temperature, they merely increased the humidity. My shirt had begun to feel like a towel I'd used following a shower. Thanks to the thick, high-topped socks I had donned, the ankle holster was no problem. I considered sitting there with the air conditioner running, but a glance at the gas gauge discouraged that idea.

As I sat there sweating, I tried to piece together in my mind where we stood. Bradley had not given up the Marathon papers before his murder, or there would have been no reason to toss Arthur Liggett's house the next day. An unknown assailant, assisted by Casey Olson, had killed Bradley. The killer then did away with Olson, his witness. Mickey Evans had identified a recent close friend of Casey's from Samran, a man known as Kayjay, who might possess information about Casey's plans and other associates. The killer had apparently dropped a Dallas Lights cigarette when leaving Bradley's home. He had also dropped or discarded a Dallas Lights pack near the scene of Casey's death. Shelby Williams' story had checked out, eliminating him as a suspect.

We now knew that Stone Hedrick was aware of the hidden papers, that he detested Arthur Liggett. And it was beginning to look like he had knowledge of what the papers contained. As I thought about Hedrick's involvement, I recalled my discussion with Camilla Rottman Friday night. I had mentioned a case where a man was killed because he had something somebody else wanted. She had picked up on our comment the day before about going to the police regarding a murder. And as we were leaving, Jill told about our plans to attend Pierce Bradley's funeral. Jill didn't mention the name, but Camilla would have known the identity of the reference. She no doubt tied it to the case we were working. Which led to the question of Camilla's involvement.

Immersed as I was in my mental ramblings and lulled by the heat, I sat up, startled, when Jill opened the passenger side door and slid onto the seat. I glanced at my watch. She had been inside for almost half an hour.

"You must have made some headway," I said. "You've got that chessy cat grin."

"You want to know who Kayjay is?"

"I believe that's why we came here."

"Okay, Mr. Smarty Pants, it's Kirk J. Rottman."

"Camilla's son," I blurted.

Jill gave me a knowing look. "I notice you said Camilla's, not Roger's."

"She's the one who seemed to be more concerned about him."

"Well, he's the maintenance supervisor at the plant. He was Casey Olson's boss."

I got a sudden feeling of apprehension. "You didn't talk to him, did you?"

"No. They said he wasn't working today. Incidentally, several people from Samran plan to be at Casey's funeral tomorrow."

How close was Kirk Rottman to Casey? I wondered. How much

had they shared about each other's lives? I decided Mickey Evans
might be the key to answering those questions. I also wondered what
Kelli had pumped out of her.

I started the car. "Let's pay a call on your young friend Mickey. I
have several more questions that she might be able to answer, now
that we have a better idea of what we're looking for."

The grin returned. "Okay, dear. You're going back into Trousdale
County. Just remember to stay out of Sheriff Driscoll's way."

I intended to. "Why don't you get on your phone and find an
address for Kirk. He could be in either Lafayette or Hartsville."

As we drove along, Jill got busy on the phone while I kept one
eye on the road and one on the huge cloud formation with its anvil-
shaped, flattened top. My pilot confidant had taught me this was a
fellow you should avoid. However, it appeared to be moving on a
track that would soon intersect with ours.

By the time we reached Highway 25 on the outskirts of Hartsville,
I had to switch on my headlights. The clock on the dash glowed 3:00
P.M., but the sky looked more like eight or nine at night. Huge
raindrops soon began to pelt the windshield, almost with the force of
hailstones.

"You'd better take it easy, Greg," Jill said. "This looks like it could
be a doozy of a storm."

I slowed to 25 as we entered the town and took the cutoff that
would become Main Street. We passed few cars as the rain battered
down in torrents, creating impromptu streams along the roadside.
Streaks of lightning burned jagged paths through the darkened sky,
and thunder rumbled like a series of explosive eruptions that shook
the earth. Wind gusts made bushes along the street sway like dancers
in a bizarre choreographed routine.

We finally made it up the hill to Mickey Evans' house, where I
was relieved to see her small Ford in the driveway. I knew we should
have called or checked the restaurant first, but I didn't relish the
thought of making more than one trip out in this deluge. Ruts in the
driveway had already become mini-ponds.

"Want to try the umbrellas?" I asked. The small collapsible jobs
were stashed behind the front seat.

"This wind would blow them apart. We might as well run for it."

I jumped out and made a dash for the porch, not in my best form with the weight of the ankle holster. Jill came behind me. She huddled close to the wall in an attempt to avoid the gusty sheets of rain.

The screen stood open, blown back against the wall, it's spring hanging down, stretched out of shape. I pounded on the door loud enough to wake the dead.

No answer.

"Maybe she's in the back and can't hear with all the racket this storm is making," Jill said. "Try the door."

I turned the knob and pushed.

The door opened.

I tugged at Jill's arm. "Get in there before you drown."

I followed her inside and closed the door. Apparently the storm had knocked out the electricity as no lights showed anywhere. With the shades drawn, I could barely see.

"What's that smell?" Jill asked.

I didn't answer. The odor had assaulted my nostrils as soon as the door closed. It was a smell you never forgot, once you'd experienced it. Shifting my eyes about the room ahead, I stepped back with one leg, went into a half-crouch, and pulled the Glock from its holster at the other ankle. I detected no movement. Turning to the nearest window, I tugged at the shade. It slipped from my fingers and clattered to the top, ending with a bang that jangled my already tense nerves. The storm had begun to pass, brightening the sky. Pale light streamed through the window.

Jill uttered a muffled cry. I saw her hand reach up to cover her mouth.

"Don't move, babe," I said, trying to keep my voice calm.

The crumpled figure of a girl dressed in a pink nightgown lay on the floor a few feet beyond us. A pair of broken glasses lay at one side. Blood spatters marked the carpet, the sofa and the wall behind, as if someone had thrown a can of paint in that direction. Her face had been beaten almost beyond recognition. But there was no mistaking the short brown hair. It was Mickey Evans.

I gripped the Glock, moving cautiously, although the brown color of the blood told me this was a crime scene several hours old. Reaching her side, I put my hand down to check her pulse. The cold stiffness of her arm told me we were way too late. Rigor mortis had done its job.

37

NO MATTER HOW MANY homicides you've seen, and for me that numbered quite a few, you're never fully prepared for the lengths to which people will go to desecrate the bodies of their fellow humans. It's especially bad when the victim is someone you've met. Someone who's already gotten a raw deal out of life.

While Jill and I stood there transfixed by the unholy scene before us, the retreating storm added its own gruesome graphic as a distant flash of lightning produced a momentary glow, highlighting the lifeless body on the floor.

"Let's get out of here," I said, keeping my voice low but determined. "Don't touch anything. I'll get the door."

She dabbed a tissue at her eyes as I held the door with my handkerchief.

Out on the porch, I found the rain had turned into a moderate but steady shower. The wind had died down a bit and the lightning had almost disappeared in the distance. In our earlier rush to get inside the house, I hadn't noticed the drop in temperature. Now the skin on my arms tingled, almost a shiver, as I hurried across to the Jeep.

After settling down behind the wheel, I got out my cell phone and punched in the sheriff's number. The dispatcher answered.

"I need to speak to Sheriff Driscoll," I said.

The guy sounded bored. "He isn't in."

"Is he still tied up with that big operation going down today?"

His attitude changed. "I can't comment on that."

"Well, you'd better get in touch with him and advise him he's got another corpse on his hands. And this one is gruesome."

The dispatcher's tone shifted from businesslike to full alert. "A corpse . . . where?"

I identified myself, gave him Mickey Evans' name and address, and explained what we had found. I suggested he have Driscoll call me on the cell phone.

"That poor girl," Jill said when I had turned off the phone. "Who could have done such a terrible thing to her?"

"Somebody who was damned angry."

"It's such a waste." She stared at the crumpled tissue. "First Casey, and now her."

"Probably the same killer got them both."

She shook her head, then turned to me. "Do we need to wait around here for the sheriff?"

I looked at my watch. It was close to four o'clock.

"No. It will take a while for the TBI forensics team to get here. Nothing will be done before that. Why don't we run over to Big Mama's and see what she can tell us about Mickey's movements over the recent past?"

I drove into town, avoiding a few fresh potholes, and turned toward the restaurant. Only two cars sat in front as we parked and went in.

"Well, if it ain't the Nashville private police force," Big Mama said in her commanding voice. "You up here for the big bust?"

"What big bust?" Jill asked.

"One that's on the TV." She pointed to a monitor mounted on a shelf above the check-out counter. It presently showed a stylish A frame house nestled in a rural setting. "The high sheriff was just on. He told about finding a cave beneath that house where they was growing marijuana. Hundreds of plants. Biggest bust ever in Tennessee."

"That should've made him happy," I said.

"Oh, he was grinnin' all right. Y'all can take that table over there."

As we headed over by the front window, my cell phone rang.

"What the hell have you done now, McKenzie?" Sheriff Driscoll asked.

"I just did my civic duty, Sheriff. We went to visit Mickey Evans and found her on the living room floor with her head bashed in. I called the local authorities as I was honor-bound to do."

He let out a noisy breath. "Well, I'm getting a little tired of all this messy mayhem. That stuff didn't happen around here until you showed up. I may have to put out an order to stop you at the county line in the future."

"I trust you're only joking," I said.

"Mostly. But it is beginning to jar my nerves."

I decided a new tack was in order. "Congratulations on the big marijuana catch, Sheriff. I just heard about it."

His voice mellowed. "Yeah, that was nice. Our multi-county Drug Task Force has been working on it for nearly five years. We finally got the bastards. You wouldn't believe what they were doing in there."

"It was a cave?"

"They built the house on top of it. Nobody lived there. They had a passage leading underground where they had the most sophisticated operation you ever saw. Lights and climate control. They could raise a crop in two months that would take four-and-a-half on the outside."

"Make any arrests?"

"Yeah. We got the three dudes that ran it." He was silent for a moment. "The TBI crew is about ready to wrap it up over here. I don't imagine they'll be all that happy about it, but it looks like they'll have to set up again in Hartsville. I'd better get with Wayne and tell him what's happened. That Evans woman was Casey Olson's girlfriend."

I looked out at the rain that continued its steady drum beat on the window. "Right. My guess is the same guy got her that killed Casey."

"Maybe so. Where are you?"

"We're at Big Mama's. Just sat down."

"Enjoy your meal, and stick around. We may need to talk again."

Big Mama came over when she saw I was off the phone. "What can I get you folks?"

"It's a little early for supper," I said. "Just bring me a cup of decaf."

"Make it two," Jill said. "No cream for either of us."

After Big Mama left to get our coffee, Jill put her elbows on the table and rested her chin on folded hands, her eyes fixed on me. "What do you want to ask her?"

"Anything she can tell us about Mickey over the last forty-eight hours."

When the oversize proprietress brought our cups a few minutes later, I asked if she'd like to sit down, that I had some bad news for her.

With the help of a little huffing and puffing, she lowered herself onto the chair across from me. "What's going on?"

"We just came from Mickey Evans' house. I'm afraid she's met with some terribly foul play."

The heavy jowls sagged as her face took on a look of dismay. "I don't understand. You mean—" She stopped as she saw tears well in Jill's eyes. "No . . . no . . . what happened?"

I reached across and took her large hand in mine. "I'm sorry, but she's dead. We found her at her house a little while ago."

She began to whimper. "I knew it. I knew that girl would come to a bad end. I tried to help her."

"You did help her," Jill said. "She told me you put her to work when everything was falling apart. Some terrible person killed her. We hope you can help us get some idea of who did it."

"We need you to think really hard and tell us everything you remember about what she did from the time she came to work Saturday," I said.

A small waitress with a slight limp brought Big Mama a glass of water. After a few minutes, she calmed down enough to begin her reminiscing. I sipped my coffee as she recalled the past two days.

Mickey had come to work as scheduled at three on Saturday afternoon. It was a routine evening.

"The only unusual thing I remember is her talking a lot to a red-headed woman who was a newspaper reporter from out of town. I had to get onto her about taking care of her other customers, but she said the woman kept asking questions."

"What kind of questions?" I asked.

"Mostly about Casey Olson's murder. Pierce Bradley, too. Said she was writing stories on the case for a paper up north."

Just what Mickey had told Jill on the phone. Big Mama said Mickey left when the café closed at nine. On Sunday, Mickey came to work at eleven A.M.

"Anything particular you recall about that shift?" Jill asked.

"That newspaper woman came back late in the afternoon. She cornered Mickey again, looking real intense, asked a couple of questions and left."

"Did Mickey say what she was after?"

Big Mama screwed up her face, thinking. "Something about Casey's boss at Samran. I think she wanted to know where he hung out."

"Did Mickey know?"

"She told her some place she knew about, but I don't know where it was."

I pushed my coffee cup aside. "Do you recall anything else?"

She shrugged her large shoulders, like a buffalo getting ready to move on. "I don't think so. She left around seven that evening. That's the last I saw of her. Oh, God, I can't believe this."

She pulled a napkin from around a set of utensils, wiped her eyes and blew her nose. Getting up from the table, she excused herself, said she needed to go to the kitchen.

That's when my cell phone rang. I made a mental note to put it on the charger when we got back in the car.

"This is Patricia Cook, Mr. McKenzie. We just got back from Lebanon, and I found your note in the door."

"Thank you for calling," I said. "I wondered when it might be convenient for my wife Jill and I to come over and talk with you for a few minutes?"

"Where are you?"

"We're in Hartsville at Big Mama's restaurant."

"That woman," she said with a chuckle. "If you'd like to come over now it would be fine. I think I have something you're looking for."

My heart skipped a beat. "What is it?"

"Some papers from Marathon Motor Works."

38

PATRICIA COOK AND her daughter, Marcie, met us at the door. Mrs. Cook's face had gained a bit more color since we'd seen her at the funeral, but her hair still resembled what my mother called a rag mop. She gave us a polite smile, though, and invited us in.

I shook my little collapsible umbrella. "We'll just leave these out here."

"Nonsense," she said. "Give them to me. I'll just set them here in the foyer. It won't hurt anything."

The foyer was floored with tile. The living room had a large stone fireplace that reminded me of our own in Hermitage. We sat on a brocade sofa with a floral design while Mrs. Cook took a chair across from us. She lifted a black leather case that sat beside it. I recognized the type used by Air Force pilots to stow maps and charts, radio frequencies and the like.

"This was Pierce's," she said. "He carried his important papers in it. I told you about the argument we had the afternoon before he . . . before he disappeared."

"Yes, I recall," I said when she hesitated, swallowing hard.

"He left in such a rush I didn't notice if he had it or not."

"Where did you find it?"

She looked across the room with a meek, tentative smile. "Behind that chair over there, where he had sat. I should have seen it, but I hadn't gone around that way, I guess. Then, after the sheriff came by, I was so upset I wasn't fit to look for anything."

"Did you just find it tonight?" Jill asked.

She nodded. "We spent a couple of days with my brother-in-law. They helped get my emotions back under control. When I read your note, I went right to it." She opened the case, pulled out a large brown envelope and held it out to me. "I believe this is what you've been looking for."

I got up and took the envelope, which had "Liggett" printed in large letters on the front. As I returned to sit by Jill, I opened it and slipped out a sheaf of yellowed paper. Clipped to it was a note bearing the signature of Sydney Liggett and the date August 7, 1914.

I looked up. "Mrs. Cook, you have just saved the day for my clients. I can't thank you enough."

"As I understand it, Pierce had intended to deliver the envelope to a Mr. Liggett in Nashville. I presume he's your client."

"Actually, we were retained by his granddaughter. But we'll see that it gets to Mr. Liggett."

Her face had a forlorn look. "Maybe, if Pierce had carried it to Nashville that night . . . ."

Her voice trailed off.

I had to agree with her, but in this case fate didn't allow second chances.

"We had better get this on back before anything else happens," I said, stuffing the papers into the envelope. I didn't mention the latest victim of the Marathon murderer. She wasn't ready to take on any more bad news.

As Jill and I got up to leave, I thanked Patricia again.

"I'm sorry my husband wasn't in here to meet you," she said. "He's out back unpacking. His sister-in-law gave us tons of string beans and corn and tomatoes she'd been canning. Lord, that woman has to clean jars off the shelf every year to make room for new stuff."

Marcie, who had sat out of the way, watching silently, all during our stay, stepped over beside her mother and waved. "Bye," she said. "Hope you don't get caught in another storm."

"We do, too," Jill said. "Bye, bye."

As we walked out to the car, I stared at the envelope. This wasn't the time or the place to start digesting its contents, but I couldn't help wondering what could be in it that warranted all the destruction of life it had triggered. I handed it to Jill as she slid into her seat.

"I feel like we should have a safe in here to put this in," she said.

"Not a bad idea. But for the moment, just stick it under your seat."

Before starting the car, I called Warren.

"I'm getting worried as hell," he said. "Kelli hasn't showed up and hasn't called. Mrs. Zander——she and her husband run the place——said Kelli's bed wasn't slept in last night."

"Did you ask what kind of car she was driving? A lot of motels require that information."

"Yeah, I checked. It was a blue Malibu."

"Did they get the license number?"

"No, but Mrs. Zander is a sharp little lady. She went out front to talk to Kelli one time and noticed the car tag was from Nashville. It had a Titans sticker on the back bumper."

"I'd better hire that lady. Most people don't even pay attention to what state's involved. What else has happened since you've been there?"

"It's been quiet, except for a wrong number. I guess that's what it was."

"On your cell phone?"

"Yeah. Guy asked who it was. When I told him Colonel Jarvis, he said, 'Oh, sorry,' and hung up."

"Well, we're presently in Hartsville. We'll keep an eye out for Kelli. Damn, I almost forgot about the good news. Patricia Cook, Pierce Bradley's sister, found the Marathon papers."

"That's great, Greg. Have you determined what it's all about?"

I looked up at the windshield as the spattering rain picked up in intensity. Although it was early evening, the dark overcast gave the landscape a look more like the fading shades of dusk.

"The papers look pretty fragile," I said. "We'll need to sit down at a table and take a close look at the whole set of documents before we can make any kind of assessment."

"What do you plan to do now?"

I told him about Mickey Evans' death and the sheriff's instructions to stay around Hartsville for the present. I also mentioned what Jill had learned at Samran about Kirk Rottman, and the word Big

Mama had given us about Kelli looking for information on Casey Olson's boss.

"Sounds like you two have been busy," Warren said. "I may head that way soon. I'll give you a call."

Closing my phone, I plugged it into the charger connected to the car battery.

I turned to Jill. "Where's our Mapquest map of Hartsville?"

Jill spread the map out in front of me as I switched on the overhead light. We had cobbled the map together by printing several scrolled out views from the computer, then taping the pages to make a single sheet. I found the street where Kirk Rottman lived running off of Old Lafayette Road east of town. It was in what you might call, for lack of a better term, the Hartsville suburbs, if a town with one traffic signal could be considered to have any such.

"You know what we haven't done?" Jill asked.

"Tell me."

"We haven't checked the office phone to see if Shelby Williams called with names of the people he gave Dallas Lights."

"Then best we do it now, babe."

She powered up her cell phone and called. After a moment, she punched in our answering machine replay code and listened.

My own phone rang about that time, and I grabbed it up and answered.

"Who is this?" a male voice asked.

I gave my usual answer. "Who wants to know?"

As he stammered around for a moment, I checked the caller ID. It showed a number in Hartsville. "I guess I have the wrong number," he said and hung up.

"Who was that?" Jill asked.

I laid the phone down and frowned. "Who knows? What did you find out?"

"There were five people on Williams's list. One was Kirk Rottman."

I swung around in the seat and stared at her. "Did any of the others sound familiar?"

"No. He said Kirk was the only person from within the company."

I rubbed the stubble on my chin. "That is troubling."

We reviewed what we knew about Camilla and Roger's son, Kirk. He had been a troublemaker as a kid, drank too much, gambled, smoked pot, had been "chummy" with Casey Olson in the past week or so. He had visited Mickey Evans' house, but she was turned off by him. And he smoked Dallas Lights.

"Let's go check out Mr. Rottman's house," I said, starting the car.

"Shouldn't we call the sheriff or Wayne Fought?"

"I imagine they're pretty busy at the moment. We'll call after we see where young Kirk lives."

I drove over to Highway 25 and hung a right. I spotted the turn-off, also known as Melrose Drive, just past the funeral home where we had attended Pierce Bradley's service on Saturday. I drove slowly, so as not to miss Rottman's street in the semi-darkness.

We found it in a wooded area with only a smattering of houses. The first one we came to was under construction. The framing and roof appeared finished, with work just beginning on the outside walls. An old portable concrete mixer sat beside the driveway, which had been covered with gravel. As I started past the house, Jill shouted:

"Stop, Greg! Back up."

The anti-lock brakes did their thing. I shifted into reverse.

"What's up?"

"That car up next to the new house. It's blue, maybe a Malibu."

I pulled into the driveway, eased toward the parked car.

I saw the Malibu nameplate and Davidson County markings on the license tag. Nashville and Davidson County were one under the Metro umbrella. The bumper contained a sticker with a T-shaped Roman sword surrounded by three stars and a trailing flame, the familiar Titans logo.

This was Kelli's car.

39

A S I OPENED THE door to go check on the vehicle, Jill poked the black umbrella at me. Mine was black, hers red. "You'd better take this if you don't want to drown."

The pesky rain had let up a bit but still posed a problem. My shirt was damp in spots from getting in and out of the Jeep. I pulled the Glock off my leg and stuck it under my belt. I could free my gun hand quickly if necessary. With umbrella in one hand and a small flashlight in the other, I walked up to the Malibu. I kept my head swiveling back and forth, checking the area for any movement. All growth had been cleared from around the house, and it was still light enough to see into the nearby trees.

The Malibu was locked, as expected. Shining my small point of light through a front window, I spotted a container on the floor that resembled Warren's description of Kelli's disguise case. The only other things I saw were a water bottle on the front seat and a copy of *The Christian Science Monitor* in back. She must have bought it before leaving Nashville.

When I returned to the Jeep, Jill gave me a questioning look.

"It's hers," I said. "No doubt about it. Even contains a copy of *The Monitor*."

"Where do you suppose she is?"

"If I had to make an educated guess, I'd say somewhere around Kirk Rottman's house. Let's go take a look."

I drove on down the street past a large frame house, a small open field, then more woods, until I saw a mailbox with Rottman's house number. I switched off the headlights and continued slowly. The house sat back in the trees, some thirty yards from the road. Blinds had been drawn in front. Light showed in a large window on the right, likely the living room.

"There's a car parked next to the house," Jill said in a hushed voice.

I eased on past until a line of tall bushes hid us from the house. Swinging onto the shoulder, which I hoped was solid enough to give the traction we'd need for a quick getaway, I pulled on the handbrake and switched off the ignition. As we sat there, something clicked in my brain.

"Didn't you jot down Rottman's phone number as well as his address?"

Jill handed me a slip of paper. I took out my penlight and held it so that only a speck of light shined on the paper between my knees. I flipped open the cell phone and checked the incoming call that purported to be a wrong number.

"That bastard has Kelli's phone," I said with a growl.

Jill gasped. "Why would you say that?"

"The wrong number I got a while ago? The caller was from Hartsville. It came from Kirk Rottman's phone. Okay, maybe he accidentally hit my number in the six-one-five area code. But Warren got the same call. Where would you find both our numbers? In Kelli's cell phone contact list."

Jill stared at me. I could barely see her eyes in the darkness. Her voice carried a new urgent tone. "What can we do?"

"I've got to know if Kelli's in there."

"And how do you propose to find out?"

"I'll have to work my way up close enough to see through a window, or find a way inside."

She clutched my arm. "If Kirk Rottman killed those three people, he's a dangerous maniac. You'd better wait here for Agent Fought, Greg."

I'd thought of that, but it seemed too big a risk.

"Dangerous, yes. But not a total maniac. I think he knows exactly what he's doing. It sounds like he's trying to get information out of Kelli. If he doesn't get it, then he could go berserk and treat her the same way he did Mickey Evans. It could be too late already. I can't wait around and take a chance."

I had shifted the Glock to a more comfortable position when I got in the car. I moved it back to the ready.

"What should I do?" Jill asked, almost frantic.

"Call Fought and the sheriff. Tell them what we learned and what's happening. Get your gun in your hand and sit tight. If anybody comes out and it isn't me, shoot first and ask questions later."

"What if you need help?"

"It shouldn't take them long to get here. Keep your eyes and ears open and let them know the situation as soon as they arrive." I leaned over and kissed her. "We'll be okay, babe. Keep the faith."

She squeezed my arm until I thought her fingers would leave holes.

"Be careful, Greg. I love you."

"I love you, too," I whispered.

I slipped out the door and eased it shut. By now the rain had dwindled to a drizzle, which wasn't the most comfortable environment, but one I could live with. I was happy I had decided on my typical dark colored shirt this morning, with navy pants. I didn't worry about being seen as I skirted around the trees toward the house. I navigated through soft, squishy soil, doing my best to avoid mud holes.

Approaching the house from the end opposite the living room, I found two windows, likely bedrooms. The structure featured brick up to the window level, wood the rest of the way. A pale glow showed through the window of the back room. The blinds fit snug, however, leaving no chance of seeing around the edges. I put my ear close and listened. I detected no sound.

Easing around to the rear of the house, I saw another window. It must have been in the same room. Since the lot sloped to the rear, I searched about, found an old concrete block and boosted myself even with the opening. This blind had not been let down all the way. A small space beneath it allowed me to view a narrow slice of the interior. I identified what I saw as the surface of a bed covered by a tan spread.

My elation at this break quickly disappeared as my gaze moved to the right. A pair of bare female legs stretched across the bedspread.

The feet were tied to what I could see of two bedposts. I had observed the same bright red toenails in Kelli's sandals on Blair Boulevard last Wednesday. Then I saw the gleaming blade of a long knife. My heartbeat went into overdrive as it dropped onto the bed between Kelli's legs. I took that as a threat of something soon to come. Too soon.

I stepped off my block perch and ran toward wooden steps at the other end of the house. They led up to a small deck. It provided access to a kitchen door. Light flowed from a window I reasoned would be above the sink. As I took the steps at a run, I noticed an overstuffed garbage can with the lid ajar. A pizza box lay half-exposed. I checked and found it relatively dry. That meant it had been discarded recently. Did it also mean the door been left unlocked?

I moved around a rusted barbeque grill and eased up to the door, which contained a window in the upper half.

By now I had virtually shut out the misty weather from consideration. The adrenaline flowed like a surging tide. I felt the tension of a race against time. Scant knowledge of the man I would soon encounter kited up the situation. The only certainty was his capability for extreme violence. I couldn't block out that image of Kelli's bare legs tied to the bed. Add to that the more gruesome picture of Mickey Evans on her living room floor. As my anger grew, I fought to keep myself calm. This was no time to get irrational.

A sheer curtain covered the window, allowing a full, though somewhat fuzzy, view of the kitchen. It included the usual appliances, along with a round wood table and four chairs. I saw a glass-covered light fixture mounted above the table. A doorway toward the front probably opened into the living room. Glancing around, I saw no one. I grasped the doorknob, gave it a gentle twist.

The knob turned.

There was also a deadbolt. Could rattling the door make enough noise to alert Kirk Rottman? This was no time for debate. I pulled on the knob.

The door came open.

Crossing the room quickly, I passed near the range. In my rush, I failed to notice a pan with a long handle that stuck out from the stovetop. My hip brushed against it. As I looked around, the pan toppled off the stove.

I grabbed at the handle but hit it instead. As I watched in what seemed like slow motion, the pan careened toward the floor.

The clatter made enough noise to wake a corpse.

I knew I'd lost the element of surprise, but I hesitated only for a moment. Maybe I could still catch him off guard. Throwing caution aside, I ran through the doorway into the living room like a rookie cop on his first crime-in-progress call.

A gunshot inside a small house makes a hell of a racket. And when the sound is accompanied by a stinging sensation in your arm, you know you're in big trouble. Especially if it's your right arm, and you're a right-handed shooter.

My Glock fell to the floor as I looked down at the blood and grabbed my arm.

40

ORTUNATELY, I HADN'T squared my body into a two-handed stance, or I'd have taken a bullet in the chest. It appeared to be only a flesh wound to my upper arm. I flexed my hand. The fingers still worked okay. But I now stood defenseless as the young man I recognized from Friday night stood in the doorway to a hall. He aimed what appeared to be a .38 revolver directly at me. I took a deep breath to calm the thumping in my chest.

"You must be Kirk Rottman," I said, hoping I sounded calmer to him than I did to myself.

I eased toward the back of a nearby chair. My Glock had landed beside it.

"Stay where you are, Mr. McKenzie. I recognize you, too. My mother told me about you."

I tried to muster a smile. "I went by to see her yesterday afternoon, Kirk. Do you know what she wanted?"

"Man, I got no earthly idea."

He wasn't a trained shooter. He held the gun in one hand, his finger on the trigger. At this range, I figured he got me with a lucky shot. I wondered if Casey Olson had been the victim of worse luck. More likely he was shot close-up as he turned to flee. I decided my best defense was to keep Rottman talking. It would also take my mind off the pain in my arm.

"Camilla wanted me to take on a private investigation for her. She wanted me to snoop around and find out who your dad has been sleeping with."

He broke out laughing. "Son of a bitch. That sounds like her. Hell, he wouldn't know what to do——"

While his attention was distracted, I dived behind the chair, reaching out to grab my pistol.

He fired two quick shots, one burying itself in the lower part of the large upholstered chair, the other hitting the floor at least a foot to one side.

I gripped the Glock, flexing my trigger finger. The arm hurt, but I had apparently suffered no ligament or muscle damage.

With as fast a move as I could manage, I stuck my head and arms out almost at floor level and fired where I knew he should have been. I heard the sound of something falling. As I raised my head just above the chair, a wild burst of laughter came from the hallway.

"Damn! You almost got me that time. Why don't you come on back in the bedroom? I have your friend in there. If you don't get rid of that gun, I'm gonna do something gross to her."

Rottman's footsteps hurried up the hallway, and I wondered where the hell Fought and Sheriff Driscoll were.. Help should have been here by now.

I pulled out my handkerchief and tied it around my bleeding arm. Walking cautiously, I held my gun out, arcing left and right, and approached the doorway. I made a quick move through the opening, ready to fire. The hall was vacant. As I edged toward the door to the back bedroom, I kept the gun in front of me. I strained to catch a glimpse inside the room.

The head of the bed suddenly came into view. Kirk Rottman stood with the long knife I had seen through the window. He leaned over Kelli's body, holding the blade against her chest just below the sternum. Even if I succeeded in killing him with a single shot, which was unlikely, he could fall and plunge the knife into her heart.

"Throw your gun on the bed," he said in a voice as icy as a glacier. "Unless you want to see this woman's guts all over the place."

I didn't see any alternative. As I tossed the Glock onto the bed, I thought of Jill out in the car. She must have heard the shots. Would she follow my advice and stay put, or would she be as hardheaded as me and wander into harm's way?

I turned my attention back to Kelli. She had been stripped to bra and panties. Her skin appeared white where it had been hidden from the sun. I'm sure her assignment hadn't given her the time to lounge around the pool like Camilla. Her face showed several bruises. She still wore the red hair we had heard about. A strip of duct tape covered her mouth. The bed was a four-poster. Strips of duct tape secured her arms to the head posts. Her brow furrowed as she looked across at me. What I saw appeared more loathing than fear. She was one tough lady.

"What do you want from us?" I asked.

Glancing around the room, I saw a small chest next to the bed. A dresser with a large mirror stood against the adjacent wall. In front of it sat a small three-legged stool.

"I want to know what the cops know about me, what you people have told them about those papers. Mostly, I want to know where the hell the papers are."

I considered whether to send him out in the open where Jill could train her .38 on him. It seemed a better idea than leaving him here to do whatever he had in mind.

"That's easy," I said. "The papers are in my car out on the street."

I saw his fist grip the knife, his knuckles turning white. "Don't shit me, man."

"I have them in my car. Pierce Bradley's sister, Patricia Cook, found them in his pilot's case that he left at her house last Monday afternoon. Put that knife down and untie Miss Kane, I'll show you where the papers are."

It had already been more than twenty minutes. If Fought and Driscoll hadn't arrived by the time we got to the car, I'd drop to the ground and let Jill take care of Rottman. She had spent a lot of time on the range and become a proficient marksman.

The young man twisted his face in an evil grin. "You aren't going anywhere, mister. I've already killed three people. Two more won't make that much difference. In fact, killing can be fun once you get into it. You're a military man. You ought to know that."

"Son, killing is never fun, especially in the military."

Without moving the knife, he reached over and picked up my Glock. "Get up against the wall and put your hands behind your back.

After I get you trussed up, I'll check out your car."

I faced the wall and held my hands back as instructed. Now I really began to worry about Jill. The window would be up in the car. Would she let it down so she could get a clear shot? Would he see her first and try to kill her?

I heard him rummaging around behind me. I turned my head enough to catch a glimpse of him in the dresser's mirror. He had laid down the gun and picked up a roll of duct tape.

"Don't get any ideas, old man," he said, moving closer.

I held my hands apart. I felt him begin to stick tape on my right hand and pull it toward the left. If I intended to do anything, it had to be now. I was no match for him physically, but at the moment he was unarmed. And I had the advantage of surprise.

Spinning, I swung my right leg around. I got my foot behind his ankle and pulled forward. At the same time, I pushed off against the wall with my left hand, leaning into him.

He toppled over backward, me right on top of him. I jabbed an elbow into his stomach. A loud grunt sounded as the breath came out of him. While he was momentarily stunned, I rolled over and began to kick his body with all my strength. After a few good blows, I jumped up and started for the Glock, which lay on the dresser.

Before I could make it, he reached out a hand and grabbed my foot, tripping me. I came down on my left side, stretched out like a ballplayer sliding home headfirst. I felt more anger than shock. Finding myself next to the three-legged stool, I grabbed one leg with my good arm, swung it forward and threw the stool at him. I heard a solid thud as it struck his head. He groaned and rolled to the side, letting go of my foot.

Scrambling onto my knees, I grabbed the gun.

"I was trained to shoot to kill," I warned him. "And I have eight rounds to do the job. Roll over on your stomach and stretch your hands out above your head."

He took me at my word, turning onto his stomach, hands outstretched. I wished I had brought a pair of handcuffs. The duct tape would have to suffice. Not wanting him to pull my trick in reverse, I straddled his body and rested my substantial weight on his legs as I applied the tape. In my anger, I wasn't too gentle.

"Did you rape her?" I demanded.

"No, no, man. I just pulled off her clothes to embarrass her. I thought it would make her easier to deal with."

I shoved my hand against the back of his head. "Stay right there. Don't move. I'm not taking my eye off you."

I edged over beside the bed, reached down and peeled the tape off Kelli's mouth. "Are you okay?" I asked.

She twitched her lips and spoke in a weary voice. "Yeah, I think so. Get me out of this."

I used Rottman's knife to cut the ropes and the duct tape, freeing her arms and legs. She stretched them carefully, then swung her legs off the bed and sat up.

"Do you know what he did with your clothes?" I asked.

"They should be in the front bedroom. That's apparently where the bastard took them off. Where's his gun? I'd like to shoot him right now."

With the determination in her voice, I had little doubt she would gladly do it.

I gave her a sympathetic shake of my head. "Can't blame you, Kelli. I wouldn't mind having a piece of him as well. But I don't believe that would be too good an idea. Go in there and get your clothes on. Sheriff Driscoll and the TBI are on the way. They should be here any minute."

I went back to stand behind Rottman.

"What do you plan to do with me?" he asked. His voice was now filled with anxiety.

"I'm turning you over to the cops. What they do is up to them."

Kelli had gone into the other bedroom. "The police are here," she called out. "We'd better signal them everything's okay. They may come in shooting at shadows."

In the heat of battle, I had forgotten my cell phone, which was stuck in the small scabbard on my belt. Surprisingly, it hadn't fallen out. I had turned it off before approaching the house, not wanting a ring to spoil my surprise. I punched in Jill's number.

"Greg, are you all right?" she asked, an anxious note in her voice.

"Kelli and I are fine. Tell the Sheriff, or whoever's out there, to come on in. All's clear."

"Agent Fought is standing beside the car. Do you want to talk to him?"

"Sure. Put him on."

I heard her say something, then Fought's voice.

"What the hell's going on in there, McKenzie?"

"We have your murderer, but I don't have any handcuffs. Better get on in here."

There was disbelief in his voice. "Who've you got?"

"Kirk Rottman, Casey Olson's superior at the Samran plant. I don't think he realized what he was doing, but he confessed to three murders in the presence of two witnesses."

41

WARREN JARVIS CALLED while we were still in Rottman's house. I told him we had rescued Kelli, that she was okay. I gave him directions. He said he'd be here as fast as his rental car would take the curves and hills.

Fought made the arrest, read Rottman his rights and turned him over to another TBI agent. They hauled him off to Sheriff Driscoll's jail in Hartsville. One of the TBI techs brought in a first aid kit and patched up my injured arm.

"You'd better stop by the ER and let them take a look at that," he said. "I notice you flinched pretty good when I tried to clean it."

I grimaced. "Yeah. Thanks a lot for checking my reflexes."

Fought joined us in the living room and queried Kelli and me on what had happened. I gave a capsule version of what we had learned, starting with the Dallas Lights, the trail leading to Hedrick Industries and Jill's visit to Samran. I described our attempt to check with Mickey Evans about Kirk Rottman, and the cell phone calls that convinced us we were on the right track.

Fought looked across with a troubled stare. "Why didn't you call me?"

"You made it pretty plain last night that you would be tied up all day today. Incidentally, congratulations. I understand you made the biggest marijuana bust in Tennessee history."

He ran fingers through hair as black as his eyes. "It was pretty spectacular." He turned to Kelli. "What was your role in this affair?"

She started out by telling him she was Arthur Liggett's granddaughter, the one who had hired us to find the Marathon Papers. She knew the problems we were having and decided to come up here and help with the case.

"Obviously you're not a reporter for the *Christian Science Monitor*. Why did you make that up?"

"I thought I could get more information as a newspaper reporter. It worked."

"It also got you in a lot of trouble. How did you wind up Rottman's captive?"

"I interviewed Mickey Evans to get information on Casey's supervisor at Samran. He sounded like a prime suspect. After I got his name, I started making inquiries around town about Kirk Rottman. The last time I talked to Mickey yesterday, she gave me the name of a roadhouse where she'd heard he hung out. I went there and found him late last night. I told him I'd heard he could steer me toward a good source of pot. He denied smoking pot or knowing anything about it, although he sat there with a joint between his fingers. I said Mickey Evans told me he'd know where I could find some."

I bit my lower lip. She didn't know about Mickey's murder.

"What happened then?"

"I thought there was a good prospect that he took the Marathon Papers after killing Bradley and Olson. So while he was at the tavern, I found his house and came inside."

"You broke in," Fought said.

She frowned. "That's being a bit harsh. The door was unlocked. It was practically an invitation to come in."

I doubted that. She was probably a good lock picker.

"What did you find? Did he surprise you?"

She looked down at her hands, shaking her head. "I took way too long. I should have been more alert. He must have suspected something, although I had parked my car down the street. I didn't hear him come in. I was on hands and knees when I looked around and saw him pointing a gun at me."

"What did he say?"

"He asked what I was doing there, repeating that he didn't have any marijuana. I decided I might shake something loose with the truth.

I told him I was looking for the Marathon Motors papers he took from Pierce Bradley. He laughed, said Bradley didn't have them, but he was still looking, too."

She said he demanded to know who she was and why she wanted the papers. She decided to play the old quid pro quo game——you tell me and I'll tell you. He said she wasn't going anywhere, so why not? Of course, he changed the order of the game. And sitting at the kitchen table with the pistol pointed at her quickly became nerve-wracking, considering how long he might have been drinking and smoking pot. The look in his eyes was worrisome.

She went first, telling him who she was and that the papers belonged to her great-great-grandfather. Rottman replied that his grandfather wanted them because they might reflect badly on Sam Hedrick, as well as the company.

Kelli said the young man had obviously spent a good while at the bar, and he seemed to relish his role in the plot. He was eager to talk about it. He said the way he heard the story, his great-grandfather, Randall, had whacked Sydney Liggett in the head and drove his car down to Dickson County. Sam Hedrick had followed and brought Randall back to Nashville. Sam had discovered some files were missing, files that could prove he stole thousands of dollars from the company. So he publicly accused Liggett of taking both the papers and the money.

The story had been handed down from father to son, and in his case, daughter, Camilla. Kirk wouldn't have known if he hadn't followed an old pattern of eavesdropping on his mother and grandfather. When Stone Hedrick learned the papers had turned up, and a guy from Trousdale County planned to give them to Arthur Liggett, he nearly panicked. He called in Kirk and asked him to find someone who would take on the task of recovering the papers for $25,000. Kirk approached Olson, who jumped at the deal. Kirk waited outside while Olson went into Bradley's house carrying a gun. When he didn't find the papers, and Bradley refused to say where they were, Olson became angry, took a cane and struck him a stunning blow the head

"That was probably payback for Bradley's breaking his arm," I said.

"After that," Kelli said, "Kirk decided they had better get rid of the man to cover their tracks. But after they drove Bradley's Jeep into the lake, Olson began to have second thoughts. He talked about turning himself in. Kirk was afraid Olson would try to plea bargain a light sentence in return for testifying against him.

When Kelli stopped, Wayne Fought stared in disbelief. "You want us to believe he voluntarily sat there and told you all of that?"

"I was astounded, too. But once he started talking, it seemed like he couldn't stop. I had the feeling he was confident I would never live to repeat any of it.

"He took me into the front bedroom and taped my wrists behind a large straight chair. Then he taped my ankles to the legs. I thought if I could get him out of there long enough, I might be able to work myself free. So I asked if he had any food, that I was hungry. He went into the kitchen and was gone only a short time, coming back with a soft drink in a glass. I told him I couldn't drink it with my hands tied like that, but he just held the glass to my lips. That was a big mistake."

"What happened," I asked.

"The drink must have contained Rohypnol, or some similar drug. It knocked me out in a hurry. When I awoke, it was daylight. I was groggy and tied to the bed. He came in to check on me after a while, sober, as best I could tell, and angry. He demanded to know what Mickey Evans had told me. He asked a lot of questions about who was looking for the papers, and what the cops knew. When I refused to answer, he slapped me around the face. Then he said he was going out, that he'd take care of me later."

"When did he return?" the agent asked.

"After the storm had nearly passed. It wasn't long before you arrived, Greg."

"Are you sure he didn't rape you while you were drugged?"

Kelli shook her head. "I don't think so, but I'd better stop by a hospital and get checked out."

Fought instructed her to visit the Trousdale Medical Center for testing. "One of the deputies can take you if you need transportation."

I assured him we would see that she got there.

"Okay," Fought said. "I'll need statements from both of you, but not until tomorrow. We still have a helluva lot of wrapping up to do tonight."

When we were finished and walked outside, Jarvis ran up to Kelli and threw his arms around her. For the first time, that hard exterior she had displayed throughout the ordeal appeared on the verge of breaking down. Before we got to the car, Agent Fought walked over.

"Do you have any idea what happened to the infamous papers?"

"As a matter of fact I do," I said, gesturing toward the car. "They're under Jill's seat. Patricia Cook found them where Pierce had left them at her house. I picked them up before we came out here."

"I'll need those for evidence."

"I know, but I'd like to bring them in tomorrow. I need to go over them for Kelli's grandfather's peace of mind. He's eighty-four and in poor health. This should really boost his morale."

Fought gave me a hard stare. I knew he didn't want to go off without the papers, but since I had caught his murderer, maybe he'd cut me a little slack.

"All right, McKenzie," he said after considerable hesitation. "Just be sure you have them with you in the morning. I'll meet you and Miss Kane over at Headquarters at nine."

42

W E MADE A PROLONGED detour by the hospital, where I got my arm checked out, and they determined that Kelli had not been subjected to any sexual molestation.

We invited Kelli and Warren to drop by our house and check out the Marathon papers after stopping by their motel. When we arrived home, the most recent message on the answering machine was in Wes Knight's annoyed, yet excited voice.

"What the hell's going on, Greg? Call me!"

For the sake of future relations, I dialed him back.

"What can I do for you, Wes?" I asked, playing Mr. Cool.

"Damn, man. We got this story out of the TBI in Trousdale County. Triple murders committed by the son of a prominent Belle Meade family. And what do I find in the middle of it? Your name and that of Miss Kelli Kane. What the hell happened to that speed dial with J for Juicy?"

"Simmer down, Wes," I said. "I just got back from Trousdale County and a little trip to the Emergency Room. I haven't exactly had much time for speed dialing."

"Okay, sorry to hear that. Was the Mrs. involved in this one like the last time out?"

He was referring to the Fed chairman affair from a few months ago. "On the case, yes. But, fortunately, not the shooting. I'll tell you what I can, but I don't want to get in trouble with the TBI. They're still investigating."

"What about Kane? Where can I find her?"

"At the moment, you can't. Why don't you tell me what you've got, and I'll fill in what I can."

Turned out he had all the basics of the story, who had been killed, who was arrested, where it happened. Agent Fought had identified me as being involved in an exchange of gunfire with Kirk Rottman while rescuing Kelli Kane. The TBI spokesperson left the facts a little loose, not wanting to give me all the credit for bringing in the killer. That was fine with me. Wayne Fought deserved a major share for feeding me information that led to tracking down Rottman.

One point totally left out of the TBI story was the Marathon Motors records. I knew Wayne Fought had purposely omitted that, both because he hadn't seen the papers yet and because he intended to use them in confronting Stone Hedrick.

I gave Wes a few choice details, including the discovery of Mickey Evans' body in the midst of a raging thunderstorm and what the scene at Rottman's house was like. I told him Kelli had become our client and got caught up in this situation while helping us investigate another matter. Wes wanted more, of course, but seemed satisfied when I reminded him about client confidentiality.

Warren and Kelli arrived shortly afterward. She had stopped by the motel for a shower and change of clothes. She appeared noticeably rejuvenated, with her original hair color back. I figured Warren had ratcheted up the charm.

Jill fixed us a snack, since a big meal hardly sounded of interest to anybody, even Kelli despite her enforced fast. We sat at the dining room table and spread out the papers. Warren picked up the first page and studied it.

"This looks like it concerns an account for something called Automotive Products Company," he said.

I read through the sheet and agreed, pointing at figures beside names like Winner, Runner, and Champion. "These are apparently proceeds from car sales. I seem to recall those were model names that went with the Olympic marathon theme."

"I'll bet that was an account Sam Hedrick set up that only he had access to," Kelli said.

As we went through the pages, we noted the dates covered a

period of nearly two years. And the total at the end amounted to more than $200,000. In 1914 greenbacks, that represented a tidy sum.

"Hey," Jill said. She leaned over one of the pages and pointed at a small group of initials at the bottom of the page. "Did you see this? It looks like 'SAH.'"

I thought about that for a moment, remembering something from Friday night's party. "Camilla told me her great-great-grandfather was named after Revolutionary War patriot Samuel Adams. I'll bet he was Samuel Adams Hedrick—'SAH.'"

Kelli slammed her hands on the table. "That cinches it for me. Sydney Liggett uncovered the secret account Hedrick used to funnel money out of the company into his own coffers. He was preparing to turn it over to the DA when Hedrick found out about it."

"Sydney got wind they were coming after him and hid the papers in his office wall," I said. "Remember those letters your grandfather had? One said something about Sydney indulging in his woodworking hobby."

Kelli looked around and nodded. "Right. It was in one of those I read to you and Jill over on Blair Boulevard."

"He managed to hide the files," Jill said, "but they got him before he could do anything about it."

We reached a consensus on the theory that Sam Hedrick used his windfall to bankroll Hedrick Industries during World War I. The possibility of the incriminating papers being brought to light, badly tainting the reputation of the company, likely led to Stone Hedrick's decision to seek Kirk Rottman's help. And then things got deadly.

WHILE JILL AND WARREN waited in the TBI Headquarters lobby Tuesday morning, Kelli and I met with Wayne Fought in the conference room. This time he brought in an agent assigned to the Nashville office to help with the questioning.

As soon as we took our places at the table, Fought looked across at me, eyes narrowed in an expression of concern. "How's the arm?"

I raised my arm, turning it one way, then the other. "Still sore, but no major damage. It'll provide a good excuse for avoiding chores around the house."

"Glad to hear some good came from the ordeal," he said, in a little more jovial mood today. "Okay, I'll switch on the recorder and we'll get started."

Kelli rehashed the account she had given yesterday in Hartsville. When it came my turn, I gave them all the information I had dug up about Olson and Rottman and our collective take on the Marathon papers. I handed the envelope full of accounting sheets to Fought.

After the two agents pored over the information for a few minutes, Fought looked up. "So you think this prompted Stone Hedrick to go after Bradley?"

"That's certainly the way it appears. In essence, that's what Kirk Rottman told Kelli. I'm sure it would help if you could pull a confession out of Rottman."

Fought shut off the recorder. "I'm not sure if we can do that. His family has already sent a big-shot lawyer up to Hartsville. We'll take these papers along on our visit to Mr. Stone Hedrick. I've already called for an appointment at two this afternoon."

"You must have been anticipating this," I said.

"I have something else to ask him about." Fought pulled an evidence bag out of his briefcase. It contained a semiautomatic pistol. "Here's the Beretta the diver pulled out of the river yesterday. It's registered in the name of Stone Hedrick."

Kelli leaned her elbows on the table, her hands folded. "After all this, I'm convinced Mr. Hedrick is the one who hired that PI character, Harold Sharkey, to tail me and go through my Grandpa's house."

"You're probably right." Fought gave me an apologetic look. "I didn't think it had anything to do with this case when Greg first told me about it."

"You might ask Kirk about that, too," I said. "Chances are he took part in creating all that mess. Also look into Camilla Rottman, Kirk's mother, as an accessory. I'd bet she was in on all of it. From what she told me about her husband, he was probably kept in the dark. But she is one certified scheming woman."

JILL AND I JOINED KELLI and Warren for lunch shortly after we wound up the session at TBI Headquarters. After we had given the waitress our orders, Warren turned on a big smile and reached over to take Kelli's hand.

"We have an announcement," he said. "Kelli has decided her usefulness as a clandestine agent is over. She plans to resign her position with the Department of Defense and take up a new role as an Air Force wife."

Jill leaned over and hugged Kelli while I congratulated Warren.

"I wish both of you all the happiness in the world," Jill said.

"Thanks to both of you for everything," Kelli said. "My Grandpa was ecstatic this morning. And we have one piece of unfinished business. Please figure up what we owe you as soon as possible. I don't want to leave any debts unpaid."

"We'll get it to you," Jill said. "But don't worry about being in too big a hurry to pay it. You'll have lots of other things on your mind in the next few days."

We said our good-byes to Warren after lunch. He had to catch a flight back to Washington. Kelli said she planned to stay around until Agent Fought wrapped up the Marathon murders case and every possibility for getting Sydney Liggett's name cleared had been pursued. Meanwhile, she'd move back into Arthur Liggett's house on Blair Boulevard and spend more time with him at the nursing home.

It was after two when we got back to the office in Hermitage. We sank back into our chairs, prepared to wrap up all of our current business and clear the way for a trip to Perdido Key, Florida and total relaxation.

All that was put on hold when the door was suddenly flung open. A fiery-eyed Camilla Rottman stormed in. You could almost see her fangs.

"I told you you would regret the way you treated me," she said. The words reflected anger, not pain. "Now you've tried to hurt my son."

Camilla had marched up to my desk.

Jill got up and came around the side of hers. "A slight correction, Mrs. Rottman. Your son not only tried but succeeded in hurting Greg. That bandage on Greg's arm is from a gunshot Kirk fired."

"Too bad his aim wasn't better."

For a moment, I thought Jill would slap her. Instead, she gritted her teeth and spoke in as icy a tone as I'd ever heard from her. "You are one sorry excuse for a mother . . . and a woman. You have caused way too much trouble already, Mrs. Rottman. I would appreciate it if you would get the hell out of here . . . now!"

I nearly went into shock. My wife never, I mean never, used profanity.

Camilla turned on her and sneered. "You pathetic people. I have powerful friends in the state government. I'll have your license suspended so quickly you won't know what's happened."

I smiled and spoke in a calm voice. "Mrs. Rottman, I hope you have some powerful friends in the Criminal Courts. Your son is charged with three murders. Murders he admitted in the presence of two witnesses. Murders he committed in an attempt to get a collection of Marathon Motor Works records that show your great-grandfather stole hundreds of thousands of dollars from the company."

Her mouth dropped open for a moment, then closed tightly and her eyes flashed again. "Liar!" she shouted.

"If you haven't seen them," Jill said, "I'm sure TBI Agent Wayne Fought will be happy to show them to you."

Camilla stood there for a moment, her expression running the gamut from shock to fear to total frustration. She spun on her heels and rushed out, leaving the door wide open. I walked over to close it, watching as her small red Jaguar spun its wheels and raced off.

I turned back to find Jill walking toward me, smiling. "I hope we didn't blow anything for Agent Fought by mentioning the Marathon papers," she said.

I checked my watch. "He's probably meeting with Hedrick right now. Incidentally, you did a magnificent job, babe. I think we can cross Mrs. Rottman and her highfalutin friends off our potential client list."

"Amen." She threw her arms around me, resting her head on my shoulder. She looked up with a failed attempt at a doleful expression. "I'm sorry you won't be sitting in the HI club suite at Titans Stadium this fall."

"Yeah. I regret that almost as much as I regret not giving Kirk

Rottman the chance to shoot me in the other arm."

     She started to giggle, then broke out laughing so hard I couldn't help but join in. After all the misfortune that had plagued Marathon Motor Works' demise and its aftermath, I relished the opportunity to wind up our involvement with a good guffaw. Wayne Fought might still have a few problems to resolve, but our case was all neatly wrapped up and ready for the archives.

Printed in the United States
107068LV00004B/55/A